THE SHADOW DREAMS

Book 1 of The Shadow Series

J. Dispenza

JADE PRESS
LITTLE ELM, TEXAS

Jade Press
PO Box 747
Little Elm, TX 75068
www.jdispenza.com

Publisher's Note: This is a work of fiction. Names, characters, places, and incidents are a product of the author's imagination. Locales and public names are sometimes used for atmospheric purposes. Any resemblance to actual people, living or dead, or to businesses, companies, events, institutions, or locales is completely coincidental.

Editing by Laura Gerrard

Cover Design by Daniel Machuca

The Shadow Dreams/ J. Dispenza. -- 1st ed.
ISBN 979-8-9854765-0-7

*This book is dedicated
with love
to
Susan Dispenza,
Adam Dispenza, &
Natalie Dispenza*

Thanks for dreaming with me.

Divine

And so we watch
The candles sprout,
The flames lick up,
Some flicker out.

Collect them quick
And help them grow,
Before the wind
Snuffs out their show.

Rise up, fierce torches.
Light the way.
The night is long,
But cannot stay.

See through the dark
And break of dawn.
Then hide away,
Yet never gone.

Whisper softly,
Truths divine.
New fates unraveled
In due time.

Breathe life, take life,
Bend the stars.
Take heed, this
Universe is ours

—ISRA KAWN,
THE ACADEMY OF DIVINE ARTS

1 OPHELIA CLARK

September 7

"You're looking a little pale, O. Try to perk up before we get there." Mom drove as she shot a disapproving glance at my slouched frame in the passenger seat of our white Ford Explorer. Her short dark hair was neatly styled in what I could only describe as a mom-cut and her collared, sleeveless blouse was firmly tucked into her tan capris. I was uncomfortable just watching her.

"God, Mom. Since when do people need to look nice when they visit the doctor's office? I mean, shouldn't they expect us to come in looking sick?" I asked, slinking down lower into the seat and massaging my temples, my brown curls becoming a mess of tangles on either side of my head.

This was the third day in a row I'd had the same headache, and I couldn't take it anymore. The sunlight pouring in through the windows felt like shards of glass piercing my eyes. I squinted and focused on my knees as we barreled down the GA-83, the lush greenery of the Monroe countryside zipping past my peripherals like broccoli in a blender. The motion of the car made me queasy and, even though my gothic clothes were loose and over sized, I felt like I was choking and did my best not to gag. I cracked the window open, hoping some fresh air would help, but the heat and smell of manure wafting from the cattle farm we were passing almost sent me over the edge. I closed it immediately, my face draining of all color.

Mom opened her mouth to say something, reconsidered, and pressed her lips into a thin line instead. After about five seconds, she said:

"You know, I started getting migraines when I was about your age. They came like clockwork every month a few days before my... woman's curse." She half-whispered, half-mouthed the words *woman's curse*.

"Mom, gross." It was bad enough I was in pain and trying to hold down my breakfast, but did she have to talk like that? What century did she think we were we living in? "It's called a period. Can you just use the right word? Jeez."

"O-phe-li-a!" She used my full name, emphasizing each syllable. Whatever she was about to say next, it wouldn't be good. "Of course, I know what it's called, but proper southern women don't speak that way. My mother raised me to be decent. It seems I have failed to pass on the same lessons to my daughter in this department." Mom inhaled deeply through her nose. "So..." She exhaled and regained her composure, possibly out of mercy for my current condition. "Is that what's going on with you right now?" She looked me over before focusing her attention back on the road. I was in too much pain to come up with something clever or sarcastic in retaliation of the embarrassing question.

"Um. Yeah, if you must know." I folded my arms around my midsection as if hiding it from view would end the conversation.

"Well, congratulations, honey. That's amazing!" Mom was beaming. "You know..." she leaned toward me. "... this is happening pretty late at your age. I was beginning to wonder if you had gotten it years ago and you just hadn't told me." She raised an eyebrow and looked me over. The suspicion on her face was unmistakable.

"I don't know what to tell you. All the websites I read said that anywhere between 10 and 15 is normal. I'm only one year older than the average range. It's not that big of a deal," I said.

"My little girl is finally a woman." Mom smiled and reached over to pat my thigh with her with her hand. "And you know what else, O? If you have questions, you can always ask me. Anything at all."

"Thanks, Mom, but I think I've got it." I couldn't even imagine trying to have a conversation about menstruation with this woman. Not with her endless code names for the human anatomy. I've already learned about how my body is a "garden" and how I need to protect my "flower". I rolled my eyes and instantly regret the movement as a fresh wave of pain crashed within my head.

"Alright then. It's just that... sometimes girls your age rely more on the information that they hear from their friends than they do on the facts, and I want -"

"MOM." I cut her off. My temples were throbbing.

"Then again," she continued, "it's been a while since I've heard you mention any of your friends." She shot me a glance, but quickly returned her eyes to the road.

She was right. It *had* been a while. Years, actually. I searched my aching head for a friend I could name, but the people I talked to the most were the school staff and some members of the faculty. I was pretty sure they didn't count, and though my classmates mostly ignored me, there was one group of girls who constantly picked on me. Breathing out a sigh, I changed the subject.

"Are we close? I don't see why we have to drive all the way down to Montibello when our family doctor is five minutes from our house."

"Because small towns like Monroe, as lovely as they are, have eyes and ears everywhere. I don't trust Dr. Mayson's secretary or that old, skinny pill-counter at the pharmacy to keep what they know about me to themselves."

I whipped around to face her a little too fast and felt another wave of pain rush into my head.

"About *you*?" I winced.

"Yes. I'm taking you to my doctor, *Dr. Li*, to give you the same prescription he gave me for *my* migraines. It's nobody's business what medications I take. And besides, sometimes Chinese medicine just works better."

I groaned in my mind. Dr. Li was born and raised right here in Georgia and had a thicker southern accent than *she* did. *Did Mom really believe that all Chinese doctors practiced Chinese medicine?* I was in no condition to get into it with her, so I kept quiet until we got there.

The appointment was quick and Dr. Li wrote me a script for the pain, though the medication ended up being different from the one Mom used after all. We headed to the pharmacy around the corner, but by that time, the pain was like nothing I'd ever felt before. I thought my left eye would pop right out of my head and there was some part of me that wished it would just happen. I'd had enough. *Mercy. Please, mercy.* In the end, it was my stomach that turned out to be the pressure release valve. We'd just pulled into the parking lot when I threw up into a canvas grocery bag Mom kept in the back seat. The sight of it made her gag and so she quickly parked the car, taking up two spaces, and flung her door open.

"You wait here. I'll go in." She slammed the door closed. I winced at the sound and hoped she wouldn't take too long.

Since I couldn't trust my stomach to keep the pills down while we were driving, I waited until I got home to my room to take them. The pharmacist told Mom that the meds would take the edge off and help me sleep, but she was only half right. I passed out within the hour, but when I woke up the next morning, I was more on edge than ever. Though my migraine was now only a dull ache, my heart was practically beating out of my chest, and I felt this sense of terror and dread throughout my whole body. Something strange happened while I was asleep. Something I hadn't thought about in years. The shadow dreams. They were back.

2 CHARLOTTE MILLER

September 7

The first night in Monroe was rough. I took a taxi from the Hartsfield-Jackson airport in Atlanta, all the way into town. Given my present financial situation, it would have been more prudent to have taken the bus, but Mr. Holland was waiting for me, and I wanted to be there on time.

"Is this the only bag you have with you, ma'am?" The stocky cab driver lifted my small carry-on into the trunk of the car, craning his body to check behind me for more.

"Yes, it's just the one for me, thanks." I slid into the back seat, hoping for a quiet ride.

The driver hopped into the front seat and I passed him a slip of paper with an address printed in block letters.

"I'd like to go here, please."

"Yes, ma'am. No problem." He punched it into his navigation system, turned on some country music, and we were off. "So..." He started as he flashed a quick glance at me from his rear-view mirror. "... where are you visiting from?"

I really wasn't up for chit chat but, not wanting to seem rude, I answered. "I'm moving here from Dallas."

"Oh, wow. The Cowboys, huh? Nice. Welcome to Georgia. Wait, did you say you were moving here? You sure packed light." He chortled.

"Yes, well... I guess I wanted a fresh start." I forced my mouth into the shape of a smile and rummaged through my purse for my phone and ear buds.

"Ah, a fresh start. I like it. That's good. It's never too late." He nodded his head in approval, shooting me a look in the mirror again, presumably to assess my age. "So, where are you staying in Monroe?"

"Actually, it's the place where you are driving me. The house was my grandmother's. I never met her, but she left it to me in her will." I popped my ear buds into my ears and scrolled through a list of podcasts on my phone, hoping the driver would take the hint.

"Oh, that's sad. My condolences," he said.

"Thank you." I muttered as I thumbed for the play button.

"So, what kind of work do you do, ma'am?" The man was not one to pick up on social cues, that was for sure.

"I'm a psychologist," I answered, instantly regretting telling him the truth.

"Really? Wow. You know, this one time..." I braced myself for the inevitable over-share. "...my cousin, Jose, thought he was possessed by the devil. He asked the church to give him an exorcism, but the priest told him he needed to talk to a therapist. Jose saw the therapist for about two weeks, but things got worse and my sister had to take him to the hospital. He was convulsing and screaming when she got him there. The doctors found an earwig that laid a bunch of eggs in his ear. When they hatched, they pierced through his eardrum and he went nuts! Haha. They took them all out, though. He was fine after that."

"Well, it sounds like he received the help he needed. I'm glad your cousin is OK. Hey, I need to catch up on some of my files now. I'll be listening to my audio and I won't be able to talk. Is that okay?"

"Yes, ma'am. Of course," he said, directing his full attention on the road ahead.

Thankfully, he didn't speak another word until we stopped an hour later.

"Ma'am? Are you sure you gave me the right address?" the driver asked, looking at me, then out the window, then back at me.

I drew the crumpled legal papers out of my purse and read the address out loud, squinting at the crooked numbers on the house we had pulled up to.

"Is this Old Post Road?" I asked.

"It is."

"Then I guess I'm home." I stared at the building, but could not bring myself to get out of the car. I was about to be sick.

In its day, the 1840s plantation-style home would have been impressive. It had a wide, sprawling front entrance with double doors in the center and two large windows, each flanked by green shutters. There were four white pillars that stretched from the bottom porch and continued to the covered balcony on the second floor. I imagined this is where planters overflowing with ferns and periwinkle would have lined the banisters and cascaded down the front like a waterfall. This house might have been a dream back then, but today the massive wooden wreck was a complete nightmare. The lawn hadn't been touched in years and had overtaken the steps to the front door. The overgrown trees and shrubs were collapsing from the weight of their own leaves. Ivy choked the white columns, snaking their way up to the second floor and along the broken shingles. I shuddered.

A person or thing left unloved for too long often became dark and bitter, but this house looked like something that had spiraled into madness. The grief and loneliness of this place was permeating through the windows. I could almost taste it. Wet moss and rot. I swallowed hard and tried to push the thoughts that were drawing parallels between this antebellum ghost of a house and my personal state of affairs from my mind. Not that I believed in fate or that the universe had a bias for irony. Still, I couldn't help but wonder if men looked at me, a single woman of a certain age, the same way I was looking at this house. *Do they see the cracks along my face and the sadness in my eyes? Do I, too, appear desperate and a touch mad?* I reminded myself that this house was the first step on a path to getting my life on track. A knock on the taxicab's back window startled me out of my daze, and I jolted.

"Ms. Miller?" A stout gentleman with round framed glasses and an unflattering suit peered through the glass.

I nodded my confirmation and paid the driver as the balding man removed my bag from the trunk. As soon as I stepped out, the driver sped off. *That was rude.*

"Ms. Miller, I'm Harvey Holland. It's a pleasure to meet you. I'm sorry it is under these circumstances. Inheritances are always bittersweet. I trust you had a pleasant flight." He shook my hand.

"Please call me Charlotte. Yes, the flight was fine. Thank you for meeting with me here."

"Oh, it's no trouble at all. My office is just a few minutes down the road." Harvey grinned, revealing a row of straight but small teeth. "So! These are for you." He slapped at the pockets of his pants and pulled out a set of house keys. "And here are the remaining documents for your records." He handed me a manila envelope that he had been holding under his arm. It was warm and slightly damp to the touch. I hoped he didn't see me cringe.

"Thank you, I think." I focused my attention back on my new home.

"I know it doesn't look like much now, but this place was a beauty back in the day," he said. I couldn't hold back my grimace. "That's the allure of Monroe. We remember our past through our architecture. With a bit of man-power, I'm sure you'll have the old gal looking better than ever!" he nodded, as if to reassure himself. Man-power was an interesting choice of words. Sadly, I was fresh out. "I'd recommend staying in a hotel for a few days, though. You'll need to call the city to get your electricity and water turned on," Harvey continued. "You'll likely want to have the pest control people out here, too. And the roofers, by the look of things." He stepped back and looked the house over, squinting at the damaged shingles. My head spun and my chest tightened. This was not the fresh start I had imagined.

"I can take you to the Red Roof Inn if you'd like. It's only a few minutes from here."

"That would be lovely. Thank you, Harvey. You've been so helpful," I said.

And that is how I spent my first evening in Monroe. In a chain motel, crying my eyes out onto scratchy sheets, questioning every life decision that led me to this moment in time.

3 OPHELIA CLARK

September 8

When I was little, I used to have strange dreams. Not all the time, but often enough to make bedtime a terrifying experience for me. One evening, I dreamed my grandma was dying. In the dream, it was the middle of the night and she was in her bed. The moonlight entering the window cast a soft white glow across her linens. I stood by her side and watched as she drew in ragged breaths. Her eyes fluttered a bit, and then she noticed me. She used all of her strength to raise her bone-thin arm; her withered hand trembling as she reached out toward me. I froze, terrified. As she got closer, I noticed there was something wrong with her eyes. They were wide open, but completely colorless. She stared out with white, glossy orbs. Her mouth drooped down into a frown, and her knitted eyebrows forced her forehead into a mess of wrinkles. Grandma looked weak and sad, and as her hand reached for me, I tried to scream, but my voice caught in my throat. I winced as I waited for her gnarled fingers to grip my nightshirt and yank me toward her, but she didn't touch me. Instead, she pointed her index finger to the back of the room. She hadn't been looking at me at all. Grandma was looking at someone or something behind me. As I turned, I noticed a person's shadow out of the corner of my eye.

I woke up screaming, and though I knew I was safe in my bed, the mysterious figure stuck in my mind. When my parents came to check on me, I told them what I saw. Of course, they tried to comfort me by explaining that it was only a dream. I wanted them to call Grandma so I could talk to her and make sure she was OK. They said that it was much too late at night and that I could call her in the morning. When morning came, Mom and I left Grandma a voice message. Mom said that Grandma was probably out at church, as she attended service every day, and that we could talk to her when I got home from school. But I would never hear Grandma's voice again. After 2 days of unanswered phone calls, Mom got really worried. She drove down to her house in Hawkinsville and found Grandma's lifeless body. She had passed away with her arm dangling off the side of the bed, her eyes open and rolled back so only the whites were showing.

They didn't let me go to the funeral. Mom and Dad thought six was too young an age for a kid to see a dead person, so they left me at home with my babysitter, Eloise. I liked Eloise a lot. She was young and fun and always let me eat ice cream. But as much as she tried to play with me and make me smile that day, I couldn't stop sobbing. She sat down on the couch next to me and rubbed my back with one gentle hand as she dabbed at my tears with a tissue in the other.

"Did Grandma die because I dreamed it?" I asked her.

"Oh, sweetheart, no. Of course not. What would make you think that?" Eloise lifted my chin with her index finger and looked into my puffy, red eyes.

I told her about my dream and the creepy shadow lurking in the corner of my grandma's bedroom.

"Ophelia, honey. Don't you pay that shadow dream any attention. Let me tell you something. You can't change the future any more than you can change the past. Everything happens for a reason, even if we can't understand it." She pulled me into a tight hug, my tears staining her sweater.

It wasn't too long before I had a similar type of dream. In it, it was dark outside, and Mom's car was on the side of a road. The windshield was smashed, and the hood was crumpled up like a cardboard juice box. Everything was silent and still except for a shadowy figure that crept along the side of the car. It made its way from the back to front, where it stopped and turned toward me. The shadow looked like a person, and though it had no nose, or lips, or eyes, I knew it could see me. Once again, I was too afraid to move, and all I could do was stare back at it. The last thing I remember was watching the shadow slowly dissolve into the air like a fine mist in the wind.

When I woke up, I told Mom about the dream and begged her to stay home from work. I heard her tell my dad that I was going through a "clingy phase", and she headed to her job at the Monroe County Clerk's office. I was a nervous wreck the whole day. After what happened with Grandma, I was positive Mom was going to die.

When the bus brought me home from school, Dad was standing in the driveway instead of Mom. I knew something was wrong, and I rushed toward him, terror crushing the air from my lungs.

"Where's Mom?" I cried, wrapping my arms around Dad's neck as he knelt down to pick me up.

"Well, I'm glad to see you too," Dad joked, though I didn't find any humor in the situation. "She's going to be late tonight. Someone hit her parked car in front of the office. She wasn't in it, but whoever hit her drove away and she had to stay to file a police report," he explained as he carried me into the house. I was never so happy to see her as when she got home that day.

That year, the "shadow dreams", as Eloise called them, kept coming. They were dark and showed me things that were about to happen. I would wake up in a panic, and Dad would try to calm me down. He'd remind me that dreams weren't real, but I knew that sometimes they were, and I could tell the difference. Whenever the shadow figure appeared, as terrified as I was, I knew that what I was seeing was something that would become true. At one point, my parents concluded I was seeing scary things in my dreams because I was watching too much TV. They banned all of my cartoons and enrolled me in a bunch of after-school activities to keep me busy. It took a few years, but as I got older, the shadow dreams happened less and less. I was so occupied with swimming lessons, piano lessons, and karate classes that when I went to bed, my head barely touched the pillow before I was out and dead to the world. I couldn't remember my dreams when I woke up anymore - even when I tried. By the time I was ten, the shadow dreams had stopped, and I never thought about them again. Until now.

4 CHARLOTTE MILLER

October 4

Restoration of the old Victorian house was going well, but the stress of the massive project was taking its toll. I needed a walk to clear my head.

The sun was bright, but the air was cool and brought the faint smell of fall; dead leaves with a hint of baking spice and cloves. The street was quiet except for the gentle rustling of the wind through the trees lining both sides of Old Post Road. Massive branches extended like hundreds of gnarled hands, their bony fingers reaching for each other across the narrow road. They were both haunting and beautiful. My white linen dress floated around me, effortlessly carried by the breeze, and for a moment I felt the weight of the world lifted from my shoulders. My bare legs bristled with goosebumps under the shade of the trees. I contemplated turning back to change into something warmer, but decided I had gone too far and would accept the minor discomfort. Besides, the house and I had seen enough of each other over the past few weeks. I was happy to take some space.

I rounded the corner onto Main Street. The large trees gave way to quaint little shops and restaurants with owners setting up for the day. There were people all around. I couldn't help but notice all the strolling couples (mostly tourists) walking hand-in-hand, casually peering into store windows, sipping coffee and nibbling on scones. I had that with someone once. Ted was probably my last chance at marriage and motherhood, but after I had to shut down my practice in Dallas (a time when I needed his support the most), he left me for a younger woman and told me he wanted to be with someone with more stability in her life. He broke my heart, and I feared I would never find another man who would make me feel special or wanted ever again. I pushed the memory from my mind to avoid crying in public and continued on my way.

It wasn't long before I got the uneasy feeling of being watched. I stopped in my tracks and looked around until I saw her. An old woman with a troubled look in her eyes stood in front of a coffee shop across the street. She was staring straight at me. Cars crossed the intersection and temporarily obstructed her view, but she remained unphased. Something about the way she looked was very unsettling. Then again, she was quite elderly. Maybe she needed some help.

"Hi there," I said. As I waved at her, a white delivery truck pulled up to the stoplight in between us. I crossed the street, expecting to find her on the other side of the truck, but in the few seconds it took me to get there, she had disappeared. I didn't think someone her age could move so quickly. Searching up and down Main, there was no sign of her. The only other place she could have gone was the coffee shop, so I stepped inside.

A bell on the door announced my entry. Everyone stopped what they were doing and glared at me. I scanned the crowd. The woman wasn't there either. *How strange.*

Dressed all in black (including an apron with a name tag that read "Byron"), the young barista spoke as if he was running on his seventh cup of coffee already.

"Hi, and welcome to Brew House Café. What can I get for you this morn... ing?" He trailed off when his eyes met mine. A flicker of recognition flashed across his face, even though I had never seen this man in my life.

"Hello," I said, growing more uncomfortable by the minute. I tried to be casual and ordered something. "Let me see..." I squinted at the over-sized chalk board mounted high behind the counter, the specials written in colorful block letters. "I would like a small dark-roast. Black, please."

"Yes, ma'am." Byron nodded and got to work immediately. He had the simple order ready within seconds and placed the cup on the counter, staring at it, silent and unmoving.

"Thank you. How much?"

"Oh yeah. Sorry. That will be two-fifty," he said, avoiding eye contact at all costs. I handed him five dollars and tried to leave with my coffee. It was scalding hot, even with the cardboard sleeve wrapped around it. I would need to let it cool for a few minutes before I could carry it with me, so I looked for a seat inside. Scowling faces peered up from their tables. One couple was whispering back and forth, and I heard the woman giggle. *Was the rear of my dress tucked into my underwear?* I gave myself a quick check. *All good.* I had met none of these people and wondered what in the world was happening. An older man with kind eyes raised his coffee cup and hailed me over, so I made my way to him. His deeply creased face and hunched body led me to believe he spent many years doing physical labor.

"May I place my cup down on your table for a few moments, sir?" I asked. In my peripheral vision, I noticed Byron the barista wince and turn away, distracting himself with a mop in the back of the coffee bar.

"Yes, ma'am. Come. Have a seat." He pulled out the chair next to him.

"Charlotte Miller." I smiled and shook the man's hand. "I just moved into the Victorian house on Old Post Road."

"I'm Bruce Swanson and I know who ya are. Yer the woman livin' in the witch's house." He cleared his phlegm filled throat in a loud theatrical "A-hem," that filled the entire room.

"Excuse me?" I recoiled. *Did I hear him correctly?*

"I said ya live in the witch's house. The one on Old Post with the overgrown yard and busted up trim. The place shoulda been condemned," he said matter-of-factly. I considered his words.

"Is that why people are staring at me?" I asked.

"It's why *I* was starin' at ya," he said as he took a deep drink from his lukewarm cup.

"Fair enough. What do you mean by 'witch'?" Surely he wasn't talking about my grandmother, Ruth. Not that I knew anything about her.

"They didn't tell ya when ya bought the place?" he mused. "They probably saw a city slicker like you coming from miles away." He half laughed, half coughed, phlegm dislodging in his throat. He swallowed it down, and I attempted to hide my repulsion.

"No. No one told me anything." I played dumb. "Who was the witch that lived there?" I smiled and leaned forward, using my body language to encourage him to keep going. It was a practical tool to get patients to open up and share, but it was useful in day-to-day conversation as well.

"Bah!" He threw a hand in the air. "You don't wanna hear about that."

"Oh, come now. I bet you know a lot about this town. Surely there is something you can tell me about that old house." I blew on the surface of the hot lava that was my coffee, never breaking eye contact with my new friend.

"Persistent!" He started coughing again, slapping his knee to soothe himself through it. "Alright, then. But once I tell ya..." He shook his head like he was trying to convince himself not to proceed. I leaned in a bit more and waited for him to continue talking. He started up again with a long sigh. "There was a woman that lived there. She moved inta the place sometime in the forties. She was 'bout your age back then, and she moved in alone, same as you." Bruce was too focused on remembering what he could about the woman to notice the smile fade from my face. *How did he know I was alone? And how dare he?* But as badly as I wanted to defend myself (and all single women over forty), I decided it was more important to learn what I could, so I swallowed my pride and forced a polite grin.

"Her name started with an R. Rachel? No. Ruby? No. Ruth! Her name was Ruth. She mostly kept to 'erself and toiled around in the garden.

One day she met a man who put a baby in 'er belly and that man was called off to war. He was shot dead out there and never returned home to see his lil' girl.

When that poor woman learned the news of 'er baby's daddy, she went a little crazy and became a shut-in. She sent the baby to live with 'er brother and 'is wife and mourned the man the rest of 'er life. She wore black every day, and she let 'er hair and fingernails grow long. The kids ridin' bikes past 'er house would see 'er sweepin' 'er porch and call her a *witch*, but she never paid them no attention." He cleared his throat and took another sip of coffee.

"That must have been horrible for her," I said. Bruce raised a wrinkled index finger at me to let me know there was more. He closed his glassy eyes for a time, as if he was working to locate the rest of the story deep within his memories.

"As the years passed, folks around town saw less and less of Ruth, but that didn't stop 'em from pointin' at 'er house. Any time somethin' went wrong in or around Monroe, people joked that *the witch* must'a done it. If there was a thunderstorm, or some freezin' weather, that was all *Ruth-the-witch*'s doin'. People didn't actually believe it, though. At least not in the beginnin'. It wasn't 'til the late fifties that folks started suspectin' she was up to somethin'.

It started out with someone's pet gone missin'. I can't remember if it was a cat er a dog. It don't matter now, I suppose, but people started noticin' new flowers bloomin' in Ruth's garden. Every time someone reported a missin' pet, a new flower bed would pop up on Ruth's lawn. Maybe the rumors were true. Maybe the woman was a genuine witch. Who knows what a wicked woman does with 'er free time? All anyone knew was that those animals never came home. Add another ten years and the *real* rumors started ta' fly." Bruce's eyes were watery, but alive now. He had my full attention.

"It was the summer of 1968 when a little boy wandered away from his front yard. Henry, I think 'is name was. The boy was three or four years old and 'is eight-year-old sister was supposed to be watchin' 'im while they played outside. Well, th' boy went missin'. It was all over the news. Police searched all of Monroe and eventually all of Morson county. They went door-ta-door, searchin' backyards and people's homes, includin' Ruth's house. After a few days went by, they was worried the boy wandered inta the lake. They sent divers to search the water, but they came up with nothin'. The boy'd vanished without a trace. The town was devastated by the loss. We all knew each other and looked out for one 'nother back then, ya know?" Bruce said, dabbing at his eyes.

"So they never found the boy?" I knew the question was unnecessary, but I wanted Bruce to continue. "What did his disappearance have to do with Ruth? You said the police searched all the homes and came up empty-handed." I took a small sip from my cup. The coffee had finally cooled to a tolerable temperature, but I wasn't ready to leave.

"Sure, the cops found nothin' at Ruth's house, but everyone noticed one glarin' change to that old woman's yard. A rosebush! A big, stinkin' rose bush right out there for all ta see." He nodded as if he had just cracked the case himself.

"A rosebush," I repeated.

"Yes, ma'am. A rosebush. That's what sealed the old woman's reputation in this town. After that, no one dared go near 'er place. Parents warned their children about 'er. Grown folks were afraid of 'er. Wouldn't even cross the street in front of 'er house lest they be struck dead by some evil force. No one visited 'er. Not even her brother with 'er daughter, but she kept 'erself busy in that garden, which was always neat 'n tidy. When people started noticin' the garden had gone ta hell, a neighbor called the police to check in on 'er. She'd been dead for weeks when they found 'er," Bruce said.

"Oh, no." I cupped my hands to my mouth. *Poor Ruth, alone in a town that didn't accept her. And for what? For planting a rosebush?*

"I'm sorry, Miss. If you hadn't realized, this place is just crawlin' with history. Ghosts 'round every corner, ya know?" Bruce rubbed the back of his neck.

"It's all right," I said. I didn't want to hear any more about the house or the misery my estranged grandmother suffered while living there.

"After that, the house just sat and rotted. People said the witch left the house to 'er brother, but 'e never came down to take it over, clean it out, or sell it or nothin'. It just fell apart for years 'n years. And now you're here. Fix'n the old thing up. Now I don't know ya and I ain't one to get inta people's business, but lemme give ya some free advice..." He leaned in close. "If I was a nice look'n lady like you, I'd cut my losses and leave that place. Go find a man ta' take care of ya' and build a life someplace else. You don't need that bad juju 'round you." He nodded and downed the last bit of coffee in his cup before standing up and patting me on the back. "Ya know, if I was a couple years younger, heh, heh..." Bruce's giggle turned into a coughing fit that followed him as he walked out of the shop.

By now, all the rubber-neckers had moved on with their own conversations, leaving me alone with my thoughts. *My house didn't have "bad juju"*. Especially not after all the repairs. In fact, the room (originally designated as the den) at the front of the house would be converted into a place of healing. After all, I had just gotten approval from the zoning commission to establish a new practice there. I was finally ready to put what happened in the past behind me.

5 OPHELIA CLARK

October 12

It was 12:30 AM and the pressure in my head felt like my brain was being separated from my skull with a crowbar. I kept expecting to hear a loud pop, followed by the feeling of ooze dripping from my ears. It was that time of the month again and the cramping in my abdomen was like nothing I'd ever felt before. And though my discomfort was mostly physical, I could feel a mental shift taking place, and it scared me more than anything. My thoughts were a mess. In my mind, I felt weak and powerful, strong and vulnerable, ordinary and mystical all at the same time.

I took my meds and hoped the shadow dreams would stay away tonight. Over the past three weeks, I had the same horrifying vision of the shadow, and as much as I tried to think happy thoughts before drifting off to sleep, my unconscious kept bringing me back to a scene that would haunt me forever.

Dressed in a white nightgown, Ophelia walked barefoot on the cold, damp grass. The sky above was overcast, but the dimness surrounded her like a blanket. She couldn't see anything beyond her reach, as the world in front of her appeared smudged and out of focus. Ophelia did not recognize where she was and an uneasiness stirred in the pit of her stomach. Compelled to move forward, she held her arms out in front of her as she slowly and methodically placed one foot ahead of the other. Two steps turned into ten and ten into twenty, but before long, she heard a sound that stopped her in her tracks; a boom so loud and enveloping she thought the sky had cracked open above her. Ophelia covered her head with her hands and crouched to the ground, the noise still ringing in her ears. Assuming it was thunder, she waited for the rain, but a gust of wind plowed into her instead, ripping her dark mop of hair loose from its tie and swirling it in every direction. She thought she heard a woman scream, but the violent gusts were whistling and distorting the surrounding sounds. The air grew colder and darker clouds rolled in. The electricity in the air was palpable, and Ophelia knew she had to keep moving.

As she groped and stumbled her way forward, her body fought against the elements which had grown so malevolent, they threatened to knock her down. As she advanced, the temperature dropped. She could see goosebumps on her bare arms and her breath appeared in little white puffs in front of her. Her fingers and toes turned a grotesque shade of blue, and her feet went numb. It was only in this moment she realized she was no longer walking on grass. The ground had turned smooth and black. Ophelia hoped this was a sign that she was on the right track; a road to follow instead of an open field. As she contemplated her next move, the wind died down and gave way to a thick fog that cascaded in layers from above. The sky brightened and a cool white mist surrounded her, but Ophelia could not see past her nose. Her heart was racing, but she couldn't turn back now. The dream was trying to show her something, and whatever it was, it was close; she could feel it.

Shuffling her feet and inching her way forward, Ophelia felt the ground become slippery. She looked down and noticed she was standing

on a bright yellow painted line that stretched on-
ward into the mist.

"What are you trying to show me?" Ophelia
shouted into the abyss. "I can't see anyth-"

Before the girl could finish her sentence, she
broke into a violent coughing fit and struggled to
draw in a breath. She fell to the ground, feeling
the air being sucked out of her lungs. Clawing at
her chest and throat, her eyes bulged as she realized she was choking. Ophelia flailed her arms
and legs, desperate for help. As she writhed on
the pavement, she noticed a burst of warm red
liquid spreading across the top of her nightgown.
She opened her mouth to scream, but could not
eek out a sound. Ophelia's life force was leaving
her body, and there was nothing she could do.

In her final conscious moments, Ophelia saw a
shadowy figure emerge from the mist. It reached
out and took hold of each of her forearms to draw
her close. She was certain this was the same dark
presence she had seen in her grandmother's room
many years ago, and she braced herself for the
end. As the figure pulled her in, an elderly woman's face came into view. They were nearly nose
to nose. The woman's eyes were not unkind, but
were heavy with the knowledge of many years
lived, her white hair framing her face in cloud-
like tufts. As Ophelia's body went limp, the
woman got even closer and whispered in her ear:

"Wake."

I sat bolt upright in my bed and coughed violently, my heart pounding in my ears. My body drenched in sweat, I fumbled for the lamp on the nightstand to check my chest for blood. There was none. *I'm alive.* But the feeling of relief didn't last. I quickly propped myself up against my headboard, pushed my damp hair away from my face and looked all around my room for the shadow woman, half expecting to find her lurking in a corner. There was no one in sight, but there was one more place I'd have to check. Trembling, I leaned over the edge of the bed. As I got closer to the bottom, my head hung upside down and my hair brushed the floor. *What if a hand pops out and pulls me under by my hair? Shut up. Shut up. Shut up. Just take a look and come up really fast.* I held my breath as my blood-shot eyes breached the side of the bed frame and frantically darted from left to right. My heart jumped into my throat when I saw a clump of white hair and my whole body stiffened. It's HER!

It actually wasn't. The white hairy clump was a dust bunny, and there was no one under the bed. I pulled myself back up and tried to collect myself. I wanted to call Mom into my room, but the last thing she'd want to hear was that the shadow dreams were back. She'd probably blame it on the Internet and take my electronics away. I grabbed my phone from the nightstand and checked the time. It was 4:05 AM. Wide awake and shaken, I lay back down and replayed the dream over and over in my head. *What did it mean? If the shadowy old woman was some kind of reaper or a symbol of warning, did I just foresee my own death? How long would I have?* Before I knew it, my alarm was going off. I swallowed hard, turned it off, and mindlessly got ready for school, wondering whether today would be my last.

6 OPHELIA CLARK

October 12

After only three and a half hours of sleep, I could barely function. I was so anxious it took me three tries to get my head through the right hole in my T-shirt. I pulled it on and stared at myself in my closet door mirror. With my finger, I traced over the spot on my chest where the burst of blood kept appearing over and over in my shadow dream, and I shuddered.

"I'm heading off to work, honey. Your lunch is in the fridge," Mom called out as she headed for the front door.

"Thanks," I shouted from my bedroom, wondering if I'd regret it if that was the last thing I'd said to her. The rest of my morning routine was a blur.

I slipped my backpack over my shoulder and started walking to school, hanging my head low, feeling like it was full of sand. Trudging along what I thought was my usual route, I looked up and noticed something was wrong. I was standing in the middle of a field with a forest of trees all around it. A fine mist hovered above the dewy grass. Panic washed over me as the shadow dream from last night snapped into memory again. I stood there, trying to figure out where I'd ended up and hoped the feeling of déjà vu would pass. Finally, a glint of light reflecting from a metal post flickered at the far end of the field, and when I turned around, I saw an identical post behind me. *Were those soccer nets?* A sudden high-pitched squeal of a child pierced my ears, and I squinted to see there was a playground nearby. That's when I realized I was standing in Armitage Park. I must have wandered past my turn at the bypass and made a left down the road leading into the park instead. Feeling like an idiot, I scuttled off the field and made my way to the path that led to the park's exit.

As I walked, a gust of wind ripped through the leaves of the tall oaks that surrounded the park like the walls of a prison yard. The dried, dead foliage skipped along the ground, and I wrapped my jean jacket around myself a little tighter. A passing cloud blocked the sun, and the slight drop in temperature gave me the shivers. I quickened my pace but kept glancing at the trees. An unsettling feeling of being watched came over me and my heart hammered behind my ribcage. *I need to get out of here. Now.*

I was nearly through the exit. I could see it from where I stood and figured if I could get to the clearing, I would be visible to the main road, and I'd be safe. But something in the woods caught my attention, and any hope of a quick escape turned into terror instead. A pair of eyes stared out at me from between the trees. Cold eyes. Unblinking eyes. I wanted to scream, but it was as if my body no longer took orders from me. It was like I was on autopilot and the only thing I could do was put one unsteady foot in front of the other and try not to do something stupid, like trip on a twig and fall. *Move forward. Don't look back,* I told myself. But my body betrayed me again. As I turned my head and peered into the woods, I realized the sunken pair of eyes that were staring me down belonged to a woman. A cloud of white hair covered in dirt and leaves framed her round, wrinkled face. A dark stone hung from a delicate chain around her neck and nestled itself in the center of her chest. She wore a long green dress, which was caked in mud and had bits of dried juniper and burrs stuck to the fabric. It looked as if she'd just woken up from a long night's sleep on the forest floor, but this didn't seem to bother her as she stood watching me from the trees a few yards away from where I walked along the path. I kept my steady pace without breaking eye contact with her. As I passed, she brought a shaky index finger up to her cracked lips as if to say "Shh". Her presence filled me with dread. *She's just an old woman out for a stroll,* I told myself. But, deep down, I knew she wasn't. There was a presence about her. She gave off a confident and powerful energy that made me understand that if she willed it, I'd be at her mercy. The feeble stance and the dirty hair and clothes were just a disguise. I was sure of it.

It seemed like forever before I put some distance between myself and the creepy old lady. I was breathing hard, and had broken into a cold sweat, which ran down my back and gave me the shivers. I was only a few steps away from the clearing now. Remembering every horror movie I'd ever watched, I had a nagging feeling to look over my shoulder. Half-expecting to see the old woman standing within inches of my face, I winced as I craned my neck around and let out a small shriek. Blinking like a maniac, I realized she hadn't followed, though her stare continued to penetrate my soul from her spot between the trees in the distance. As soon as I rounded the corner of the park, I ran as fast as I could.

It took me eight minutes to reach Morson County High, though I was so out of shape, it felt like much longer. I rushed past the massive pillars and through the heavy doors. They slammed behind me with a thud and I was safe, but I couldn't get the image of the old woman in the woods out of my mind. *Who was she, and what was she doing in there?*

I slipped into first period and slumped down at my desk, still fighting to catch my breath. Mrs. Goldfinch (or Mrs. Oldfinch as some kids called her) started the day by calling her students up to the front of the class, one by one, to pick up our graded geometry tests.

"Brenda H?" she announced, scanning the room for her student and holding the piece of paper in her outstretched, age-spotted-hand. Brenda stood up and collected her test, dragging her feet to the teacher's desk, then back to her own.

"Marcus?" Mrs. Goldfinch called. I heard a chair being pushed back, but didn't look up. The florescent tube lights were hurting my eyes, so I closed them to give them a rest. "Ophelia?" she said. I didn't answer. "Ophelia?" she tried again. "Ophelia Clark, it is time to wake!" she shouted louder. I snapped out of my semi-conscious state and jumped out of my chair as the other kids snickered.

"Sorry, ma'am," I said when I got up to her desk. She furrowed her brows together and handed me my test, tapping on the circled D+ written in thick red marker at the top of the page. On any other day, my poor grade would have devastated me. I might have even cried about it. But today something scary, something crazy, something impossible had happened. Mrs. Goldfinch's words repeated in my ears as the image of the old woman in the woods flashed in my mind. *Wake, wake, WAKE*. At that moment, I knew exactly who the lady in the green dress was. I just wasn't sure I could believe it. The shadowy figure from my dreams. The force that showed me things that hadn't happened yet. She was *real*, she was *here*, and she was *watching*.

7 OPHELIA CLARK

October 12

When the second period bell rang at Morson County High School, everyone dashed for their classes. I struggled through the student-packed halls like a salmon struggling to swim upstream. Since I was smaller than most kids my age, I had to weave my way through the masses. The door to my computer science class was in sight when Jessica James (MC High's self-appointed mean girl) stepped in front of me and blocked my path. Her mean girl crew flanked her.

"Hey, freak." Jessica eyed me up and down, smirking. Her beautiful skin and flawless makeup were the perfect mask for her cruel intentions.

"Excuse me," I muttered as I tried to go around them, never making eye contact. The four girls formed a human wall and wouldn't let me pass.

"Do you have an extra pen I can borrow?" Jessica twirled a lock of her blond hair on her middle finger.

"Umm. Yeah. I guess," I said. Confused and suspicious why she'd ask *me*, I rummaged through my bag and pulled out a pen.

"Thanks!" She snatched it out of my hand and threw it down the hallway. Her friends burst into laughter as I turned to watch it land. "Go fetch," Jessica said as she shouldered her way past me. The girls broke formation to chase after their leader, leaving me speechless, my blood boiling. I headed straight to class and sat down, cutting my losses on the pen. *Try to calm down, O. You have much bigger things to worry about right now.*

"Alright, class," Mr. Everets said as he smacked his bony, wrinkled hands together in one loud clap. He stood in the middle of the room wearing his usual over-sized glasses, tweed jacket with elbow patches, and forest green corduroy pants. Everyone was sure they were part of his original wardrobe from the '80s. The murmuring sound of thirty-three kids chatting stopped immediately. "We'll start off with a pop quiz!" The entire class broke the silence with a groan. *What? How could I pass a quiz when the creepy shadow woman from my dreams had stepped out of my unconscious and into real life?* My chest was feeling tight, and I couldn't take a deep enough breath to fill my lungs. The thought of the old woman in the woods, only minutes from the school, had my stomach in knots.

Mr. Everets walked down my aisle and placed a quiz face-down on my desk, as he did for all the kids behind me. I picked up my pen, and it immediately felt wrong in my hand, like the first time I tried to use chopsticks. My head wasn't in the game, and as soon as I turned that piece of paper over, I knew I was in trouble. I read and re-read the same question at least four times, rubbing at my bleary eyes and fighting fear and exhaustion just to focus.

When it was over, the only thing I was sure I got right on my test was my name. Even worse, we had to hand our quizzes to the person behind us to grade. As distracted as I was, I don't remember being more embarrassed in my life. Blake Jones, one of MC High's major rejects, was sitting behind me and had to grade my test. The mop of greasy brown hair across his face couldn't hide how confused he looked when he handed it back to me with one check mark and nine X's on it. Blake's own test was lying on his desk and I could see that even *he* got four answers right. *This is completely unfair.* I approached Mr. Everets about it after class.

"Sir, can we talk about the quiz?"

"We can." Mr. Everets held the stack of tests in his hands and thumbed through them until he found mine and looked at it. "Whoa! This isn't like you. What happened here?" he asked.

"I really don't know. I got very little sleep last night and I'm having a rough morning. Is there any way I can re-take the test tomorrow? I don't want this to wreck my grade point average."

"I see. Well, I'm sorry, but if I did that for you I would have to do it for the rest of the class too," Mr. Everets said, tucking the tests into a folder and preparing his desk for his next class. I squirmed.

"But, sir, can't you make an exception just this once?" I hated how whiny my voice sounded, but I was not above begging at this point. Mr. Everets stopped what he was doing so he could look me in the eye.

"Ophelia, you are a bright young woman with an incredible future ahead of you. There will be plenty of opportunities to bring your grade back up," he said, taking notice of the look of despair on my face. "I know this isn't what you want to hear right now, and don't tell anyone I said this, but life isn't all about getting the highest grade, you know."

I opened my mouth to argue, but he raised his hand up to silence me. "Yes, of course, good grades are important to help you get into a top school, but in the grand scheme of things, the people who are the most successful are the ones who try, fail, and get back up again," Mr. Everets said. He was looking deep into my soul, and I turned red with embarrassment.

"I'll think about that, thanks," I said. If I stayed any longer, I would get emotional, so I gave him a quick nod and bolted from the room as fast as I could.

"Ophelia, wait. Is everything OK?" Mr. Everets called after me in the doorway, but I was already down the hall and headed toward my next class. *Forget him. He just doesn't understand.*

I went through the rest of the day without incident, but when I got home, Mom could tell how upset I was.

"Ophelia, what's wrong? You look like a wreck. Is that girl, Jessica, bothering you again? Do you want me to call her parents?" she asked.

"Oh, please no!" I dropped my backpack on the carpet beside the desk in my room and flung myself onto my bed. I actually forgot all about the encounter with Jessica this morning.

"So what is it then?" Mom followed me into my room and sat down next to me. "Obviously, *something* is bothering you. Talk to me, honey." She stared at me as I wracked my brain and fidgeted with my hair. I really didn't want to tell her the truth, but I was too tired to make something up.

"Do you remember when I was a kid, and I'd wake up in the middle of the night? I'd come to your room and tell you that the shadow showed me something that was about to happen?" I asked. Hot, stinging tears pooled in my eyes.

"I remember," she said.

"Well, the shadow dreams are back. Only this time..." I rolled to my side so Mom couldn't see my face. "... I think *I'm* the one the shadow is after." My voice cracked, and I sobbed as the image of blood bursting from my chest flashed across my mind. "I don't know how or when it's going to happen. It's all so confusing and... I'm just so... I'm so TIRED." My tears spilled over and rolled down my cheeks.

"Oh, honey. I thought you got over that shadow nonsense ages ago. I think you're right. You're so tired you don't even know what you're saying. We need to see Doctor Li again. Maybe he can give you something to help you relax. I'll call right now and see if we can get an appointment for the morning," Mom said. She didn't believe me, but I lacked the energy to object, so I just curled up on my bed and buried my face in my pillow. Mom got up and rubbed my shoulder. "Just try to get some sleep, honey," she said, though sleep was the last thing I wanted.

8 CHARLOTTE MILLER

October 17

I awoke to the sound of knocking at my bedroom door this morning. My eyes flew open, though I kept still as I lay in bed. My heart was racing at the thought of an intruder in my home. I propped myself up and listened for another knock, or perhaps some footsteps, but none came. Fifteen minutes later, I mustered enough courage to slip out of bed and approach the door. I pressed my ear against it and listened again. Nothing.

"Hello? Is anyone there?" There was no answer. Renovations on the second floor had been on hold for days, as the crew waited for baseboard and trim materials to complete the job. The house felt eerily quiet, though the phantom echoes of all the sawing and hammering still rang in my ears. *Is that what I'm experiencing now? Was the knocking just a lingering dream?*

I flung the door open and stood back before peeking my head into the hallway. Beams of sunlight were creeping through the windows and spilling onto the newly installed floors. The remaining bedroom doors were ajar, just as I had left them. As I inspected each room, my adrenaline came down. I was the only one here.

I spent the rest of the day arranging office furniture in the front room on the main floor. My practice. The design was clean and minimalistic, contrary to the house's traditional antebellum style. The geo-print area rug and silver-gray walls were a pleasant contrast to the espresso-stained hardwood. A gray cloth armchair faced a matching loveseat that backed up against the window. I dressed the glass with a simple sheer curtain to let the light in, though it was dark by the time I finished hanging it. A potted ficus and a brown bookshelf nearly completed the look. There was just one last thing to do. What therapist's office would be complete without an inspirational and uplifting slogan on the wall? I pulled out the picture I had bought. It depicted a dark landscape with rolling hills, illuminated by the faintest sliver of dawn creeping up on the horizon. Large white letters ran across the top and read: The darkest of nights always give way to the rising sun.

I hung the picture opposite the couch and sat down to study it. A rush of memories from my former practice came to mind. The long nights, the people I helped to find their inner light, and the individuals I couldn't reach. I knit my eyebrows as my thoughts spiraled into self doubt. *Am I ready to start again?*

As my chest tightened, the loneliness crept in, and my mind shifted to memories of Ted. Maybe I was missing human connection or the physical comfort of being held in someone's arms. *Don't do it Charlotte*. Against my better judgment, I picked up my phone and scrolled through old photos until I found one of the two of us on vacation. I stared at his handsome, smiling face and longed for the days of sharing intimate moments with a partner. The screen flickered and the phone vibrated. I jolted, and it took me a few seconds to realize that I was receiving a call.

"Hello?... Yes, this is Gentle Rivers Psychology. My apologies. The phone caught me by surprise. Yes, I'm Dr. Charlotte Miller. Am I accepting new patients? Actually..."

A few moments later, I was writing the name of my first patient in my scheduler and was back in business. "Sounds good. I look forward to meeting you then." Just as I hung up, there was a loud bang from inside the room, startling me out of my wits. The picture had fallen off the wall. It dropped straight down but didn't break. Curiously, the nail was still firmly embedded in the stud and the wire backing on the frame was perfectly intact. An uneasy feeling washed over me as I hung it back up and checked that it was secure. Giving the picture a suspicious stare, I crept out of the office as quickly as I could, reaching my hand inside to turn off the light.

Shaken, I walked into the kitchen to prepare dinner, and I reminded myself that I was a licensed therapist and a grown woman, repeating the mantra: *there is nothing wrong with this house, there is nothing wrong with this house, there is nothing wrong with this house.*

9 OPHELIA CLARK

October 17

"Open up and say ah for me." Doctor Li peered into my mouth with a small flashlight and a tongue depressor. He had to stand on his toes to get a better look.

"Ahhh." I tried not to gag and distracted myself with the gallery of thank you cards and photos of patient's children that were thumb-tacked to the corkboard in the cramped, tiffany blue exam room.

"Looks good," he said, taking the wooden stick out of my mouth and jotting down his observations in my chart. I sucked on the inside of my cheeks to get rid of the taste. "Well, Ophelia.

Everything we tested today is completely normal and wouldn't explain why you are having trouble sleeping through the night. I do see signs of fatigue, though." He looked genuinely concerned as he reached for his rolling chair and sat in front of me like someone who was about to share some tough news. I braced myself as he got comfortable and continued. "Often we don't sleep well because of our anxiety. I'm sure you are under a lot of pressure with your school and homework. Your thoughts are running wild, even through the wee hours of the evening. It's an exciting time, but it's also a stressful time for you and many youngsters your age."

I stared blankly, waiting for him to tell me what miracle drugs he was going to prescribe.

"Ophelia, I'm writing you a referral to see a psychologist," Doctor Li said. *What?* "There is a new practice that just opened up not too far from here. She's in Monroe. I think working through some things with a professional who can give you the tools you need to cope with what you're going through should help with the disturbing dreams you're having, and your overall quality of sleep." He paused and stared at me as I digested his words.

Psychologist? I think I might be psy-chic, not a psy-cho. I shifted, crinkling the sheet of protective paper on the exam table. Doctor Li turned to Mom as if I wasn't there and continued talking about the potential benefits. I didn't hear a word of it, but I could see the tension growing on Mom's face. She wouldn't even look at me.

"What if I don't want to go?" I interrupted. They both fell silent. Doctor Li looked at Mom and then over at me.

"That is certainly an option. My patients always have autonomy to choose what is best for them. This is just my recommendation."

"Of course you're going, O-phe-li-a." Mom shot daggers at me out of the corner of her eye. "We are going to follow the doctor's orders. Why would you say something so ridiculous? I'm so sorry, Doctor Li." She peered up at him, her cheeks flushed.

"It's quite alright. I encourage my patients to ask questions," he said, giving a thin smile as he stood up. "Annette at the front desk will provide the contact information you'll need to make an appointment."

"A *psychologist*? Good gracious, Ophelia. All over those silly dreams of yours. I hope you are pleased with yourself." Mom huffed as we walked to the car.

"Totally!" I blurted in defiance as I got into the passenger seat. We drove home in complete silence as I stewed over the realization that Mom was embarrassed by me. Going forward, I knew I couldn't talk to her about the dreams again, no matter how terrifying they were.

10 CHARLOTTE MILLER

October 18

I took a sip from the glass of Chardonnay I had been nursing since noon, having spent the better part of my day on my laptop, surfing the Internet from my living room sofa. The knocking and banging noises in this house kept me awake all night. I got up to investigate some time around 1:00 AM, terrified that I would surprise an intruder, but there was no one here and no obvious cause for the sounds. Now I was on edge and needed some answers, as my imagination was running wild. I kept thinking about the man at the coffee shop and how he said that Monroe had "Ghosts 'round every corner", and though I knew this was the house that Ruth Rivers died in, I needed to find a more logical explanation for the disturbances. As if on cue, there was a tap at the large bay window to the left of the room. I jerked my head up to see who was there, my fright nearly ejecting me from my seat, but it was only the wind toying with an overgrown branch from the large oak tree at the side of the house. The sight of it painted a dreary picture of a day cloaked in gray clouds that masked the brilliant colors of the garden. Everything out there looked dull and muted, from the orange mums to the violet pansies. Even the boxwood hedges had lost their waxy sheen and looked more like carefully clipped boulders than greenery.

"This is definitely a day to be indoors." I sighed and drew a long breath before returning my attention to my laptop. I typed "home making strange knocking sounds" into the search bar. Several articles discussing air in the pipes, expanding and contracting wood during a change in seasons, and other naturally occurring noises in the home popped up. As I read through them one by one, my concerns melted away. I took another deep drink from my glass, feeling the effects of the alcohol combined with my fatigue setting in.

I set the glass down on the coffee table, my arm feeling heavy. I fought through the fogginess in my head to type: "Tree trimming services near me" into the search bar and glanced out at the imposing oak tree again. This time, what I saw made me jump out of my seat.

I struck my foot on the coffee table as I made my way toward the window. My glass toppled to the floor and shattered in all directions, but I would need to deal with it later. An old woman was standing beneath the tree and staring at the house, her white gossamer hair floating about her face. My feelings of dismay returned within an instant, though I think what disturbed me most were her eyes and how they rolled back into her head. With my shoulder against the wall next to the window, I peeked out just enough to watch her without her noticing me, my adrenaline pulling me out of my tipsy state. The woman's arms were resting at her sides, palms upturned, and she was completely still, except for her lips. I couldn't see who she might have been talking to, nor could I make out anything she was saying through the glass, so I eked my head out a little further to get a better look around. She appeared to be alone. *Was she praying?* My heart was racing. I squinted to read her lips and, and as her face came into focus, it alarmed me to see that she was glaring at me. Her silvery gray eyes, now facing forward, locked onto mine, which sent a jolt through my core, and I realized where I had seen her before. Not knowing what to do, I raised my hand up in an awkward greeting.

"Hi, please wait right there!" I shouted from behind the window, though there was no telling if she heard me. Tearing out of the room, I hurried out of the front door, down the steps, and cut through the flower beds that wrapped around the house. Red mulch crunched under my shoes and as I struggled to maintain my balance, I regained sight of the oak tree and came to a grinding halt. There was no one there.

"Hello? Ma'am? Is there anyone out here?" I walked around the entire house, but once again, the woman had vanished. When I gave up and returned to my front door, I hesitated before turning the knob. *Could she have slipped in while I was in the back?* My stomach dropped.

I flung the door open and remained outside, peering into my home. I listened intently for any hint of movement, but I couldn't make out anything except for the sounds of my surroundings outdoors. Lawns being mowed, airplanes overhead, dogs barking and the like. *What am I so afraid of? She's just an old lady.* Stepping into my home, I closed the door behind me. I pulled out my cell phone and keyed in "9-1-1" on the dial pad, hovering my thumb over the "Send" button. *Better safe than sorry. If she snuck inside, she doesn't want me to know, and things could get dangerous.* Just as I had done in the wee hours of the night, I searched the house, room by room, and found that I was completely and decidedly alone. Wherever the mysterious woman went, she wasn't here.

After cleaning up the broken glass in the living room, I poured myself another drink and sat down. *Keep it together. There must be a logical explanation for everything. The house is old. It makes noises sometimes. That lady is probably someone's elderly parent who lives in town. Once again, there is absolutely, positively, nothing wrong with this house.*

11 OPHELIA CLARK

October 18

"Out of the way, NERD!" a boy shouted from on top of his friend's shoulders as they knocked into me in the school hallway. A group of kids were messing around and jumping onto each other's backs, laughing as they clumsily ricocheted off the metal lockers and bumped into other students. I felt my cheeks get hot, and I wanted to yell something back, but I was too flustered and before I knew it, they were down another hall. I dusted myself off and headed for home.

By the time I had reached the Monroe Bypass, a cool wind had kicked up, and the clouds looked like they'd bring in the rain. It was much darker than usual for this time of day, and I knew I needed to get home fast, especially because I didn't have an umbrella with me. But there was something about the woods on the opposite side of the road that captured my attention. Of course, just beyond the row of pines was Armitage Park - the place where I saw the old shadow woman. Every day since then, I hurried past this section of road and kept watch for her, half expecting to find her standing in between the trees, staring at me. Thankfully, I hadn't seen her, but I knew that didn't mean she hadn't seen me. *What could she want from me?* I swallowed hard and took in a deep breath. The thick scent of the woods filled my nostrils. The dampness of the tree bark, the rotting of fallen leaves. Peat moss, earth, insects, puddles, everything. I inhaled all of it and felt the energy within my mind and body shift all at once. A calming oneness with nature washed over me and, intoxicated by the alluring scent, I crossed the road and headed into the woods.

Pushing past branches and stepping over wild shrubs, I made a path through the dense brush. *What the hell am I doing? Have I lost my mind?* Alarm bells were going off in my rational brain, but something compelled me to push forward, and I let the woods guide me. I nearly reached a clearing when something clawed at the sleeve of my jean jacket. My brief connection with nature ended abruptly as I whipped around to face my attacker. My terror, too much for my body to contain, released itself as a scream from my lips. A flock of cardinals in a nearby tree flew off all at once, leaving me alone to face the thing that had taken hold of my arm. By the time I turned all the way around, I felt the sharp sting of my flesh being torn open, and I flailed and thrashed until I was free. It was only then that I realized I was the only one there. The sleeve of my jacket had caught on a locust tree thorn, tearing a hole in the fabric and giving me a small gash on my left elbow. The two-inch spike that got me dripped with blood. I covered my wound with my hand and continued walking toward the clearing, careful not to rub up against any more branches and thinking about how to hide the damage to my jacket from Mom. She would think I was rough-housing or some other unladylike thing (*like traipsing through the forest*) and I'd never hear the end of it. Just like that, my enchanted walk through the woods was over. I didn't know what I was thinking, but I wanted to get out of there as soon as possible.

"Ophelia," a stranger's voice called out from the opening just a few steps ahead. I froze at the sound of someone so close by, and I stopped dead in my tracks. *Oh, no. What do I do?* It wasn't long before I heard the voice again. "Come on out, child. I've been expecting you."

Whoever it is, they know I'm here. There's no use trying to hide. The sounds of my shoes crunching along the dried leaves and packed dirt was deafening, as I was the largest (if not the on-ly) thing disturbing the woods. My eyes wide and on the lookout for anything that moved, I slowly stepped into the clearing. That's when I saw her. Standing in the center of the paved trail, her gray eyes measuring my timid steps, was the old woman from my shadow dreams. As I ap-proached, I could see that she was smartly dressed in a black pantsuit, accented with a warm knit scarf loosely wrapped around her neck. The hint of a necklace carrying a blue stone peeked out above the wool. She loosely clasped her hands in front of her and gave a slight smile.

"Who... who are you?" My voice trembled.

"My name is Isra. Isra Kawn," the woman said, rolling the r in Isra. Every line and every wrinkle on her face told a story. She was old, but her skin seemed to glow, and her eyes sparkled with wisdom.

"I'm Oph -"

"I know who you are, child," Ms. Kawn cut me off. I put out my hand, but she only stared at it. "I have been watching you for some time now."

Her admission made my palms prickle with sweat. *What did she mean she was watching me?* Feeling uneasy, I thought about running, but I figured it wouldn't do much good if this woman could infiltrate my dreams. If I ever wanted things to get back to normal, I had to face her and learn as much as I could.

"I've seen you too. You were here... in the park." I must've sounded like a toddler to her. *Use your words, O.*

"That's right. And you've seen me somewhere else, haven't you?" Isra leaned in closer, staring, and I could smell hints of lavender oil drifting from her décolleté. I stared at my shoes until I could gather the courage to answer her, as if saying it out loud made it more real than it already was.

"You're the shadow in my dreams."

Isra nodded but said nothing.

"Every time I've seen you, the vision from my dream came true. The dreams have a very different feel to them, too. When I wake up, it's like I just remembered something that already happened. My parents never believed me and I used to get in trouble whenever I'd talk about it, but I knew it was real. You eventually stopped coming, though," I said, finally looking up at Isra, who was listening intently with compassion in her eyes.

"But I came back," she said, continuing the story where I'd left off. "And once again, your psychic gifts have sparked a flame in your third eye." Isra reached out and gently tapped the space between my eyebrows. Though she hadn't touched me for more than a second, I felt a cool rush of energy from her finger flow from my forehead down to my toes. Isra cocked her head to one side, as if she had expected something different to happen. "Only this time, your vision is blurry, you are completely lost, and you've become so self-absorbed that you've confused yourself for the actual subject," she frowned.

Stunned, I attempted to say something, though the sound that came out only slightly resembled a "Yes." She patiently waited for my next question:

"So, in my dream, the blood on my chest - it's not mine?" I asked.

"No, child. Even the most talented of us cannot see our own deaths. The will of the universe makes it so," she said. This should have been a comfort to me, but I was still unsettled.

"Is it someone from my family, then? I don't understand what any of it means. Why am I having the dreams again? Why did you come back? Why are you here in Monroe?"

"Ophelia." Isra put a tentative hand on my wounded arm. Another surge of energy coursed through me. Miraculously, the cut began to heal. "I have returned after many years because there is something very special about you. Yes, you possess some raw and unpracticed psychic abilities. We call people with these skills 'diviners'. But you, dear girl, have the potential to develop something exceptional," she said. I stared at her, blinking. "Ophelia, I'm here to see if you have what it takes to be a divine *bender*."

12 OPHELIA CLARK

October 18

Isra's words were rattling around my head like marbles in a tin can.

"Sorry, I don't understand," I said, shaking my head in bewilderment.

"It's quite alright, child. Walk with me," Isra said as she turned on her heels and strolled from the clearing to a path that led into the main area of the park. The clouds overhead grew darker. A storm was near, but it didn't phase her. "Well, don't just stand there," Isra said, looking over her shoulder. I leaped into motion, catching up to her with a few quick steps, and apologized again. But Isra waved it off with her hand.

"Let me explain," she began. "Many children are born diviners. They can see bits and pieces of the future. Some of them have additional abilities, like communicating with animals or interacting with the spirit world. As time passes; however, most of them get conditioned to ignore their gifts. The mundane tasks of everyday life cause their talents to atrophy, and the children forget how to see with their third eye." She tapped the center of her forehead in demonstration. "When these children grow up, they become the people who tell you they were just thinking of you right before you called them and the ones who have déjà vu all the time," Isra smirked. "But the word 'coincidence' is never far from their lips as they explain away their suppressed talent.

Then there are children who exhibit all those qualities and more. These have the potential to be divine benders. Divine bending is a unique skill that not only requires the ability to see into the future, but to *change* it. If destiny is a divine plan, these children can set off a chain of events that bend it to their will. My order is most interested in finding this talent. Many years ago, we learned *you* were a divine bender, Ophelia."

My eyes went wide. It was the first time anyone acknowledged that something special had happened to me - that my premonitions were more than just frightening dreams. "I... changed destiny?" I asked, thinking back on my childhood, unable to connect the dots that would support Isra's assessment of me.

"You did, child. You saved your mother's life. It was the day you woke up after dreaming about her car being smashed." Isra took one look at me and let out a small sigh when she saw I needed more. "You begged her not to go to work and, for all your pleading, she still left the house. She was late, though, and had to park farther down the street than she normally would. This one change caused a three-minute delay for her getting into her building and (more importantly) another three-minute delay for her to get back to her car when it was time to leave. That small window of time saved her life. Had she parked in her normal spot in front of the Clerk's office, she would have been in her car and on the road at the time the other car crashed into it and sped away. She would have suffered extensive injuries and would have eventually succumbed to them in the hospital." Isra watched me as I replayed the events of that day in my head. I was speechless, so she continued explaining. "Obviously, your mother being alive instead of dead has had a significant ripple effect on the lives of everyone around her - especially your own. After that event, my mission was to monitor your progress for a few more months before approaching you and your family. Unfortunately, I was called away from my post and our resource based in Monroe had already been relieved of her duties. By the time I returned, you were 10-years-old and the light from your third-eye had dimmed so much that I had to remove you from my list and move on to the next candidate."

"I dimmed?"

"Yes. Dimming happens when a diviner neglects to practice their skill. It's like lighting a campfire. The fire may burn brightly at first, but if no logs are added, the fire weakens until there is nothing left but glowing embers. Even the embers turn to ash, and once that happens, the fire is completely out. What happens so often with diviner children is that their day becomes so heavily regimented with school and other activities, they don't have a waking moment to reflect inward or relax their mind to receive other signals and frequencies. If I had gotten to you before the years of swimming, dance, piano, and karate lessons on top of your schoolwork, you would have been invited to join the Academy of the Divine Arts during the school breaks in the winter and summer. There, you would have benefited from a decade of my guidance in working with the energies of the universe." Isra looked saddened by guilt. "But something very unusual has happened." Isra stopped walking and turned to face me. "After all these years, your light has flickered again. I've only ever heard of this happening; I've never seen it for myself. From what I understand, when a child reaches an age of maturity and begins menstruation, the hormonal and chemical changes that occur in the body and mind can be so intense and abrupt that it introduces something akin to adding dry kindling to the dormant campfire. We call this a 'second flame'. This, Ophelia, is why you are having those dreams. It is the reason I have returned to Monroe." Isra waited patiently while I considered what she had said.

"So, you are here to teach me? Do I get to join some kind of academy?" I asked.

"No, child. I'm afraid things are not as simple as that." She frowned and gave me a sympathetic look as she wrung her age-spotted hands together. "You see, you are far too behind to join the other students, and becoming a divine-bender takes a great deal of practice, commitment, and sacrifice. It wouldn't be fair to bring you in now. That being said, the order has reviewed your case and wants to give you a chance to earn your place," she said. I shifted my weight on my feet and listened intently. "Ophelia, I want to talk to you about that dream that you started having. The things that happen in it are *real* and they will happen to someone right here in this town. Someone is on a course that will lead them to die a senseless death," Isra explained as I squirmed. "It sounds horrible, I know, but this is how their destiny is written. Your third eye is flickering, but if you want to understand the true strength of your power and learn to unlock the secrets of the universe with us, you will need to pass a test."

"What kind of test?"
"Decipher your dream. Bend the future. Save a life."

13 OPHELIA CLARK

October 18

"What? That's not fair. What kind of test is *that*? If you know what's going to happen, why don't *you* save them?" I asked, not realizing how loud I was talking. A couple glared at me as they walked past quickly to avoid the coming storm.

"You have a lot to learn, child," Isra said. "A watcher like me cannot go around interfering with the lives of everyone she meets. People die every day. Lots of them. Even the ones that don't deserve it."

My head was spinning. This was just way too much. Maybe I'd feel differently if the situation was more specific to me or my family, but this was a complete stranger we were talking about. This was none of my business.

"What if I don't want to be a diviner or a bender, or whatever? What happens if I say no?"

"Of course you are well within your right to decline. You can ignore the dreams and focus on other things until they stop appearing to you, though it could take a while now that you've become a woman." Isra looked me up and down and continued her slow and steady walk toward the parking lot by the front entrance. I followed her, cautiously glancing at the blackening sky that looked like it could crack open any second. "You will eventually lose your gift, live a regular life, and destiny will take its course, as it usually does. But ask yourself this:" Isra pointed a bony finger at me. "How will you feel after all is said and done, after you've lost your special gift, after the person you've been dreaming about is dead? Will you be able to face yourself in the mirror, knowing that you might have made a difference? Would the mysteries of this world and the next torment you? Are you such a spoiled child you won't even try?"

"No, that's not it at all!" I shook my head, my eyes wide. *I'm not spoiled.* She had me all wrong. "Obviously, I don't want anyone to get hurt, and I'm not ungrateful for my dreams. That's not what I'm saying, but... I'm just not *ready.*" I felt like I was falling.

"You might not think you are," she said flatly, "but I believe in you. And *you* must believe in *yourself*." She drew a thin smile. "More than seeing with the third eye, being a divine bender requires instincts, problem solving, and courage. You posses these traits already."

"I don't know about all that, but what if I agree to do this and I *still* fail? How will I look at myself then?" I thought I had given her a clever answer, though her expression told me otherwise.

"It is risky business; *trying*." Isra nodded. "I suppose you will never know until you do it." She raised her chin and looked down her nose at me. "Ophelia, this is the point at which *your* destiny diverges into two paths. The first requires no effort, no risk, and no rewards. The second requires hard work, a leap of faith, and promises to answer the question: *what if?* What will you choose?" she asked. I thought about it in silence as the woman watched me.

"I don't even know how to start." I threw up my hands in frustration. *Am I really considering this? This is just crazy.*

"What you need to do is to keep focusing and remain vigilant," Isra instructed as we walked toward the few remaining cars that were in the lot. She pulled her key out of her pants pocket. "Your power will find its way back to you. Follow your instincts and always do what your gut tells you."

I stared at her helplessly. *What do I know about any of this stuff?* I flinched at the sound of a thunderclap booming overhead.

"Oh, and one more thing..." Isra said, completely unphased by the weather. By this time, she had unlocked her car, a black Lincoln, and opened the driver's side door. Tossing the key into one of the cup holders, Isra reached both hands behind her neck and unclasped her necklace. A stone about an inch long dangled from a silver chain. "Take this." She placed it in my hand, and I inspected it. The pendant was dark blue, with swirls and specks of gold marbled throughout the piece. I ran my thumb over its surface, finding appeal in its sleek texture.

"What is this?" I asked, without taking my eyes off it.

"That, my child, is one of the first covellite stones ever found. It was mined from Mount Vesuvius, a volcano in Italy. During the nineteenth century, diviners discovered these stones carried metaphysical properties and could enhance psychic visions and manifestations. Lucid dreaming, astral travel, inner vision, and improved intuition are well known side effects of having a covellite stone nearby. Some diviners have even been able to use the stones to look back in time and see their past lives." Isra's eyes twinkled as she spoke, adding magic to the gift she handed me.

Another thunderclap rumbled, though it didn't frighten me as much as the first few had. "Keep it close to you when you sleep. Under your pillow or under your bed would be best. Don't expect too much. Covellite will only amplify the talent you already have. In your case, I imagine it will clear up some of the mental clutter that is blocking the light from your third eye. Allow a couple of days for it to take effect and make sure you go to bed at the same time every night. Consistency and rest are key." She closed my fingers around the necklace and patted my clenched hand.

"Wow. I don't know what to say," I stammered, still trying to process the situation, my new bobble tingling in my palm.

"Say yes. Say you accept this challenge."

I stared at my fist, the thin silver chain dangling out of one side.

"If I agree, and I successfully bend this person's destiny this one time, they'll live a good life?" I asked.

"They will live out their lives as if what you saw in your dream never happened," Isra said.

"And if I do this, I'll get to meet others who are like me? Other divine benders?"

"From all over the world."

I stood there, contemplating. *All my life I thought I was different, and now I have confirmation that I am. Am I really going to walk away from the only person who believes in my gift?*

"You have little time, child," Isra pressed. A flash of lightning lit up the sky.

"OK," I said. "I'll do it!" More thunder rolled above us. This time the rain fell all at once, rushing down in sheets.

"Get in. I'll take you home." Isra slid into the driver's seat as I scurried to the other side of the car and hopped in.

14 OPHELIA CLARK

October 18

The rain raged with a viciousness that distorted the world beyond the windows of Isra's Lincoln, smudging the colors and reducing my view of the neighborhood homes, trees, and lawns to blobs. As Isra brought the car to a stop in front of the blurry shape that was my house, I psyched myself up to get soaked while getting to my front door. Before I made a run for it, I turned toward her.

"So what happens now?" I asked.

"This is the part where you get out," Isra answered with a coy smile. I gave a reluctant nod as I took my jacket off to use as a make-shift tarp over my head. I reached for the door handle, but stopped when I felt Isra's hand on my shoulder. "Just one more thing," she said. "Always trust your intuition. It will keep you safe." I nodded once more and stepped out into the storm.

"When will I see you again?" I asked, peering into the open passenger door, the cold shower from above hitting my back and running down my legs.

"Complete the challenge. I will find you. Now hurry on inside, child. You'll catch your death out there." Isra shooed me away with her hand. Still confused and overwhelmed, I gave her a strained smile, swung the heavy door closed, and dashed into my house.

"Ophelia, is that you?" Mom called out from the kitchen. She had started dinner, and the smell of chicken and potatoes roasting in the oven filled the entire house. My stomach rumbled in anticipation. After the day I had, I was starving.

"Hi, Mom," I shouted back as I slipped off my sopping shoes and threw my jacket onto the coat rack to dry off.

"I was just about to call you. It's raining cats and dogs out there." She looked up from her cutting board as I poked my head into the kitchen.

"Is it?" I played dumb.

"Very cute, O. Why don't you take that smart mouth of yours upstairs and get yourself washed up? Dinner will be ready in twenty minutes." She continued chopping, tossing tomato slices into the salad bowl beside her.

"Uh huh," I grunted, disappearing around the corner and making my way to my room.

I closed the door behind me, pulled the dark blue and gold stone necklace out of my pocket, and looked for a good place to put it.

"Please let this work," I whispered to no one as I lifted the top corner of my mattress and stuffed the stone as close to the center of the bed as I could. As I changed out of my school clothes, I heard Mom yelling my name from the hallway.

"O-phe-li-a! What happened to your jacket?"

Crap. I had completely forgotten about the tear on the sleeve. In fact, I had forgotten about the wound on my arm. As I looked over the area, I could barely find the mark. It had healed. The only thing that remained was some dried blood, which I wiped away clean in the bathroom. *Incredible. Could Isra really teach me how to do this one day?*

"Ophelia!" Mom shouted again.

"Yeah, mom. I'm sorry. I don't know how that happened."

"I'll patch it up, but you need to be more responsible for your things. You're not a child anymore." I could hear her shuffling into the laundry room where she kept her sewing kit.

By the time I came downstairs, dinner was ready and Mom, Dad, and I ate with no further mention of the jacket or criticisms of my character. After I cleared the dishes, I told my parents I had a lot of homework to do and headed back up to my room for the rest of the night so I could be close to the covellite stone.

Ophelia stood in a patch of grass, her feet bare, the edges of her toenails caked with dirt. The white nightgown she wore remained pristine. The clouds, once again, loomed in ominous shades of gray, and the world as she saw it was veiled in shadow. Ophelia measured each step forward with care.

"Hello?" she called out. "Is anybody out there?" There was no answer. "Can you hear me?"

After a long moment of silence, she heard a dreadful, yet familiar, booming sound crackling through the air. She plugged her ears as the wind tousled her hair and ripped at her gown from every direction. Then there was another sound, and she stopped moving so she could listen. It came from far out in the distance and sounded like a woman's scream; faint at first, but growing louder and louder. Within seconds, the noise was so loud Ophelia thought a freight train would come roaring past her. She let the fear wash over her trembling body as she spun around, trying to pinpoint the source of the noise. But it was no use. The horrible shrieking was coming from everywhere and in every direction. She covered her ears with her hands, cowered to the ground, and waited for the unseen terror to pass.

Wincing and puffing, the girl slowly lifted her hands away from her head as the sound faded. Ophelia wanted nothing more than to curl up on the cold, wet sod, but knew she had to keep going. Summoning every ounce of courage, she stood up and shouted: "I hear you. I'm coming!" As she continued forward, the breeze softened, but the temperature dropped. She watched as the color of her fingers and toes transitioned from pink to gray to blue. She reached the smooth black ground with the yellow line. A white mist cascaded down around her. "Oh, no. Not again. The stone isn't working," Ophelia muttered to herself. But before the mist obscured her vision, she noticed the ground she was standing on was asphalt. "The yellow strip looks a lot like... I'm in a parking lot!" she said. Though she could no longer see what lay ahead of her, she quickened her steps, arms outstretched, until her hands touched something solid. She pounded her fist against it until a light flickered on. "A window maybe?" She cupped her hands around her eyes and tried to peer into the room beyond, but all she could make out were some blurry shadows. "Hello? Who's in there?" She shouted right before her coughing fit started. She was out of time, and it would be a matter of seconds before she'd be writhing on the ground. As she fixed her eyes on one spot inside the room, she struggled to draw breath, but something came into focus. The blurry shadows became silhouettes of people kneeling in a circle. Ophelia gasped.

The world disintegrated around her, and as her eyes strained to capture any and every detail, an image flashed before her. A white square with the number 7 printed in a large font in the center. In her last moments, she saw a pool of blood blossoming across her white nightgown, and she dropped to the ground. As she lay there dying, Isra's shadowed visage appeared through the mist.

"Wake," the old woman whispered.

At 3:33 AM, I woke up to the sounds of my own gasps. Propping myself up on one elbow, I turned on the lamp on my nightstand and reached for my journal. Still half terrified, I forced my shaking hand to scribble the words: *parking lot, window, circle of people, #7.*

I supposed the stone was working. In just one night, I extracted four more clues than I had any other night since this dream started over a month ago, but I was no closer to figuring out the identity of who I needed to save or how I would save them. Time was running out. I could feel it. I'd need to come up with something, and fast.

15 GLORY WALKER

October 18

We were late for Trent's appointment with Doctor Mayson today. It took me almost five minutes to convince him to get in the truck, and then there was an entire battle just gettin' him to buckle his seat belt. Lord knew he was gettin' pretty big, and it was becomin' harder and harder for me to control him; especially when he knew he was goin' somewhere he didn't wanna be. The only reason we made it to the appointment at all was because I bribed him with a trip to the ice cream shop afterward. That seemed to do the trick.

"I'm sorry, Mrs. Walker, but we called Trenton's name at 9:00. You weren't here, so we took the next patient," Norma, the receptionist, said as Trent and I approached the front desk. The heavy-set, tired woman took one look at my face and knew she was about to get an ear full. I'd be damned if I didn't see her face twitch as she mentally braced herself.

"Don't you 'Mrs. Walker' me, Norma. We are FIVE minutes behind schedule. Five!" I said. Norma pursed her lips and stared at somethin' behind me. I followed her eyes and realized that we weren't the only ones in the small, run-down clinic. I leaned over the reception desk so I could continue expressin' my frustrations more discretely. "Do you have any idea how hard it is to drag a ten-year-old autistic kid away from the T.V.?" I asked. Norma opened her mouth to say somethin', but I cut her off. "The answer is NO. No, you don't! So exactly how long do you plan on makin' us wait in here?" I held onto Trent with one arm and gave Norma a wide-eyed stare.

"Mrs. Walk-, excuse me. *Glory,*" she corrected herself and looked me in the eye. "Trenton is very next on our list. It shouldn't be more than another five minutes. Please have a seat and Doctor Mayson will be with you shortly," she said. I could see her strugglin' to keep her cool, and I knew there was nothin' to be done about it now, so there was no sense in carryin' on.

I kept my eyes on Norma but spoke to my son. "Go on, baby. Take a seat in one of the chairs." Trent stood next to me and rocked himself from side to side. He eyed the colorful bead maze sittin' on the floor by the children's corner. Norma busied herself with some paperwork and, seein' that I'd won the stare down, I guided Trent to one of the brown plastic seats. His rockin' got more intense and his fingers started flailin' as if he were physically touchin' the bead maze, spinnin' and movin' the wooden shapes across the wires.

"C'mon, Trent. You've got to sit or no ice cream," I said, rubbin' his arm. Trent started hummin' to himself. This usually meant he was gettin' agitated. I didn't blame him. I felt agitated too.

It was times like these I missed Cooper the most. Sure, the nights were tough, but the days were tougher. The times where nothin' seemed to go right were the worst - and man, there were a lot of them. It had been two years since Cooper's deployment to Syria. He would send me emails and we would video chat every chance he could, but it wasn't enough. I prayed for his safe return every day, and though I was proud to have a husband brave enough to serve, there were just some days when bein' a single mom to a special needs child was too hard. It didn't seem fair to me either. Sure, Coop was at war, but what about the war that I fought every day? No, I wasn't gettin' shot at, but I was dealin' with violent temper tantrums, emotional explosions, and melt downs on the regular. Every day with Trent was like bein' at war. Even for somethin' as simple as sittin' in this watin' room for a few minutes. Yes, my baby boy suffered a lot, and it broke my heart, but no one seemed to remember that I suffered too.

"What are *you* starin' at?" I asked a mother with her young son sittin' across from us. Trent didn't notice, but they were both watchin' him as he rocked and hummed in his chair. The mother quickly buried her nose in her magazine and instructed her son to play with the doll he brought with him.

"Thought so," I said, strokin' Trent's light brown hair. He didn't seem to notice that either.

"Trenton? The doctor will see you now," Norma announced, usherin' us through the heavy door beside her desk enclosure.

We were in and out in no time. Dr. Mayson said that Trent was physically developin' like any boy his age and that everythin' was progressin' as expected. Each time we visited his office, I secretly hoped that Dr. Mayson would tell us about some new advancement in science; some miracle drug that would help Trent live a more normal life. But he never did, and today was no different. The war at home raged on.

With Trent full of ice cream and happily back in front of the T.V. in our livin' room, I sat on the couch holdin' a partially knitted throw project that my nanna started about a year ago.

She was a resilient woman and would've never let those people at the doctor's office get to her. Nanna raised six children on her own and didn't take crap from no one. She could be soft too, though. I remember how she'd bake oatmeal-raisin cookies every time I visited her when I was Trent's age. She would time them perfectly, so they'd be sittin' on the coolin' tray as soon as I walked in the door. I'd eat at least eight of them before the cinnamon, sugar, and gooey chunks of raisins felt like lead in my belly. Then I'd sit with her in her livin' room, where she'd be knittin' up a storm. I'd help her by unravelin' her yarn and keepin' it slack while she clicked her needles together and made entire blankets in just days.

She taught me how to knit too. Well, just the basic stitches, but I still remembered how. She never came right out and said so, but I could tell that I was her favorite grandchild. Whenever I was in a room full of my cousins, she always called me over to help her in the kitchen or to show me this or that. Maybe it was because of how much time I spent with her on my own, or maybe it was because we looked exactly alike. We shared the same shade of cornflower blond hair, the same turned-up nose, and the same full apple cheeks. As I got older, it only seemed right that I inherited her pear-shaped figure, forever cursed with tryin' to buy a pair of pants that fit. But that's life, I suppose.

When she passed away last year, I found a partial blanket she'd been workin' on, just sittin' there in her knittin' basket. Her needles were still in place, and she'd bought enough yarn for the whole thing. Momma told me I should take it. She said that Nanna would be so proud if I finished her project for her. I loved the idea, but in all this time I hadn't been able to bring myself to start.

The pattern Nanna had stitched up was simple enough for me to copy. As I sat there rememberin' her, and thinkin' about Cooper bein' away, and how far Momma and Daddy were livin' from us now, I realized that the only thing keepin' me sane was that pile of yarn. I held the soft wool to my cheek and smiled, breathin' in a faint wisp of Nana's signature perfume; White Diamonds.

16 BLAKE JONES

October 18

Mom and Gary were fighting again.

"I... DON'T... CARE, Jolene! The school don't need to be call'n me at my JOB!" Gary emphasized the word 'job' by slapping a can of beer off one of the end tables. I heard the can hit the wall that separated the living room from the den, and I cringed. Mom was smart enough to never come home with beer in glass bottles. She learned that pretty early on after Gary moved in. In fact, she learned many new tricks, like how to avoid making eye contact to appear less threatening, how to take Gary's side no matter how stupid or wrong he was, and how to cover up bruises with drug store makeup.

I turned down my music and pressed my ear to the wall, careful to avoid the spot where the dingy wallpaper had peeled.

"I'm sorry, babe. I must have been in the shower when they called me. I told them to only use your number for emergencies. I *told* them." Mom sounded tired. It didn't surprise me she went straight to trick #2 and tried to put the blame on someone else. It was the smartest move to deescalate situations like this.

"And what do I care that Austin's drawin' pictures? He's in kindergarten, ain't he? He's supposed to be doin' pictures and paints and shit!" Garry huffed.

"You're right, hon. When I asked him what happened, he told me that the entire class was drawing pictures," Mom hesitated, then added, "I'm guessing his teacher was expressing concern for the *type* of pictures Austin was drawing. She seems to be on the sensitive side, though he showed me what he drew, and the images *were* pretty violent." She was walking a tightrope with that one. I held my breath in anticipation of what would come next.

"That's what little boys do. They're rough. They break things. They smash things. They draw things. He's got a good imagination." Gary seemed to calm down now, but I knew that the smallest thing could set him off again.

"I'll take care of that tender-hearted teacher of his tomorrow. I'll set her straight," Mom assured him. They continued talking, but lowered their voices. Then someone flicked on the T.V. which was sitting in a console just opposite the wall I had my ear to, and all I could hear was the theme song to *Family Feud.* I concluded everything would be fine in there and went back to messing around on my computer.

Austin was going to be messed up when he got older. I didn't see things going any other way. How was he supposed to amount to anything when his dad was a drunk-ass, violent piece-of-crap who barked out orders to everyone and never lifted a finger? I was sure the only reason that asshole married my mom was so that he could have someone wait on him and his kid hand-and-foot. She'd never admit it, but I bet if my dad had life insurance, Mom would never have looked twice at this guy.

Things would have been better if Mike was still here. Yeah, he put me through a lot of crap when we were growing up, but that's what big brothers were for, right? Mike left when Mom and Gary started dating about a year ago. He knew the jerk was bad news and packed up all his belongings in a bag, hopped on a greyhound, and traveled halfway across the country. The last I heard, he got a job as a mechanic and was living with a girlfriend he met online. The day he left, we got into a nasty fight. I hated him for abandoning Mom with this loser. Mike was the big, strong jock of the family. He could've protected her. Not like me and my skinny ass. For all the horrible things I said to him before he took off, I hoped he was OK and that he knew I didn't mean it. Looking back on it, I can admit that I was jealous, and if I could disappear like he did, I probably would've. But my time would come. In two years and thirty-six days, I'd be eighteen and out of here for good. I'd have my bag packed the night before my birthday and disappear before dawn. I would start a whole new life and leave all of this crap. Sure, I'd feel bad about leaving Mom and Austin, but they needed to make their own choices. We all did.

"Dinner will be ready at 6:30," Mom smiled as she poked her head into the den. She held a basket of dirty laundry against her hip, though the days-old t-shirt and sweatpants combo she was wearing should have been in the pile too. Her greasy blond hair was in a messy bun and her smudged eyeliner weighed heavily on her bottom lids. Mom was beautiful, but the time she spent with Gary was chipping away at her, and it showed. Before I could respond, she was already halfway down the hall, clearly on a mission to get the wash started before she had to cook. My stomach growled, and I looked at my watch. I definitely needed a snack, so I headed to the kitchen.

"Why don't you keep your li'l brother in line?" Gary asked, clearly drunk and hanging onto the kitchen's door frame to steady himself.

"Huh?" I pushed the hair out of my face. *Was this guy still talking about the kid's drawings?*

"You heard me, you li'l shit," Gary spat. He slurred his speech. *Note to self: proceed with caution.*

"You know that me and Austin don't go to the same school, right?" I slipped past him and grabbed a Coke from the fridge. He stunk of stale booze, body odor, and loads of cheap cologne. The hairs on the back of my neck stood up. Major red flag. Before I could close the fridge door, Gary's hand was swinging through the air and caught me on the side of the head. I stumbled backward.

"Don't you talk back to me, you fairy." Gary's hulking frame loomed over mine like a bear staring down a rabbit.

"I wasn't talking back." I threw my arms up to protect my face as Gary took another swing. This time, he connected with my forearms and sent me careening back. I toppled over a kitchen chair. The son-of-a-bitch stood over me and scoffed as he watched me scramble to take cover under the table. *Does he really expect me to fight him?* He was huge and crazy as hell.

"That's right, folks. He's hiding like a li'l sissy coward," Gary announced to no one as he sauntered out of the kitchen. "You'd better toughen up, boy. There's a lot meaner things in this world than me," he called out over his shoulder from the hallway. I remained shaking under the table until I heard him settle into his reclining chair and start flipping channels on the T.V. Then I slinked up to my bedroom. There was no way I was coming down for dinner tonight.

The entire rest of the evening, I kept thinking about how much I hated him. I prayed and prayed that something would happen to him, and he'd be gone. Anything would do. Liver failure, car wreck, lightning strike; I'd take it. Then there was a knock at the front door. I peeked out the window and saw a cop car parked right out front. A neighbor must've heard the yelling from earlier. This wouldn't be the first time someone called the cops to check in on us.

I opened my bedroom door as quietly as I could and crept across the carpeted hallway until I reached the staircase so I could see what was going on. Mom answered the door, but she only opened it wide enough to fit her face through. I couldn't make out what she and the cop were saying. It was raining pretty hard, and the downpour was drowning out their voices. When Mom opened the door wider, I got a good look at the officer, and he got a good look at me. I froze. *Would he take Gary away if I said something right now? Would mom ever forgive me?* Gary started shouting from the family room, demanding to know what was happening. When mom told him a cop was at the door, he stumbled his drunk ass into the hallway to join her. I stared silently through the spindles of the railing as

Mom and Gary convinced the officer that everything was fine. And just like that, the cop left. I went back to my room and, since the cops weren't taking Mom's boyfriend to jail, I resumed my prayers for cirrhosis to take him to the grave.

17 CAMERON CAITIFF

October 19

"Calling O-four-seven, calling O-four-seven," Marge's elderly voice crackled more than my truck's radio equipment. She'd been working dispatch in Morson County for thirty-eight years and had been a smoker since she was fifteen.

"This is O-four-seven. Go ahead." I held the radio close to my mouth and talked slow and loud so the old bat could hear me. There was nothing more frustrating that having to repeat myself.

"Cammy, we got a call from Mayor Winnifred at his house. He sounded distressed. All I could get out of him was that he needed an officer right away. Can you get over there real quick?" she asked.

"Marge, I told you to quit calling me Cammy. Do you think the dispatch out in Atlanta addresses their officers that way?" I warned, but I knew she didn't respect me, even with the badge. Boomers had a hard time working with people my age and there wasn't much we could do about it except wait for the old farts to die off. I made a U-turn on Main Street and headed to the mayor's place. "Is someone still on the line with him? What am I getting myself into?"

"He wouldn't say - just asked for us to send a car. He sounded real shook up before he hung up the phone, though," she said.

I flipped on my truck's red and blue flashing lights and hit the gas.

"O-four-seven responding." I put the radio down, turned the siren on, and sped toward the mayor's house. These were the calls I became a cop for.

I was in the subdivision within minutes. I turned off the siren, but kept the flashing lights on. Though it was a sunny day, there were very few people out. I was hoping there'd be a couple of bystanders near the mayor's home. People loved filming officers in action and posting it on social media, so I ran a hand through my hair just in case. I parked my truck on the road and made my way up the long driveway. Everything was quiet out there. The lawn was pristine and the evergreen shrubs leading up to the blue colonial looked freshly clipped. Two white columns and some fancy window trim framed a red door painted the exact color of Winnifred's 2010 Corvette Stingray. The man had great taste in cars. I'll give him that. I peered into the tinted windows, but no one was in it. A house like this sent a message. It was a signal to the world that an important man lived here. *And I'm here to save that man.* My adrenaline was pumping. I couldn't wait to see what was going on in there. From where I stood, the possibilities were endless. I rested my hand on my firearm and knocked on the door. *This is it. It's GO time.*

The heavy-set mayor opened the door dressed in a navy wool suit, white cotton shirt, and a red silk tie. He was out of breath and had small beads of sweat running down his forehead.

"Officer! I'm so glad you're here. Please come in." Mayor Winnifred stepped back so I could enter. My heart was racing, but something felt off. The house was too quiet. The mayor removed his glasses and wiped a tear from his eye before it could roll down his cheek. He shoved the frames back on, took a deep breath and put a hand on my shoulder. I stiffened, but when I realized it was just us, I downgraded my assessment of the threat level to yellow.

"Mr. Mayor, are you alright? What's happened here?"

"I desperately need your help." He stared into my eyes.

"How is that, Sir?" I could feel the man's warm, meaty hand squeezing my shoulder a little tighter and resisted an outward cringe. *Why was the man still touching me?* Mayor Winnifred struggled to get the words out while I waited, feeling irritated and intrigued at the same time. Finally, he blurted out the reason he dialed the Morson County Police.

"Snowball is *missing*!" he said.

"I'm sorry. Did you say a snowball?" I realized my hand was still on my holstered weapon and let it go, though the temptation to use it on myself was growing. This was obviously a bullshit call. I reached for my notepad and pen.

"Snowball is my chocolate Labrador. She's gone." The mayor pulled out his handkerchief and dabbed at his eyes again.

"And you believe someone stole the dog from your home?" I asked, still hopeful that there was a valid reason for me to be there.

"I don't think so. I let her out into the yard this morning. When I called for her to come inside, she didn't respond. I asked my wife to bring her in so I could get ready to go into the office. Larissa went outside and came back yelling that the gate was open. That was at 8:00 AM." The lump in his throat strangled his voice. "My wife and my assistant have been out looking for her all morning. I'm supposed to be giving a speech at the town's square this afternoon, but I can't concentrate on anything while my little girl is still out there."

This guy has got to be kidding me! Am I seriously here to look for a runaway dog? How humiliating. I did my best to keep my composure as I noted the details of "the case". I heard the front door open behind me and turned to see a well-dressed, ample woman in her fifties and a much younger woman with stunning eyes and a short skirt walk into the house. The mayor's face twitched with a flash of hope until he saw both women had entered without Snowball.

"Officer, this is my wife, Larissa, and my assistant, Lanore." The weary mayor introduced the ladies. We exchanged greetings. I guess I held my handshake with the assistant a little too long, but she had my full attention. *Maybe this wasn't a total waste of time.* She pulled her hand away and wouldn't look me in the eye the entire time she stood there. *Shy. I like that.*

"I'm sorry, honey. We covered a lot of ground, but didn't see any sign of her. It's time for us to get you ready and start heading to the square. I'm sure the officer will handle the situation quickly and with care. Won't you?" Larissa said, looking up expectantly. *Am I being pranked?*

"Well, actually..." I said, struggling to find the words to explain that this was not a police matter.

"Here, take this." Larissa handed me the dog's leash. *This is truly an elaborate joke.* I looked around for hidden cameras. *I swear, if I find out this is some kind of prank - if someone is messing with me to make me look stupid on the job, I'll break every bone in their body.*

"Umm. Yes, ma'am," I said. "Not to worry, Mr. Mayor. I'll do my best to bring your do- I mean *Snowball* home safely." *Why did I get out of bed this morning?* "Can I get a phone number from you, ma'am?" I asked Lanore, flashing her a smile. "I won't be able to reach the mayor if he's giving his speech." Licking my lips, I looked her over. She had nothing but daggers in her eyes for me. *So it's like that, huh? You think you're too good for me?* I pitied any sucker who tried to approach her in a bar. The mayor's wife stepped between us.

"Here, take mine." She handed me her business card. *Strike 2. I bet God is having a nice little chuckle at my expense right now.*

I fed Winifred a bunch of bull about how he'd be hearing from me soon, shook the man's hand, and headed to my truck. I tossed the leash onto the passenger seat, then drove around the neighborhood for two hours, slowing down to peer into bushes and around trash bins while praying for Marge's voice to come squawking through the radio with some urgent call. That call never came.

Assuming the Mayor's speech would be over soon, I went back to his house to check the fence one last time before calling it quits. I remembered how, when I was a kid, we had this dumb dog, Russ. That mutt would take off all the time, but he would always find his way home, and I figured it was worth a shot. When I got there, I headed straight for the mayor's backyard, leash in hand, and I closed the gate behind me.

"Snowball? Come here. Wanna go for a walk? Snowbaaaaaaalllllll." It didn't take more than a few seconds for the chocolate lab to come bursting out from underneath a tree in the yard. She was panting and dehydrated, but otherwise fine. "There you are, you miserable thing," I muttered as I clipped her leash onto her collar and led her to the garden hose to let her drink. When she finished, she soaked my hand with a slobbery kiss. *Gross.* I wiped my wet hand on my pants as the dog took off, running back to the shady spot under the tree, dragging her leash behind her. I called the mayor's wife and let her know Snowball was safe in the yard, and she thanked me for the outstanding police work. *Was she serious? That's strike 3. I need a scotch.*

I headed straight to my ranch in Costwick and figured I'd fill out the paperwork on Winifred's dog tomorrow. Though my place sat on two acres, the house itself was only 1000 square feet and, since I lived alone, that suited me just fine. Grabbing a glass and a bottle of cheap single malt out of the kitchen cupboard, I flipped on the TV and plopped myself down onto the uncomfortable15-year-old sofa my parents sent me off with when I moved out. A breaking news report came flashing across the screen and I turned the volume up.

"The SWAT team was called to the quiet neighborhood of North Buckhead in Atlanta after a local resident opened fire in his yard. A witness heard gun shots around 2:00 PM and called police. Before the officers could arrive, the man barricaded himself, his wife, their two children, and a neighbor in the suburban home." An expressionless female reporter held a bulky microphone and spoke into the camera. Behind her was a ribbon of yellow police-tape and the house where the shooting occurred. I leaned in closer, mesmerized by the news story, and absentmindedly chewed off all the fingernails on my right hand.

"Police arrived on the scene and established contact with the man via his cell phone and, after three hours of negotiating, they coaxed the man into releasing the neighbor. Once freed from the home, Mrs. Keswicki could explain to the officers that she was visiting with the wife in the backyard when the husband came home. The husband and wife got into an argument and tensions ran high. The husband became frustrated and when he walked away, the two women laughed. When the husband returned to his back-yard, he had a gun with him.

The two women attempted to escape by running to the front lawn. This is when the man started shooting wildly, stopping the women in their tracks and forcing them to get inside the house. Once inside, the wife, children, and neighbor were told to remain in the kitchen while the husband blocked the nearest exit; the front door.

With this information, police could surprise the husband by throwing a smoke bomb through a plate-glass window opposite the kitchen. They broke down the front door, where they apprehended the man and took him into custody. The wife and children were directed to safety.

Tonight, officers Billy Rushford and Chuck Benson are being hailed as heroes for their leadership and ability to diffuse the situation without the loss of life or serious injuries to any of the parties involved," the reporter said. The station flashed portraits of the police officers and before I knew it, my teeth were gnashing at the nails on my left hand. I tore off a sliver and spit it out onto the shag rug, staring at the officer's faces. Those cops were in their 30s, just like me. We were in the prime of our lives. And what was *I* doing? I was here, in Morson County, looking for lost dogs. I didn't sign up for that crap. What was the point of going to police academy training if I never got to use it on the job? Yeah, I looked bad-ass in my uniform, but the only time I ever got to draw my weapon was at the gun range. I got into the best shape of my life going through the academy and for what? To help old broads cross the street? I didn't want to end up like those other guys at the station, waiting out the clock until retirement. I had way too much time between now and then. I needed excitement and action. I needed to move to the station in *Atlanta,* where *real* cops did *real* hero shit.

18 OPHELIA CLARK

October 23

As soon as I walked up the steps to Dr. Miller's place, I knew I didn't want to go inside, despite the inviting front yard. The trimmed hedges were neat and square, and the fall flowers were in bloom, but there was something ominous hanging in the air. Maybe I was just remembering the way the house used to creep me out before the doctor moved in and fixed it up. All the town gossip about the witch who died there didn't help either, but there was no getting out of this now. I needed to get this session over with.

I waved at Mom, who was sitting in the car, but she refused to drive away until she saw me go inside, so I knocked at the door. The second I did, I felt something curl around my right ankle, and I gasped. The thing slithered a figure eight formation around each of my legs and made a soft rumbling sound. My body froze in panic, but when I finally worked up the nerve to look down, I realized it was a cat. A gray and black striped Shorthair with bright yellow eyes.

"Hello there!" I said, nervously laughing away my fear. The cat let out a soft meow and hopped onto the steps of the porch, never taking its eyes off me. If I didn't know better, I would've thought it was signaling me to follow. I crouched down on the top step to give it a little pat, and as I did, the cat continued to purr, squeezing its eyes closed in pure bliss. I smiled as I rubbed the tips of my fingers around its ears and down its neck, happy for the furry and calming distraction.

As soon as the front door opened, the cat jumped from the step and took off like its tail was on fire. And when I stood up to meet the doctor, I understood why. Remembering Mom was watching, I took in a deep breath and tried to keep calm.

19 CHARLOTTE MILLER

October 23

It was mid-afternoon when there was a knock at the door. I opened it to find a teenage girl sitting on the top step of the wrap-around porch. She appeared to be petting a small animal on a lower stair, but I couldn't see it.

"You must be Ophelia. I'm Doctor Miller, but you can call me Charlotte." The girl stood up to face me, but when I extended my hand, she did not reciprocate the greeting. Her eyes were wide, like she had seen a ghost. A car slowly inched across the road and a woman waved from the driver's side. I waved back, and the car drove away. "Was that your mother?" I asked. The young girl flicked her eyes to meet mine for a second and gave a curt nod, which seemed to help her gain her composure.

"I, um, I like your cat," she said.

"Oh?" I raised my eyebrows and looked around the yard. "I don't have a cat. It must belong to a neighbor. Come on in." I ushered the girl inside and led the way to my office. Ophelia followed tentatively and sat on the very edge of the love seat cushion. She looked like she was ready to make a break for it. I closed the door to the office, grabbed my stack of forms and notebook, and took a seat on the wing chair in front of her. Coming face to face with a patient again felt surreal. I had forgotten how much I loved helping people and was eager to get back to my life's work. "Let's start with some simple questions." I tried to put her at ease. The poor thing was practically shaking. "Have you ever met with a psychologist before?" I opened up my pad and began scribbling notes - patient's name, date, etcetera. The paper felt good in the crook of my arm and the ink from my pen flowed with grace and precision. The muscle memory filled me with a renewed sense of purpose and control.

"No," Ophelia answered.

"A first-timer!" I smiled. "Not to worry. Let me explain what I do." I leaned back in my seat, attempting to get my patient to mirror me, but Ophelia remained uncomfortably perched on the small couch. "I talk with people to assess, diagnose, and treat them for issues with their mental health to improve their overall quality of life. The men and women that I work with are just everyday people. There is a common misconception that only crazy people see doctors like me." I emphasized the word crazy with air quotes. "Mental health is very important to maintain, and the issues I treat people for are often temporary. It's like to going to the doctor when you have a broken leg. The major difference is that the problems I help with are not something you can see from the outside. Some people take longer to heal than others, the same way that some people take longer to heal physically than others. Does that make sense?" I watched for understanding, trying to project a cheerful demeanor.

Ophelia made brief eye contact with me and gave a nervous nod in the affirmative.

"Good. I will ask you to fill out this questionnaire when you get home so I can better understand your specific situation." I handed her the pages. She was reluctant to take them from me, but once they were in her hand, she folded them in half and stuffed them into the inside pocket of her denim jacket. "For now, I'd like to start with an open dialog. Let's try this one first: Why are you here?" I asked.

Ophelia's face twitched. New patients always had a hard time with that one. They thought they had already given the reason at the time they made the appointment, but there was always more to the story. I waited for her to answer, but she just stared at the wall-hanging behind me. As I studied the girl's appearance a little more closely, I noticed Ophelia looked forlorn. Her eyes were heavy and burdened, like the eyes of a much older woman. I shifted uncomfortably. *Why is this girl's stare so unnerving? Why isn't she responding?*

"Ophelia? Are you alright?"

20 OPHELIA CLARK

October 23

A wave of nausea washed over me the moment the therapist opened the door. The pungent odor of rotten meat mixed with urine and feces was overwhelming. I knew the previous owner had died in the house, but it smelled like she was still in there. I didn't blame the porch cat for taking off in such a hurry. The blood drained from my face, and I thought I'd be sick on the spot, but as soon as the therapist spoke to me, the horrible stench vanished. It didn't fade or get carried off in the breeze. It just wasn't there, as if I'd only imagined it. I followed Doctor Miller inside and tried not to think about it, though I wondered if Isra's crystal was messing with my perception of places and things.

I didn't know anything about Victorian style, but the inside of the house looked more modern than the outside. Even Doctor Charlotte was a lot younger than I thought she'd be. She had kind eyes and a pleasant smile, but when I sat down on the couch, I struggled with how much I should say to her. On the one hand, I wanted to confide in her and tell her all about the shadow dreams, and how I met Isra, and the huge challenge I was facing in order to prove myself as a divine bender. *Doctor-patient confidentiality, right?* On the other, I felt like there was something off about her. She seemed nice enough, but my gut told me not to trust her so quickly.

As Doctor Charlotte gave her song and dance about what she does, I couldn't take my eyes off the picture that was hanging on the wall in her office. It was a photo of some hills at dawn. I thought it was beautiful, but it made me sad at the same time. As I continued staring at it, an image popped into my head. I daydreamed about a boy who looked like he was around my age, and he was running down a street as fast as he could. He had acne all over his face, and dark circles under his eyes. The kid was wearing a dark hoodie and jeans, but the most memorable thing about him was how terrified he looked. I didn't need to see who was chasing him to understand that he had seen his last sunrise - and he knew it. As he ran, the image of his face faded away into the darkness of the picture, and my vision disappeared.

Snapping out of my daydream, I tried to refocus on what Doctor Charlotte was saying, but something else caught my attention. Out of the corner of my eye, I noticed a dark, shapeless shadow oozing up through the floorboards and then creeping up to and along the wall. At first, it reminded me of the dark figure from my dreams. *Could there be another like Isra? How am I seeing this while I'm awake?* Then the shadow swelled to the size of an extra-large bedspread and crawled along the ceiling. *Woah. Whatever this is, it's nothing like Isra.* I was both confused and fascinated by it. My heart pounded and my body shook. There was something very disturbing about this place.

"Ophelia?"

I heard a muffled noise that sounded like my name, but I continued watching the shadow until it squeezed into the tiny crevice between the light fixture and ceiling and disappeared.

21 CHARLOTTE MILLER

October 23

"Ophelia, are you alright?" I repeated. Ophelia met my eyes as if she had just woken from a dream.

"Oh, um. I'm sorry, what was the question?"

"I was asking you why you are here. Why did you come to therapy today?"

"I guess it's because my mom made me?" she answered as a question and cast her eyes downward.

"And why do you think she did that?"

"Dr. Li told her I should see a psychologist, and she believes he is right about absolutely everything."

"I see." I scribbled in my notepad: *Smart. Critical thinker*. "And what do *you* believe? Do you think you need to see a psychologist?"

"No, not really."

"Why is that?"

"Because I don't think what's happening to me is in any of your textbooks." Ophelia's words were blunt, though she practically whispered.

"I see. Well, why don't you tell me what is happening, and we will see if we can work through it together. How does that sound?" I knew I had to maintain control of the conversation. I wasn't about to let my first patient in Monroe write me off before I even got started.

Ophelia shifted her gaze from her shoes to my face and sat staring at me for what felt like minutes. *Steady now. She needs to be the next to talk.* It took all my strength not to break the silence.

"You wouldn't believe me if I told you," the girl finally said, though she was so quiet I had to strain my ears to hear her.

"That's the beauty of our relationship, Ophelia. I don't *need* to believe you. All I need to know is that *you* believe it. This will be the source of truth that I work with," I said, internally questioning the appropriateness of my response. *Wasn't the plight of all 16-year-old girls to be taken seriously? Did I just ruin that for her?* Ophelia took in a deep breath as my self-doubt crept into my head.

"It's too crazy. You wouldn't understand." She shook her head and fidgeted in her seat.

"Look, Ophelia. I'm not here to judge you. I'm only here to help," I said, struggling to keep a calm, controlled, and friendly demeanor.

"Really? Do you know how to change someone's *future?* What can you tell me about how to cheat death?" Ophelia asked, visibly distressed.

"Ok. Let's talk about that. I can tell you it's perfectly normal to be afraid of dying. No one knows what the future holds. Life is full of uncertainty and mystery. That's what makes it interesting. What happens tomorrow has yet to be written."

"And *that's* why you can't help me," she said. Her tired, upturned eyes were full of disillusionment. She stood up from the love seat. And before I could react, Ophelia dashed out of my office and out the front door. I tried to call after her, but I struggled to find the right words. My mouth still agape, I watched through the window as the girl hurried down the porch steps to the sidewalk, where she disappeared from sight.

Staring through the glass and contemplating what I should have done differently, I saw something that tore me from my thoughts, and I gasped. I held my breath as I watched, paralyzed by fear. A shadow stepped out from behind one of the oak trees in the front yard and walked along the side of the house toward the back. *Who is in my yard and what do they want?* I forced myself away from the window and ran to the back door in the kitchen. Setting the lock, I yanked on the handle to make sure the entry was secure. My heart pounding in my ears, I leaned against the door and listened for the potential intruder. The sound of birds chirping alerted me to a window I had opened to freshen the house with the fall breeze. One thing I enjoyed about this house was how much light the large windows let in, but all I could think about now was that they were big enough for a person to crawl through.

Peeling away from the door, I crept toward the window by the breakfast nook. As quietly as I could, I slid it down, but it got stuck halfway. *Damn these old things.* Stepping back, I peeked into the yard, but from my vantage point, I could see no one. Gripping my fingers at the top of the window frame, I pulled it downward, using all my weight. The window moved a few more inches and jammed only a foot away from the sill. Shaking off my fingers, I tried one more time, and as the window moved down the casing, a dark object appeared from the sky and rushed straight toward me. The window came down with an audible thud as flecks of blood splashed into my face. I screamed in terror.

A Mourning dove's head fell to the floor while its body twitched and flapped grotesquely on the other side of the glass. I stood there, watching it in horrified disbelief. Before I could catch my breath, a loud bang from the front of the house snapped me out of my state of shock. Wide eyed and trembling, I made my way across the kitchen and into the hallway with careful, silent steps so I could listen. As I inspected each room, all appeared to be in its place until I got to my office, where I discovered the source of the loud noise. The picture on the wall had once again fallen straight down to the floor. I inspected the nail and even tried to wiggle it, but it stayed firmly embedded into the wall, and I hung the picture back up with extra care. *What in the world is going on here?*

Once I was sure there was no one was in the house, I went back into the kitchen to perform the grim task of cleaning up the mess with the bird. Wincing, I swept the head into a dustpan and sponged up the blood with a wet paper towel. Forcing the window back open, I picked up its decapitated corpse with a pair of salad tongs and discarded both the bird and the tongs into the waste bin and then brought the bag out to the garage. I was still shaking when I returned to my office to finish my write up on Ophelia's session, but the bottle of Cab Franc I brought with me worked wonders. The first drink made my cheeks flush, but the second one settled my nerves. I was ready to focus.

As I replayed the session with the girl in my mind, a strange feeling settled over me like a fog. I wrote in my notebook, my hand tingling and operating as if possessed by an unseen force. I observed my movements with detached fascination. The loops and swoops of the pen against the paper were smooth as the words formed on the page: *Guarded, fixated on death, resistant to therapy. Visible physical signs of stress and fatigue. Behavior is reminiscent of former patient Daniel Larson. Tread carefully.* The tingling stopped there, and as I gave myself a shake, I snapped back into concentrating on the task at hand and completed my assessment of Ophelia.

By the time I finished, I felt exhausted, and not at all in the mood to prepare a proper dinner - not after what happened in the kitchen today. Shrugging it off, I brought the remaining wine and a sleeve of crackers up to my bedroom, where I retired for the rest of the evening. As the hours passed, dusk gave way to night and, in the darkness, the wind at my windows sounded like whispers and giggles. I couldn't help but think about the Larson boy. When my bottle was empty, I tucked myself into bed and pulled my comforter up over my ears, the ghosts of my past swirling and dancing across my dizzied thoughts of the strangeness of the day.

22 GLORY WALKER

October 25

Trent was already watchin' cartoons in the family room when I woke up this mornin'. I swear, I could set my watch by this boy. He got up at 6:30 AM every day. Now that he was older, he could fix himself a bowl of cereal and flip on the T.V. on his own (thank the Lord).

I walked down the steps in my blue terry-cloth robe, coverin' my ratty white tank top I used as a nightshirt and my pair of boy shorts. The carpet absorbed the sound of my steps, but Trenton was so focused on his program he wouldn't have heard a cannon if it went off beside him.

"Mornin', Trent," I passed behind him and made my way to the kitchen. Trenton sat cross-legged on the floor and gently rocked himself, completely unaware of me. I set the coffee to brewin' and opened the kitchen window to get some fresh air. When the warm sun touched my face, it gave me an idea and as soon as the coffee was ready, I grabbed the pot and poured as much as would fit into a thermos. The last few drips hit the warmin' plate with a hiss and scattered about until they burned away.

"Trent? Get dressed, honey, we're goin' to the park today," I hollered over the sound of the T.V. There was no way we were gonna spend this beautiful Saturday mornin' indoors, so I packed my coffee, Nanna's knittin' project, and a juice box for Trent, and off we went. Halfway to the park, I realized I was still wearin' my nightshirt and hoped the gray sweater I threw on top of it covered me enough. Trent looked sweet in his red windbreaker and jeans, and when I realized the top of his head now reached the height of my chin, my emotions got the best of me, and I had to fight back a lump in my throat. When did my boy get so big? I ruffled his hair with my hand. He smoothed it again, and we just kept walkin'.

Trent squealed with excitement once he could see the playground. It was buzzin' with children all around, their mothers all sittin' in clusters. He picked up his pace.

"Hold on, hon." I reached for a tissue in my bag and pulled Trent's face toward me. Holdin' his chin up with my fingers, I dabbed the saliva that pooled at the corners of his mouth. Over the years, I've learned that parents can be crueler than kids. I looked into his eyes, wishin' for him to look back into mine and smile so we could share a moment, but he was in his own world - a world I could never reach. I stuffed the moist tissue into my sweater pocket. "Ok, go on." I didn't need to say it twice. Trent ran across the field and headed straight for the swings. I took the longer way along the paved pathway. When I got to the benches where the other mothers were sittin', I pretended not to notice the way they glanced at me and cringed. I didn't feel like knittin' anymore. I took in a deep breath. *Just enjoy the day, Glory.* I pulled out Trent's juice box and offered it to him, but I couldn't get his attention, so I pulled out my thermos and poured the coffee into the cap and felt better. Why was holdin' a steamin' cup so comfortin'? I gripped onto that thing as if my life depended on it.

Trenton stood to the side, hypnotized by three little girls who were swingin' forward and back. They squealed each time they went up high and gasped for air when they swung back down. As I took in the scenery, my eyes landed on another nearby bench, and I recognized a lady named June. Her son went to the same school as Trent, though he was a year younger, and they didn't share any classes. She got up from the bench and stood next to the leftmost swing.

"Good mornin'," I said, eyin' her chestnut hair. She'd styled it into a perfect French braid.

"Hi," she said, stiffly. But there was somethin' about seein' a familiar face that made me feel less awkward and out of place.

"How are ya?"

"I'm alright. Keeping busy, rushing around like crazy. You know how it is," the small woman answered. This is when I noticed the little girl on the swing was dressed like a miniature version of her mom. Right down to the cream sweater and pearl earrings.

"Of course. A mother's work is never done, right?" I smiled, hatin' myself for playin' along with the superficial chit-chat, but I did it for Trent. "Anyway," I continued, "I'm glad I bumped into you. My boy has been talkin' about how your Thomas is havin' a birthday party at Pizza Play Palace. Trent is really sweet, but he keeps forgettin' to bring the invitation home so I can properly RSVP."

"Ah, right. Our kids's school. That's where I know you from. I'm such a scatterbrain. I'm sorry. What's your name again?" June asked.

"Oh, you're fine. It's Glory." By this time, the other mothers had shifted their attention to our conversation and started creepin' over.

"Glory, of course. And your son is Trenton?" June looked around, possibly searchin' for the words to end the conversation. Failin' to find any, she said, "You know, we didn't send out paper invitations. The party is next Saturday at 11:30 AM." She strained a thin-lipped smile.

"June." A woman with a slicked back ponytail stepped forward from the small group of mothers that had gathered around us. "You know her son is *sick*, right?" She whispered the word "sick" and gestured at my boy not just ten feet away from me. My body stiffened. I knew people talked behind my back, but I was standin' right there, for heaven's sake.

"My boy ain't 'sick'. He's autistic," I said, glarin' at her. June glanced around and realized that all eyes were on the two of us. I continued my conversation with her, but didn't take my eyes off the woman with the ponytail. "June, I fully intend to accompany my son, so you wouldn't have to stress about watch'n over him."

"Well, I think that would be helpful -" June started, but was quickly cut off.

"He *bites*, June," ponytail lady said. "I don't think it's fair to put the other kids in danger. You don't want to deal with that kind of drama on Thomas's birthday, do you?" She cocked her head to the side. I thought about the time Trent actually bit another boy. I met the boy's mother, and this wasn't her. Word sure got around. My face was gettin' flushed and my cheeks were burnin' up. This wasn't an argument I would win, so I switched my attention over to June.

"My son doesn't bite. He had ONE incident last year in the classroom, but he was bein' provoked and didn't know how to defend himself. Plus, I wasn't there to settle him down. I promise I'll keep an eye on him. He really needs to be around other kids. I'm tryin' to help him with his social skills." I felt like I was beggin' at that point.

"Not around *our* kids," another voice shot out from the group.

"My kid doesn't need to catch whatever her son's got," another woman murmured. My heart dropped. I couldn't believe what I was hearin'. How could these women be so ignorant? Before I could even say anythin' else, June looked around and spoke.

"I'm really sorry, Glory. I just remembered that I only reserved a table for 10 and I don't think there would be enough space. Maybe you can bring your son by another time?" The tiny woman gave me an apologetic look. "OK, Tiffany. I think it's time we move over to the slides," she said to her daughter.

"Noooooooo," Tiffany argued as June scooped her out of the swing and dragged her to the other side of the park.

All eyes were now on Trenton who was droolin' again. He was holdin' his fists as if they hung onto the chains of his own imaginary swing and though I tried to fight it, my embarrassment and shame crept in. All those mothers had average, healthy, easy-to-care for kids. As much as I hated those women, I envied them even more. Trent smiled and ran to the vacant swing, and as he climbed onto the rubber seat, he began makin' his happy hummin' noises. Not knowin' what else to do with myself, I got behind him and pushed. The two children swingin' beside us were called away immediately. *Would life always be like this for us?* The rest of the women moved closer to the jungle gym where their kids were playin'. They continued chit chattin' amongst themselves and shootin' the breeze, as if they hadn't crushed my very soul and made me question all my life choices.

As I pushed Trent on the swing, I noticed someone watchin' us from the wooded area off in the distance. I wouldn't have noticed her if it wasn't for her white hair. That's all I needed was another gawker. Fightin' my frustration, I swiped at my watery eyes with the sleeves of my sweater and focused on the back-and-forth motion of the swing. She stood there for about fifteen minutes before she made her way toward the playground. As she got closer, dark clouds rolled in and fanned out behind her, makin' it look like she was wearin' an enormous cape that floated across the sky. Though she dressed sharply, she wore the signs of many hard years. I could see the deep lines and age spots on her face from yards away. Somethin' about her made me think of death and decay. I shuddered.

"Ok, Trent. Time to get goin'," I said, feelin' more uneasy as the woman stepped into the play area and walked over to the children at the slides. The other mothers didn't seem to notice. When I looked back at Trent, he was furrowin' his brows and frownin' as he swung. "OK, honey, just a few more minutes, and then we'll go get a popsicle. Does that sound like fun?" Trent seemed to like that plan. He unscrewed his face and went back to a happier state as he moved through the air, forward and back. My eyes returned to the slides. The children gathered around the old woman, who now stood in the center of the circle they made around her. She was smilin' and movin' around to each of them, pinchin' that one's cheek, and touchin' another one's braid. Once she had addressed every child, she snapped her fingers and the mood suddenly changed. The kids screamed and scattered all at once. The mothers finally took notice and got up to intervene, but it was too late. Their children were already upset, clingin' to their legs, askin' to be taken home.

I shook the remainin' drops of coffee out of my thermos onto the patchy grass and put it in my bag. It was time to go, and the old woman was already walkin' toward us. I tried not to pay her any attention, but our eyes met, and she smiled and waved. I raised my hand and returned the greetin' out of habit.

"Hello there," the old woman said. She stood next to me as she watched Trent in the swing. "How are you on this fine day?"

"Hi, ma'am. We're doin' alright, aren't we, baby?" I asked Trent, rhetorically.

"I'm glad to hear it. I was watching you for a while and couldn't help overhearing what some of those awful women said to you about your brave little angel over here," she said as she nodded toward Trent.

"Oh." I was embarrassed again. "Yes. Unfortunately, there are many people who don't recognize that we are just as human as they are. Their foolishness makes them say and do some pretty hateful things. Wait, did you say you *heard* what happened? From all the way over by the tree line?" There was just no way she was tellin' the truth about that. I kept my guard up as we talked.

"Yes, dear. Some would say I have a gift." She smiled and pushed her hair back to reveal her perfectly normal sized ears. I nodded, but was unconvinced, so I changed the subject.

"Forgive me for sayin' so, ma'm, but I've grown up here all my life and you don't look like a local. What brings you to our little town?"

"You have a keen eye," she said with a slight smirk on her lips. She looked off into the distance and measured her next words with care. "I'm here to restore balance."

"Sounds cathartic," I said, unsure of what she actually meant.

"Mama!" Trent shouted as he leapt from the swing. He held out his hand, waitin' for me to take it - his way of tellin' me he wanted to go home. As I reached for him, I looked over my shoulder and said, "That's my cue. It was nice meetin' you. I hope you enjoy your stay here and find that balance you're lookin' for." I took Trent's hand. As we began our walk home, the old woman said:

"He forgives you."

"Excuse me?" I turned back to her, puzzled.

"You should know that in the end, he forgives you." The woman stared at me and Trent solemnly, and I felt a chill run down my back. I didn't know what she was talkin' about and didn't want to find out. Without another word, we left the park. *Lord bless and keep the crazies out there. And especially keep them away from me.*

23 OPHELIA CLARK

October 25

I lay awake in bed, thumbing the smooth surface of the covellite stone. The small crystal was definitely influencing my gift. In fact, it might have been working too well. Isra said it would enhance my dreams, but did she mean daydreams, too? It was bad enough that I was barely getting any sleep trying to solve this awful challenge, but having psychic visions while I was awake seemed like more than I'd bargained for. I couldn't stop thinking about the skinny boy that popped into my head while I was sitting in Doctor Charlotte's home office. In my vision, he was running for his life, and though I'd never seen his face before, I was positive he was dead now.

What does it mean? Is it like this for all diviners? I wish I could just focus on one freaky vision at a time.

I was living in a state of information overload, with one foot planted in reality and the other foot rooted in an entirely different realm with a whole new set of mysteries to solve. There were so many questions. I wish I would've asked Isra when I had the chance, but I was so overwhelmed with the idea I might be someone special, I couldn't think straight. *What kind of organization spies on young psychic children and how did Isra find out about me in the first place? If Isra recruited me as a divine bender when I was a young kid, what powers would I be capable of right now? How many divine benders are there in the world? I imagine there couldn't be many if Isra came all the way to this tiny town in Georgia just to put me to the test. If I somehow pass, how would I convince Mom to let me go to diviner school?*

I glanced at my phone on my night table. It read: 2:33 AM. If I ever wanted any answers, I would need to get to sleep and concentrate on sorting the details of my shadow dream out. I pressed the covellite stone in the center of my forehead, just between my eyebrows, and squeezed my eyes closed. I had no clue what I was doing, but I had seen Isra touch this spot when she was referring to the "third eye".

"Show me what I need to see. Divine vision, come to me," I whispered into the darkness. I felt a little foolish for the rhyme, but the words just popped into my head, and they felt right. Isra said to follow my intuition, after all. I repeated the mantra a few more times before removing the stone from my forehead and tucking it under my bed. Closing my eyes, I waited for sleep to carry my consciousness to the next dimension.

Ophelia walked along a field of grass, her bare feet caked with mud, and her toes calloused and bloodied. The edges of her white nightgown carried flecks of soil and grime. Each step she took sent a shock of pain up her legs and exploded like fireworks into her hips. She felt as if she has been walking for days - every tendon and every muscle stretched to capacity. Ophelia rubbed at one of her bare arms and, to her surprise, felt something warm and soft draped around her. A small knit blanket covered her shoulders, but threatened to fall away. She quickly wrapped herself in it to stave off the chill of the day transitioning into night. Ophelia took in her surroundings and stopped dead in her tracks. Suddenly, the dense fog that inhibited her sight in this place time after time had completely vanished and she could see.

Evergreens and oak trees lined a winding pathway to a playground.

"I'm at the park!" she said aloud, her eyes glistening and a smile spreading across her lips. She forgot her physical discomfort, if only for a moment. "I remember walking onto yellow lines on dark asphalt." She spun around to re-orient herself. "The parking lot is just around the bend!" Ophelia limped along the pathway, her clean line of sight giving her confidence and a new ability to cut across the winding trail to quicken her arrival. Time was of the essence, and she knew she only had a few minutes to observe and take note. She reached the parking lot in no time. Her eyes darting back and forth, she found nothing but disappointment; a crumbling, ill-maintained parking pad with no painted spaces. Something wasn't right. She wracked her brain to retrieve the four clues she noted the last time she was there. "Parking lot, window, circle of people, the number seven." She counted each one on her stiff and aching fingers. "The nearest parking lot where there are windows nearby are the shops on Main Street." Ophelia forced her tired legs to move, kicking one foot out in front of the other. She exited the park and headed straight for the busy part of town.

The gray clouds rolled in on cue as the row of shops and other businesses appeared in the distance. Ophelia kept focus on her mission, determined to witness the horrible scene that undoubtedly lay ahead. As she walked along the windows of each establishment, a sense of familiarity and belonging filled her core.

"I'm getting closer, I can feel it." She ran her hand along the buildings, peeping into the windows but finding nothing. There were dozens of units to look through, and Ophelia knew she could never cover enough ground before her vision came to a painful and gruesome end. Standing at the corner of Main and Jefferson, the girl reflected on her list of clues. "Where would people go to gather in a circle? It wouldn't be a place with tables and chairs." Ophelia strained her eyes to read the store signs around her, quickly dismissing restaurants, cafes, and furniture stores. "It needs to be an open space," she murmured as she continued looking. Then she noticed an establishment on Jefferson Street - The Happy Lotus Yoga Studio. As she moved toward the unit, she could see the freshly painted parking spaces. They were bright yellow. Her heart raced. "This *has* to be it!" Ophelia rushed to the glass doors as the familiar thunderous sound echoed overhead. She knew her time was nearly up. Cupping her hands around her face, she peered into the dimly lit yoga studio, eager to discover the scenario she would need to prevent inside, but it was empty.

"But... no. I don't understand. This *has to be* the right place." She rubbed at her temples in frustration, her reflection in the glass mocking her. Then there was another familiar sound. It was a woman's scream. This time, Ophelia could pinpoint where it came from. "I'm close!"

The wind tore at Ophelia's blanket and the bottom of her dress. She clung to the knitted loops, her fingers poking through the gaps like hooks into a net. Ophelia ran to each of the nearby units, frantically pressing her face up to the windows in search of the next clue. She could feel her body getting stiffer as the temperature dropped. She was down to her last few seconds, and as the red sticky mess of blood oozing out of her chest seeped through the blanket, she drew one last ragged breath and flung herself against the window of the last place on the block. It was a bank. Her vision was dimming, but her eyes landed on a white 6x6-inch flip calendar sitting on the front courtesy desk. She fought to read the black print: Today is the 7th. Ophelia's mouth gaped at the sudden realization that this was the place she had been looking for. Then everything went dark.

24 BLAKE JONES

October 25

It was mid Saturday morning when I woke up from the unusual sound of laughter coming from the kitchen. Still groggy from sleep, I cocked my head to one side to hear what was going on downstairs, and when I recognized Jay's voice, I jumped out of bed. The last time I'd seen my older cousin in person was at my dad's funeral. We used to be pretty close when we were younger. Our mothers are sisters, and me, my brother Mike, and Jay would get to hang out all the time when we all lived in the same town. Then everything changed overnight. Jay's dad took a job in the big city, and they moved away to Atlanta. It crushed me and Mike when he left. We both looked up to him as the older kid who knew all about everything. Music, video games, cars, girls (not that I was interested, but Mike seemed to have a lot of questions). Now, after all this time, he was here in my house. I pulled on a pair of jeans and an okay-smelling T-shirt from the floor and ran downstairs as fast as I could. From the kitchen doorway, I watched Gary, Mom, Austin, and Jay having breakfast at our table. The four of them looked so happy - almost like a normal family. It was bizarre.

"There's my man! What's up, small fry?" Jay put down his fork, letting the scoop of scrambled eggs fall back onto his plate. His lips broke into a bright smile, and as he stood up, he pulled me toward him for a half handshake, half hug. At six-feet and three-inches tall, Jay completely dwarfed me.

"Hey, man. What are you doing here?" I asked, still confused, but happily surprised. We'd been video chatting online for the past few months. He kept saying that he'd come visit, but I never thought he'd do it.

"I'm here to chill with you, bud," Jay said as he clapped me on the back. He was so charming, even Gary seemed to be in a good mood. "What do you say we go for a cruise in my car?" He knew the answer, but seemed to be amused by the look of shock and excitement on my goofy face.

"Hell, yeah!" I said as I leaned over the table, grabbed a fist full of bacon, and darted for the front door.

"Ha, ha. I guess breakfast time is over. Thanks, Auntie Jo. See you around, Gary. Later, little man," Jay said before taking one last sip of his coffee and chasing after me.

"Don't keep him out too late," Mom ordered, having to shout so Jay could hear her from the front of the house.

"I won't." Jay winked at me with a look of mischief on his face, and we left.

When I stepped outside, the reflection of the sun glinting off Jay's car nearly blinded me. It was the most beautiful thing I'd ever seen up close. A chorus of singing angels sounded off in my head as I stood in front of the vintage red Firebird parked in the driveway.

"It's unlocked, buddy. Get in." Jay climbed into the driver's seat and started her up. He revved the engine a few times before peeling out of the driveway and speeding out of the small subdivision. The smell of burnt rubber filled my nostrils.

We mostly drove around all day. He took me on the interstate and opened up the Firebird. *Wow, this car can move!* With hardly anyone on the road, it really felt like we were flying.

It was around 1:30 when we stopped for lunch at a Sonic Drive-In so we wouldn't have to get out of that heavenly machine. I was nervous about spilling something in there and spoiling the day, but Jay insisted I shouldn't worry about it.

"So ..." Jay started, as he took a big bite out of his cheeseburger. "... is Gary still an asshole?" he asked through a mouth full of food.

"Mmhm." I nodded my head and swallowed what was in my mouth. I put my half-eaten burger down on the wrapper I'd unfolded across my lap and pointed out the bruises on my forearms. "His handy work from a couple days back." I picked my burger back up and took another bite, not wanting to talk about Gary. I didn't want to think about how I didn't feel safe in my own home, or how ashamed I was for not being man enough to defend myself. Swallowing hard, I bit off another chunk of burger goodness and stared at the station wagon parked in front of us. I could see the silhouettes of a man and a woman in the front seat and three small children bouncing around in the back and thought: *whatever*.

"Yeah, I don't miss my old man. I'll tell you that. Ever since that fat loser grabbed at his chest and croaked at the dinner table, life has been MUCH better." Jay's voice was distant, and he stared out the front window as well.

"Gary's *not* my old man," I said. This shook Jay out of his own trip down memory lane.

"Oh, man. I'm sorry, Blake. Your dad was a great guy. You're starting to look a lot like him, you know." Jay put his arm around me and gave my shoulder a little squeeze.

"Yeah, he was." I forced a smile and stuffed the last bite into my mouth. "But I guess both our moms ended up with assholes in the end," I added as I chewed.

"I heard that when our moms were young, they used to fight over boys. Those crazy chicks have a type, I guess," Jay said. We looked at each other and exploded in laughter.

"I miss you, Jay."

"I know, bud. I miss you, too. Don't worry. You'll only need to be there a while longer."

"Yeah, but I need to plan my exit. I need a job. I want to save money."

"For real?" Jay raised an eyebrow. I could tell Jay's mind was working. He started the car and the two of us were on the road again. "Did you know I paid for this car in *cash*?"

"What? No, you're messing with me."

"Legit! Fully restored and everything." The look on Jay's face was convincing enough.

"How? Where'd you get the money? Your dad's life insurance?"

"Pffff. Hell no! That sad sack didn't leave us with a cent. After I became the man of the house, I realized I needed to earn some serious money. None of this minimum wage crap. I know a guy that could use a man in Monroe and the surrounding area. He pays well, and he pays cash. The only thing is that you'd have to do exactly as you're told and keep your mouth shut." He gave me a good, long stare.

"What does he tell you to do?" I asked. Jay had my full attention.

"This is the part where I need to keep *my* mouth shut. But I can tell you I run some simple errands. It's fast, and it's easy. I can put in a good word for you if you're interested."

"Hell ya!" I was smiling ear-to-ear. Jay punched the gas, and we were flying down the interstate again.

As we cruised along, a can of black spray paint rolled out from under my seat and tapped my shoe. I picked it up.

"Hey. What's up with this?" I asked, giving the can a little shake. It felt full.

"Oh, yeah. I almost forgot. That's for later to-night, if you're up for it." Jay winked and brought my memories back to the times he, Mike, and I used to go around tagging mailboxes, sheds, and abandoned buildings. We'd draw something dumb and then run like hell when someone saw us. It was thrilling. "And that's not all that I brought. Check the back seat," he said. Stretching awkwardly, I grabbed the plastic shopping bag sitting on the floor behind me and looked inside.

"Ha ha ha. Yeah, man. We gotta do it for old times' sake," I laughed.

"Well, alright!" Jay's face beamed as the wind tossed his hair all around. He looked happy in a way I didn't know a person could be. Maybe that's because he was free and, for the first time in a long time, I felt like I was free too.

25 CAMERON CAITIFF

October 25

With a few more hours of my shift to go, I sat in my car, writing my report on yet another domestic disturbance call to Jolene Jones's house. Marge said a neighbor heard yelling and the sound of glass breaking, but when I got there, the visit went exactly as it always did. The sight of me irritated Jolene, and she insisted nothing was wrong while Gary, drunk and stinking to high hell, stumbled to the door to explain how his shitty neighbors enjoyed wasting my time. I hated these two people more than anyone in Monroe. I felt sorry for the kids, though. It wasn't their fault their parents were losers.

The sun was getting low, and having accomplished nothing but drive around all day, I took my dinner break at "the bottle". The signage outside said "Bar on the Lake", but the locals came up with a nickname based on the first letter of each word: BOTL. After that crap with the Jones call, I deserved a drink, a no-no for on duty officers, but who was going to say anything to me in this nothing town?

I walked into the place and took my usual seat at the bar near the beer taps. This was where the cute bartender, Lucy, spent most of her time and even though we were in a "been there done that" situation, I still appreciated the view. The lighting was soft and dim, and the speakers were flooding the room with the sounds of contemporary top 40. Harry Styles' "Watermelon Sugar" murmured in the background. Settling in, I undid the top button of my collar and placed my hat on the bar.

The place was only about a quarter full, with a table of college boys, a few couples on date night, and the usual bar-flies who just came to drink quietly and watch whatever sports game was on the big monitor.

"I'll be right with you," a young woman who was *not* Lucy called over her shoulder from the opposite end of the counter. I nodded in response. But not-Lucy had already turned her attention back to stacking the remaining few glasses she had pulled from a clean dish rack.

"There!" she said to no one in particular and came back my way. "What can I get you?" She looked at my hat, then back at me, and smiled as if I were her first high school crush. Not-Lucy was in her early twenties and had the body of a cheerleader. She wore a tight-fitting black tank top that showed off some significant cleavage and low-waisted denim jeans that were cut to show off a belly ring. Her red hair was wild and framed her face like a lion's mane. She had almond-shaped, hazel eyes that sparkled with excitement and soft pink lips that glistened in the room's dimness. Maybe my day was about to get better.

"Well, hello there!" I grinned like a wolf overlooking a field of grazing lambs. "Where's Lucy tonight?" The best way to get chicks like this eating out of my hand was to make them feel like I'd rather be talking to someone else.

"She's got the night off. She hired me to help part time. I'm Jenna." She swept her hair from front to back to reveal a small name tag pinned over top of her left breast. I took my time reading it.

"I see. Well, Jenna, I sure hope you know what you're doing, 'cause I'm in a bit of a rush." I gestured toward my hat and looked up at her. "I'll start with a Fiddler Bourbon."

"Coming right up!" She blushed and poured two drinks. The uniform was working.

"Cheers!" We clinked our glasses and downed the shot.

"You did pretty good there, Jenna. I'll take another," I said while the warm, slow burn of the liquid was still making its way down my chest.

"You got it." She grinned and filled only my glass this time. I took more time with this drink and watched the bubbly bartender as she worked. Whenever she wasn't with a customer, she chatted with me. I knew I had her right where I wanted her.

"So what time do you get off tonight?" I asked.

"I finish at 12:00. Is that too late for you?" She bit her lower lip and looked up at me through her long eyelashes.

"Are you kidding me?" I laughed. "See you at twelve." I winked as I pulled a few bills from my wallet and tossed it on the bar before replacing my hat on my head and heading back out to finish my patrol.

I ran out the clock rolling around Armitage Park Circle. It didn't take much effort, but wasn't a complete bullshit task. After dark, the baseball diamonds, football fields, and playgrounds became an attractive place for teenagers to engage in underage drinking, pot smoking, and other inappropriate behavior. The presence of my truck usually kept the area clear. I parked in front of the playground and the glow of the yellow streetlamps lit the park's featured attractions: a dome-shaped jungle gym, a plastic tube slide, a wood-and-rope obstacle course, and a set of swings. There was something about the way the wind pushed the rubber seats back and forth that gave me the creeps. It made me imagine invisible ghost children playing on them, and the noise of the rusty chains creaking with the movement gave me goosebumps. Maybe it was the dark, maybe it was the alcohol, but something felt off about this place. In the academy, they tell you to trust your gut and as I debated with myself whether I should take off or stay put, something caught my eye.

A shadowy figure approached from the walkway that carved through the park. I sat up straight and watched the shape lumbering along, shoulders hunched forward and head down. It stopped under the yellow lamp and lit a cigarette. By the size and shape, I figured it was an elderly woman wearing a long, dark coat with a hood covering her head. In the dark, it was impossible to see her face, though the tip of her cigarette glowed cherry red. A cloud of smoke rushed out from where her mouth would be. The hair on the back of my neck stood on end. *Come on, I'm the cops. I need to get it together.* She continued along the path toward me. As she got closer, the park lights lit the features of her face, casting harsh shadows under her eyes and nose. *She's just an old woman. Ignore her. She's not doing anything wrong.* My heart was racing.

She reached the road where I had parked and passed the front of my F150. Nervous, I kept my head down and chewed on my thumbnail while pretending to scribble something down in my notepad with my other hand. My insides tightened up as I waited for the old bat to leave. When enough time had passed, I looked back up and, to my relief, she had gone. The park, to my right, was empty and the road up ahead was still. When I turned to my left; however, my body jerked in terror. I heard a strained yelp escape from somewhere in my throat and felt immediately embarrassed. I was now face-to-face with the old woman who was peering in at me through my driver's side window. She didn't flinch, but she took a step back, realizing she had startled me. Her pale, but sharp, eyes never looked away. My hand over my heart, I drew in a long breath and stepped out of the vehicle.

"I'm sorry for scaring you, officer..." She leaned closer to me to read my name tag. "... Caitiff."

"That's quite alright ma'am. I guess I should have been paying closer attention. It's just that I wasn't expecting you to be standing there is all." I caught myself raising my thumbnail to my mouth, but diverted my hand to fake a scratch to the back of my neck instead. I could feel the warmth of the blood rushing to my ears and hoped the darkness would disguise how red my face was. "Is there something I can help with, ma'am?" I asked.

"No. Not really. I was just on my way home, and I saw you in your truck. I thought to myself, it must get lonely sitting in there with no one to talk to."

"Ah, well, that's mighty considerate of you. I'll be alright." I grinned politely and added a head nod, hoping that would prompt her to go off on her merry way.

"This career of yours..." she started as she lit another cigarette. The smoke rose slowly around her face, creating a veil that made her look even older. "... you really should consider something else." She rushed her speech.

"Ma'am?" *Did she just say what I thought she said?*

"Don't get me wrong, son. You look great in that uniform, but it's wrong for you. I can smell it." She tapped the tip of her nose with her little finger, cigarette still in hand.

"Alright, ma'am, have you been drinking to-night?" I straightened my posture and leaned in toward her. The only smell I caught was her smoke and something earthy, like baking spices.

"No, Officer Caitiff. Not a drop. Not tonight. But when I sense something, I like to share it. There are many people in this world who suffer through a life they were not meant to live. I try to offer some advice when I can. I meant you no offense." She took a long drag of her cigarette.

"What is your name, ma'am?" I picked up my notepad and pen again, my face now burning with outrage. This old woman had no clue how good of a cop I was or how good I could become. This was the only thing I'd ever wanted to do outside of playing professional football. *How dare she? I should throw her in the drunk tank, anyway. That might teach her how to speak to an officer of the law.*

"My name is Isra, Isra Kawn. K-A-W-N." She took another puff.

"You're not from around here, are you?" I scribbled her name down, a wave of nausea passing through me.

"That's right," she said. "I'm renting a house off of Vine St." She smirked as I wrote this down too and struggled to keep from gagging. If I didn't feel so damn awful, I might have slapped the smugness off her face.

"I think it's time for you to head over there. It's not safe to be walking around alone after dark." I swallowed hard. I didn't even know what I was saying anymore. The only thing I was sure of was that I wanted her gone from my sight.

"That's where I was heading, Officer Caitiff, though I should tell you that a woman like me is not afraid of the dark." She put out her cigarette. "Have a good evening." She turned and walked away, dragging her feet and shifting her weight with some effort from side to side. "One more thing, Cameron." She turned her head and called over her shoulder. Her eyes seemed to glow. "Leave the therapist alone. The bar maid is more your speed." She continued walking and disappeared around the corner.

Therapist? What therapist? I was about to ask her what she meant, but Ms. Kawn was already out of sight. The old broad was probably going senile. *Wait, did she call me Cameron? I never gave her my first name.*

Shaken and at a loss for how to interpret the strange encounter, I glanced at my watch. It was 11:45 PM. I decided it would be best to forget about it and go claim my reward for a long day's work. Jenna, the bartender, would be waiting and there was nothing like a redhead to take my mind off things.

26 OPHELIA CLARK

October 26

I woke up coughing and gasping for air, but I felt incredible. For the first time since meeting Isra in the park, I felt like I actually had a shot at figuring this thing out. I now knew the location and day of the month the event would take place. I reached under my mattress, pulled out the stone on the silver chain, and clenched it in my fist. "Thank you," I whispered to it before laying back down and doing my best to get back to sleep. I'd have to be up and ready for school in a few hours.

Lost in thought, I walked down the drab gray hallways of Morson County High as I fingered the covellite stone dangling from the chain around my neck. Isra told me to keep it under my bed, but it was obviously meant to be worn. Why else would it be on a chain? In my dream, I saw a calendar that was flipped to the seventh. Not wanting to take any chances, I had to assume that whatever was going to happen at the bank would happen on day seven of next month, and I was running out of time. Even though I knew the where and when, I still needed to figure out the what and who, making planning how to stop it a major hurdle. Things were looking pretty grim, and as much as I wanted to earn the opportunity to mentor under someone like Isra and learn about what it means to be a diviner or a bender or whatever, it was so much more important to me to save someone's life. If I was ever going to piece this puzzle together, I would need every bit of magic this crystal could give me. I would wear it at all times.

I was nearing my class when one of my shoe-laces came loose and I stumbled. Wincing, I'd hoped no one saw it, aware that I wasn't cool enough to live down something this embarrass-ing. I tucked into the nearest corner by a tiny window so I could kneel and tie it without being trampled, though the rush of kids trying to get from one room to another was dying down with only about a minute or two before third period started. Once I finished, I stood up to see that Jessica and her bitch squad had me surrounded.

"I need to get to class." I tried to step around them, but the four girls blocked my path. "Please, Jessica, I need to go," I pleaded, my imagination running wild with thoughts of what they might do if I didn't get myself out of there. As I moved to push between them, my hand accidentally brushed against Stephanie's arm. That's when things got weird.

A flash of images filled my head, as though I were suddenly remembering something. In my mind's eye, I saw Stephanie with her curly blond streaked hair tied up in a high bun. Her tall slender frame was wearing a bikini, and she was in a backyard hot tub kissing some guy whose face I couldn't see. She was smiling and giggling and looking over her shoulder.

"Don't *touch* me!" Stephanie shrieked. She used her body to block me, her tall frame looming. The images vanished as I snapped out of my daydream, dumbfounded and curious about what just happened.

"Did she try to push you?" Jessica feigned a look of shock and offense. Things were about to turn nasty. I looked around, but there were no teachers in sight and there were no students crazy enough to intervene and ruin their reputation - at least not to help someone like me. I was on my own.

"I just want to get to-" I started, but Stephanie shoved me against the wall while Rachael (the quietest and least influential of the group) stood behind her and made faces. My backpack cushioned the impact, but it was way too heavy to run with. I thought about ditching it, but remembered the paperwork I had filled out for Dr. Charlotte was in there. If the girls rifled through it, they would tell every kid in school, in town, and possibly even the universe that I was a head case.

"What do you want from me then?" I searched their faces for any sign that I might walk away from this without further injury and wondered why the bell hadn't rung yet.

"What do we want?" Rebecca (Jessica's number two) mocked. "We want to know if you did it on purpose." She folded her arms and looked down her nose at me while Stephanie pulled a piece of paper with red marker scribbled over it from her tote bag. It was a test. The scribbles read "46%" at the top right corner.

"What? I - that's not mine," I said, completely clueless about what she was showing me.

"No. It's *mine*. I've been cheating off you since last year. I avoided summer school because of it. But now look at this." She held the test up again. "Did you fill in the wrong answers on purpose? What kind of freak does that?" Stephanie spat. The girls laughed.

"What?" *Oh, no.* I didn't know she was copying my work. With everything that was going on, my grades were suffering, and I genuinely flunked that test. Now she thought I was sabotaging her. "No. I -" Rachael grabbed me by the shoulders and pushed me into the lockers. Hard. The girls laughed again as I ricocheted off the metal and fell to the floor.

Another vision rushed through my mind before I hit the ground. This time, it was Rachael, and she was sitting on a toilet in a bathroom stall. Her brown, almond-shaped eyes were red and puffy from crying. A plastic pregnancy test was resting on top of the metal toilet paper dispenser, and her attention moved back and forth from the stick to her watch. When the image vanished, I found myself on my hands and knees.

"Oh! You're not going to cry now, are you?" Jessica taunted. What she didn't realize was that I was more stunned about the visions than being tossed to the ground. I touched the blue stone around my neck. What the hell was I seeing?

As I attempted to pick myself up, I noticed Blake Jones approaching from down the hall, his unmistakable mop of shaggy brown hair bouncing in his face. *Oh, great.* Aside from being a horrible student, he always walked around with scrapes and bruises. He probably smelled this fight from a mile away and wanted in on the action. More than outnumbered and out-muscled, I didn't know what to do besides go into protection mode. I slunk back to the floor and tucked my head and knees into my chest and covered myself with my arms.

"Yes?" Jessica asked, an obvious tone of irritation in her voice. Peeking up, I could see that

Blake was standing next to her. She looked him over with disgust.

"I think you're done here. You should go now," Blake said as he wedged himself between me and the girls.

"Excuse me?" Stephanie placed her hand on her hip. "Are you the new hall-monitor or something?" I caught her looking down at me and watched her face light up. "Oh, wait. Is this your *boyfriend*?" she asked me, then looked at her friends for approval. They didn't disappoint as they all burst out laughing.

"Get OUT!" Blake yelled so loud all of us flinched. Jessica gestured with her head, signaling her friends that they should go.

"Nobody threatens us, you weird psycho," Jessica hissed as they walked away. "You'll see," she added over her shoulder as Stephanie turned around to flip me and Blake off.

One of the most notoriously violent kids in school actually came to help me. Confused, I eked out a small "Thanks" as I unfolded myself and faltered. *Was I wrong about him?*

"You OK?" He looked down at me and offered his hand. He appeared calm - a stark contrast to how shaky and unnerved I was.

"Yeah. Those girls aren't as tough as they think they are." I gave an awkward smile as I took hold of his wrist and allowed myself to be grateful for this small kindness. Then it was flash, flash, flash - one scene after another.

The first image was Blake's shadowy face behind a staircase banister. He grasped at the spindles as if he were a prisoner peering hopelessly out of a jail cell. In the second flash, Blake stood in front of a big guy with a maroon and white varsity jacket. I only saw the back of varsity guy's head, but he towered over Blake who looked terrified. The last vision I saw was the same varsity guy swinging a backpack over his head like a cowboy with a lasso. There were some girls standing around, but all of them were facing a lake or a pond. There were tall trees in the background. When varsity guy let the bag go, it hit the water, which splashed up on the girls. They squealed and giggled. Then the vision stopped.

The next thing I knew, I was back on my feet. The bell was ringing, and Blake was tugging his hand away. He gave me a strange look, and I wondered if I'd done something wrong. I blushed, muttered something about getting to class, and took off in the opposite direction. *How embarrassing.*

27 BLAKE JONES

October 26

I walked away from that thing with the nerd girl feeling pretty good about myself. It wasn't my style to get into someone else's business, but when I saw her curled up on the floor, surrounded by those horrible girls, all I could think of was Gary and how unfair the world was to people with no power. The weak, the defenseless, the unpopular. We had nothing our bullies wanted, but they preyed on us for the fun of it - like it was sport to them. I knew that one day I would get away from the man that was making my life a living hell, and though that day couldn't come soon enough, I'm glad I was here to stand up for someone who needed it. I hope she didn't take my action to mean anything more that it was, though. I was only trying to be nice, but the way she held onto my hand and looked at me afterward was a little... cringe. Not that she was gross or anything. I just wasn't into her.

After the 3rd period bell rang, the teachers closed their classroom doors in near perfect unison to begin their lessons. The hallways went dead quiet, and I was officially late. I'd need to knock on the door to get in and I just knew my teacher would give me a hard time and would make me apologize to the entire class for the disruption. As I stood in front of the metal door, fist raised and head hung low, my back pocket vibrated. It was my cell phone. There was a text message from Jay that read: "I'm out front. Make an excuse and meet me." *That guy always has perfect timing.*

I walked out to the parking lot, the smell of fall filling me with an excitement I couldn't explain. When I spotted the Firebird, I made a beeline for it, the call to adventure drawing me in like a dog sniffing out a steak. As I got close to the passenger side, the door opened and a tall, lean guy stepped out and folded the seat forward to let me in the back. He had dark, wavy hair, green eyes, and bronze skin. *Wow.*

"Hey. You must be Blake. I'm Paul, a friend of Jay's." He shook my hand, and I blushed. This was the most attractive guy I'd ever seen in real life. He looked like he'd just stepped out of a magazine, and he had a silky smooth voice to match.

Is my hair OK? I can't believe I'm wearing this hoodie for the fourth day in a row. I hope it doesn't stink too bad. Should I be saying something right now?

"Hey, bud! Get in!" Jay leaned forward in the driver's seat so he could see me through the open door. I realized I was still staring at Paul with my mouth open like a trout and snapped myself out of it.

"It's nice to meet you, Paul," I said, the words rushing out of my mouth as if I could fix the long awkward silence. "Hey, Jay!" I slipped into the back.

Paul returned to the passenger seat and Jay hit the gas, cranking Marilyn Manson's cover of "Cry Little Sister" on the stereo. He said they released the original song as a backdrop to a classic vampire movie that came out in the 80s. I let the music wash over me and lost myself in the magic of the moment. There was something about being nostalgic with older guys that made me feel grown up - cool even. Jay was the coolest guy I knew, and though I didn't know a thing about Paul, I could tell he was somebody I *wanted* to know. *I really hope he doesn't hate my shoes.*

We drove for a while before anyone spoke again.

"Got some good news, man," Jay said. "Paul here is going to be your new boss."

"What? Are you kidding me?" My eyes went wide and my heart started racing. "That's awesome!" I wondered if my smile looked weird and tried to pull myself together. "Wait. Umm." I wiped nervously at my mouth, which was now producing way too much saliva. *Get your shit together, man.* "What do I do? When do I start?"

"Eager! I like it." Paul turned back to look at me. His smile revealed perfect teeth and the most interesting dimples. I tried not to stare. "The job doesn't really have a title, but you'll have one of the most important roles in the business. I'm really counting on you to put your best foot forward and Jay says that I can trust you."

"For sure. Absolutely. I'll do whatever it takes," I gushed, nodding enthusiastically. *Oh my God, stop it. He'll think you're a psychopath.* I dialed it back.

"Alright. Well, rule number one - you can't talk about this with anyone - and I mean *anyone*. All of this is off the books, and you'll get paid cash. Are you good with that?"

"Yeah. Sure. Of course!" *Keep dialing it back, you idiot.*

"Good. So, it's a simple gig. I'm going to drive some soccer-mom looking car - a Honda CRV or some shit to your school and hang out in the parent pickup area when class lets out for the day. You'll come out (as usual) and get into the back of my car. I'll hand you a nylon backpack with some small, addressed packages. You get out of my car with the bag and deliver the goods. Jay says you don't have a car, but you have a bike. It would be like having a paper route. Easy, right?" Paul said. His emerald, jewel-like eyes had my full attention. I think I nodded again, though I might have still been nodding from before. "You *never* open the packages. You make your deliveries. You get paid one K a week. Sound good?"

"Yeah. I mean, yes! I mean... wow. Thank you!" I didn't know what I'd just agreed to, but I let it go and kept my focus on the big picture. Paul was gorgeous, and I was going to be rich.

28 GLORY WALKER

October 26

The Walmart checkout line moved faster than I thought it would. I was hopin' to catch up on what the Kardashians were doin', but didn't want to add the Star magazine I was flippin' through to my cart. The cashier was a heavy lookin' guy with ginger hair, light brown eyes, and freckles on his pink splotched cheeks. He was breathin' through his mouth and was makin' a kind of snortin' sound that made me want to wretch. I watched him as he scanned my things and didn't imagine the look on his face would be any different if he were shovelin' piles of manure from one corner of the room to another. His name tag read: Hi, My Name is Corey.

"That'll be eighty-nine dollars and sixty-seven cents," Corey said without lookin' at me. I handed him my credit card. He swiped it through the machine twice before he spoke again. "Sorry, ma'am. It says it's declined." He raised his eyebrows and slapped the card between his fingers.

"Oh. There must be some kind of mistake. Maybe the card reader is dirty?" I forced a polite smile and looked at the line that had been formin' behind me. The woman who'd be next after me lifted a huge frozen turkey onto the counter and rolled her eyes in my direction. "Try it again," I said. Corey swiped it as I watched nervously.

"Declined. Do you want to try another card?" Corey offered, cockin' his head to one side like he was talkin' to a child. At that point, I couldn't tell whose face was more red, mine or his. I could've sworn I made a payment last week. *Was it maxed out already?*

"No, I don't have another card. I'll just pay with cash." I scrambled to find my wallet in my over-sized purse and pulled out every bill I had. The sighs from the folks behind me were gettin' louder, and I didn't dare glance back. "… eighty-one, eighty-two." I had laid down my last dollar. *Now for the humiliatin' part.* "Um. I guess I'll need to put somethin' back." I took a peek at the items in each of the bags and removed the only thing I didn't need for Trent. It was a box of tampons.

"No problem." Corey looked disgusted to be handlin' the cardboard box of cotton for ladies for the second time in less than a minute. He punched somethin' into the register and grabbed the microphone. "Bob to cash nine, please. Bob to cash nine." He stared off into the distance until Bob arrived.

The customers behind me groaned. Some of them dramatically pushed their carts over to a different cashier line. Frozen turkey lady stayed put. Bob, a middle-aged man wearin' a crooked toupee, showed up, and Corey handed him the box. When he realized what the product was he, recoiled as if Corey had tried to hand him a live grenade and then looked at me as if I was the one who put him up to it. The man entered his special supervisor code and walked away, leaving the box with Corey, who finished the transaction and handed me some sweaty change. I tossed the loose coins into my purse and marched out of the store, forcefully pushin' my cart full of bags in front of me.

My eyes stung with the prick of tears as I loaded my truck. I wish Coop would let me get a job. He really didn't understand how expensive Trent's medical bills were gettin' and there was only so much budgetin' I could do. I couldn't bring it up with him, though. The last time we fought about it he said that havin' me work made him feel like less of a man, like he wasn't providin' for his family. I tried to reason with him and told him it'd be temporary and that I'd quit as soon as he came back home, but he swore up and down that the neighbors would look down on him. I didn't know why he cared so much. Most of the neighbors looked down on us already.

With the truck loaded, I pushed my cart to the carriage-return area, and though I kept my head bowed low to hide my watery eyes, I felt someone starin' at me. A smartly dressed white-haired woman leaned against a nearby lamp post and lit a cigarette. I could feel her eyes penetratin' the cloud of exhaled smoke that billowed from her lips, but it wasn't until the breeze carried it away that I got a good look at her face and saw she was the same senile woman who talked with me and Trent in the park. *Did she drive herself here? Is the poor thing all alone?* I thought about askin' her if she was alright, but as I went to approach her, a red vintage sports car full of young men blastin' god-awful music came barrelin' down the lot. I had to jump out of the way to avoid bein' hit. *The nerve of some people!* When I looked back at the light post, the woman wasn't there anymore. There was no sign of her (not even her cigarette) and I wondered if I had even seen her at all. The image of her face weighed heavy on my mind the entire drive home. *Who was she?*

It would be an hour before I had to pick Trent up from school, and I plopped down on the family room couch and threw my head back. *Why is life so hard? Why is everythin' so unfair?* Feelin' sorry for myself, I glanced down and noticed the basket with Nanna's knittin' inside. As I picked it up, the softness of the yarn took me back to memories of her, and I managed a short-lived grin. I laid the small bit of stitchin' out on my lap and wondered if Nanna knitted because she enjoyed it or because it gave her somethin' to do when she just couldn't pray anymore. I picked up the needles and started knittin'. My hands were awkward at first, but after a while, they found a rhythm. I must've added a good three inches before I got the surprise of my life.

"Good Lord!" I yelled into my empty house as my cell phone lit up with a message from Coop. All I saw was the subject line, which read: *Coming Home.*

29 CHARLOTTE MILLER

October 26

Getting out of bed this morning was a challenge. My head ached from the wine I drank the night before. I shuffled to my bathroom, pinching the bridge of my nose to suppress the throbbing pain that was boring a hole in the spot between my eyes. There were some extra-strength ibuprofen capsules in my medicine cabinet, so I popped two of them in my mouth and leaned into the sink, slurping dripping handfuls of tap-water to help the medicine go down. Closing the cabinet, I faced myself in the mirror and stared. I looked exhausted, if not haggard. *When did I get so old?* I barely recognized myself.

As if having a silent conversation with the woman in the mirror, I kept eye contact with her as I brushed my teeth, washed my face, and applied my collection of face creams. Our back and forth sounded like this:

"Ophelia will be back today. Do you really want to continue treating her?" the old mirror woman said.

"No, but what choice do I have? She's my only client right now. I can't afford to refer her to someone else. It wouldn't look good from a professional standpoint either."

"The girl has trouble written all over her. You need to be careful not to get sucked into her delusions. You remember what Daniel Larson-"

"I don't want to think about Daniel right now. Ophelia is a different patient. This is a different place. Everything is different."

"But *you're* not different. You're the same woman you were back in Dallas. Only this time you're completely alone-"

"That's ENOUGH!" I set my bottle of cleansing oil down a bit too hard, sending a large dollop flying up and onto the counter with a splash. "Shoot," I muttered to myself as I wiped up the mess with a face tissue. I took in a deep breath and finished up without so much as a glance at the mirror again. It was the only way to keep the woman behind the glass quiet, and I didn't want her looking back at me.

I went downstairs and headed to the kitchen, hoping that a cup of coffee would provide some relief. As I crossed the hall, I noticed something strange floating just outside the bay window in the living room. I squinted to get a better look.

"You have got to be kidding me!" My eyes were wide as I stared at the large oak trees on my lawn. They were beautiful and majestic and also covered in toilet paper. The coffee would have to wait. Pulling a trench coat over my short night-gown, I burst through the front door to investigate. Of the four massive oaks on the property, two of them were completely littered with white bathroom tissue.

I scurried down the steps as fast as I dared in my slippers and made my way around the over-grown shrubs along the side of the house. As I rounded the corner, I came face to face with an unexpected visitor and I let out a short, ear-piercing scream.

The white-haired woman was standing just inches away from me, her gray eyes looking me over with a non-plussed expression on her face. The tissue fluttered in the tree behind her, and I suddenly grew angry.

"Did *you* do this?" I pointed at each of the trees and looked at the stranger expectantly. "I've seen you here before," I added, never taking my eyes off her out of fear she might vanish like she had done the last time. The thought of her disappearing into thin air while she stood directly in front of me sounded both absurd and possible at the same time.

"Of course not," she answered matter-of-factly. "And yes, I have visited before. My apologies if I frightened you. My name is Isra Kawn. I'm a teacher of sorts, but I also have other talents and I have a message for you."

A message? My mind switched over to therapist mode, and I proceeded with caution. As old as Isra appeared, I thought she might be dangerous, and took a few cautious steps back and a deep breath before continuing to engage with her.

"It's nice to meet you, Isra. I'm Charlotte. I must admit that you caught me off guard this morning, but I'm glad to be speaking with you. You have my full attention. What would you like to tell me?" I asked, leaning into the universal truth that most people simply wanted to feel heard and understood. I brought my face to a well-practiced neutral state and stared at the woman until she spoke again.

"I can see that you have put a lot of work in restoring this house, but sometimes homes as old as these need more than plaster and nails to rehabilitate them. Much like a person, sometimes a home cannot let go of the past, and the trauma it witnesses stays with them forever. Such afflicted things can influence others and impact their health as well. But, as a therapist, you already know all of this." Isra glanced at my business sign on the lawn and then turned her attention back to me. Lowering her voice, she continued. "I am someone who is very sensitive in detecting such things in objects, and I am here to tell you that there is much confusion and anguish in this place. It's palpable from down the street," Isra said.

"That is a very interesting observation." I nodded and backed a little farther away. *This lady is clearly delusional.* I wondered if she was on medication, or worse, *off* her medication.

"You don't believe in such things. I see. That's alright," Isra said. "But let me ask you this: have you experienced anything strange since you moved into the house? Have you seen things out of the corner of your eye? Are you hearing unexplained strange noises? Have you even met your neighbors? My guess is that you haven't." Isra looked at the houses to the left and right. "There is a repelling force that keeps people away. Bad for business if you ask me." She nodded at my sign again. A cool breeze kicked up and my bare legs broke out into goose pimples as a chill ran through me. *How did she know about the noises and that I haven't met my neighbors yet?*

"This is all very interesting," I placated. "But you said you came to give me a message." I rubbed at my arms to disguise my agitation as I pressed for Ms. Kawn to get to her point so she could be on her way.

"This house is poison. You have been good at resisting its influence so far, but it is taking hold of you bit by bit. I can appreciate how much effort you have put into it, but the sickness is well into the soil the house sits on." Isra cast her eyes down as she spoke. "I want to buy it from you. I am prepared to pay full market price."

"What? Is *that* what all of this is about? My house is not for sale, and how dare you make up a story like that to manipulate me!"

"I promise you, I come with the best of intentions. I need a place to open up a school for... special children. I am skilled at treating spaces and objects with ailments such as the one that plagues this place. It would take a considerable amount of time; however, I know I can heal it. And you would feel so much better in another home. I can't imagine things have been easy for you here." Isra glanced at the toilet paper in the trees and then pointed at something I hadn't noticed on the side of the house. I leaned forward to see the words "WITCH!" scrawled in sloppy black spray paint on the white wooden exterior. My jaw dropped.

"YOU did this! I *knew* it. Get out of here right now. I'm calling the police!" I stormed up my front steps, my body trembling. Isra nodded, holding her hands up and shuffling away as I flung the front door open and slammed it behind me. *The audacity of some people! I don't care how out of my mind this house makes me feel sometimes. This lady has crossed the line.* Marching into the kitchen, I made myself a pot of coffee and phoned the local sheriff's office.

There was a knock on the door at 4:00 PM. I opened it to find Ophelia clutching a pile of forms, her arms crossed against her chest.

"Ophelia, what a pleasant surprise. I'm so glad that you're here and that you filled all of those out so quickly. Come on in so I can have a look and make sure I have everything I need," I said.

Ophelia reluctantly stepped inside and followed me into my office. I reached out to receive the paperwork, but she made no move to hand it over.

"Is everything OK?" I asked. After a long pause, Ophelia answered.

"The things in these forms... they make me sound like I'm crazy. I'm *not* crazy. You know that, right?"

"Of course I know that. The questions in these forms are specifically designed for me to assess the state that you are in at this specific point in time. I understand your concerns, but please rest assured that no one, and I mean no one, will ever have access to your information except for me," I explained. And though she was hesitant, she gave me the forms. Before I could say another word, Ophelia bolted out the door. *I have my work cut out for me with this one.*

A moment later, there was another knock at the door, followed by a man's voice coming from the front of the house. It was authoritative and velvety, breaking the tension that loomed over me for the last few hours.

"Hello? Is anyone here? I'm Officer Caitiff - responding to a vandalism complaint."

"Yes, officer. Please come on in."

I walked into the foyer to find the man of my dreams standing in the open doorway.

30 CAMERON CAITIFF

October 26

I thought Marge was joking when she read me the address of the vandalism complaint call on Old Post Road. I knew the location well. Everyone did. It was the old Victorian house, smack dab in the middle of town. When I was growing up, all of us kids were certain that the old woman who lived there was a witch. She terrified us; always dressed in black, her gray hair long and wiry. We would ride our bikes down the narrow road past her house and see her glaring at us from her porch, her withered body hunched over so she had to turn her neck to the side to look up. Her features were as crooked as the branches on the trees that surrounded the place.

Vines and twigs crawled up the porch, up the walls, and along the faded and chipped shutters along the windows. No one ever came to visit her, and if they did, rumor had it they were never seen or heard from again.

One time, when I was twelve, my friends dared me to walk up the steps and knock on the door. I was petrified and didn't want to do it, but the only thing worse than certain death (if the witch caught me) was being laughed at and made fun of forever. Even back then, my reputation meant everything to me.

When we peddled our bikes over there, the sun started setting behind the house, silhouetting the crumbling chimney and crooked roof. My heart was racing and my palms were cold and sweaty when I dropped my bike at the edge of the driveway and made my way toward the front door. I could hear my friends whispering from where they waited on the road.

"Cam, be careful!"

A sinking feeling came over me as I walked past the trees with branches that looked like withered hands clawing their way out of the ground. To this day, I don't know how I mustered the courage to make it all the way up the steps, but when I got to the door, I froze.

"Hurry up and do it already," one boy yelled.

"Shh!" another one ordered.

Swallowing hard, I stared at the door and, just as I raised my fist to knock, it opened and my fist struck nothing but air. I was face to face with the witch and knew that I would be food for her rose bushes if I didn't act fast.

"RUN!" my friends screamed, as they hopped on their bikes and took off down the road, leaving me for dead. With no time to think, I ran down the steps as fast as I could, mounted my bike, and sped away.

That was the last time I stepped foot on the property at Old Post Road. Until today.

I parked the truck in the driveway and looked at the house. I could tell the new owners had put some work into fixing it up, but to me, it would always look like something out of a horror movie.

Biting off the jagged strip of fingernail I was chewing on, I hopped up the two creaky front steps and felt like I was a boy again. Before I could knock, the door flung open. I froze as a teenage girl with long brown hair and a jean jacket burst out of the home without giving me a second glance. She nearly hit me with her backpack as she flung it over her shoulder and marched straight to her bicycle, which was propped up against the side of the house. By the time I gained my bearings, she had gone.

I poked my head into the entrance and knocked on the door, which remained wide open. To my surprise, the home looked stylish and well kept.

"Hello? Is anyone here? I'm Officer Caitiff - responding to a vandalism complaint," I announced. There was a long pause, but the soft voice of a woman responded.

"Yes, officer. Please come on in," she called out from another room.

I took a few steps into the home and stopped in the center of the red embroidered carpet in the foyer. There was such a disconnect between the outside and the inside. New, shiny espresso-colored hardwood floors, tall ceilings with a grand crystal chandelier. The room to the left of the foyer had a beautiful bay window that was dressed with some kind of expensive drapery. *Velvet?* Double glass doors separated a smaller room to the right of the main entrance. One of them was slightly open. I could hear rustling from inside that room, followed by footsteps. I didn't know what kind of woman I was expecting to see, but the one that came out of the room surprised me.

She walked out of her office with such grace I thought she was floating. She wore a black turtleneck and tight jeans, which suited her slender figure. Her jet black hair framed her porcelain, oval face, and her hazel eyes sparkled when she looked at me. She wore no makeup and didn't need to. She was beautiful. *I bet she's a lace bra and matching thong kind of gal.*

"I'm sorry to keep you waiting. I'm Charlotte. Thank you for coming." She shook my hand.

"You probably noticed the T.P. in the trees out front. There's some spray-painted graffiti around the side. I can show you if you'd like."

"Sounds like a teenage prank." I pulled out my notepad and wrote while straightening my posture.

"Well, I suspect an older woman. I think she is trying to intimidate me so she can buy my house. She was here when I discovered this mess outside. Her name was... just a moment, I wrote it down." She fumbled for her phone and scrolled through her notes. A sobering thought came lurching to the forefront of my mind. The old woman in the park from the other night. Her voice played inside my head with haunting clarity: *Leave the therapist alone. Stick with the barmaid.* I cringed as Charlotte read the name aloud. "Isra Kawn."

"I see. I'll swing by her place and have a talk with her. Do you have any other evidence to support your suspicion?"

"Not physical evidence, no. She just talked about how this house was poison, which was hard for me to hear because the former owner - she died here. She was my grandmother."

"Ah, this was your grandmother's house?" *Holy shit.* I snapped right back into my twelve-year-old self.

"Yes. She lived here all her life and passed away a few years ago. Did you know her?" Charlotte cocked her head, and I swear it was like she was staring at my naked soul.

"Not really," I said, clearing my throat. "I knew *of* her," I offered, but prayed she wouldn't push for more.

"Hmm." She pressed her lips together, never breaking eye contact with me. *Could she tell that talking about her grandmother made me uncomfortable?* "Well, I know it sounds silly calling you over here to investigate toilet paper and spray paint, but the fact is that I have a business practice here. I'm a psychologist. My patients are troubled. You can appreciate that they need to feel like they are coming to a safe space," she said. I nodded in agreement and was grateful for the change of topic. "Living here alone, I also need to consider my own personal safety. I can't have people lurking around and scaring me out of my wits," she added. *She lives here alone? No husband, no boyfriend? Interesting.*

"Certainly, ma'am. I'll do my best to track down the person or people who did this." I flashed her my most confident smile, though it felt forced.

"I appreciate that, Officer Caitiff." Her face remained soft, and her eyes were kind, but she didn't react to me the way most women did. Most women got giddy and flirtatious. Charlotte, on the other hand, seemed to study me like some kind of specimen under a microscope.

"Uh. In the meantime, can I help you get the T.P. out of the trees? All I need is a stepping stool and a broom if you've got them." I had no idea why I volunteered to do that.

"Yes, that would be very helpful." Her lips formed a tight smile.

It took me less than 10 minutes to remove the paper from the trees. Charlotte followed me from branch to branch with a plastic garbage bag to collect the pieces.

"I am so grateful for your help, officer." Charlotte extended her hand once again, but seemed to change her mind mid-thought. "Would you like to come in for some tea?" she asked. *No one has ever asked me inside for tea before. I know being asked inside for a drink means sex. What does tea mean?* As I contemplated my response, all I could think about was Isra Kawn's withered face, smoking her cigarette and staring at me with her cold, gray eyes. My jaw hung open as I struggled to come up with something to say. "What am I saying? You're probably still on duty. Thanks again, officer." Charlotte shook my hand goodbye.

"Yes, ma'am. I'm sorry. Thank you. Maybe another time." I flashed another awkward smile and got into my car.

The entire way home, I thought about Charlotte and how much I wanted to be with her. The crazy thing was that I wasn't really into older chicks. Sure, Charlotte was attractive, but not like the hot, bouncing babes I normally picked up. *Did I only want her because some crazy old bat told me to stay away? Or maybe my twelve-year-old self wondered what it would be like to be naked in the witch's house.* I spent the next 40 minutes sorting it all out under a hot shower.

31 OPHELIA CLARK

October 26

After my weird afternoon of spontaneous flashing daydreams, I dropped off my patient forms at Dr. Charlotte's house. I felt like I needed help now more than ever, and since the only psychic I knew had disappeared until I proved myself worthy, maybe seeing a psychologist wasn't such a bad idea. Thankfully, nothing strange happened over there this time, but that place gave me the creeps, and I got out of there as quick as I could.

With my jacket still on, I marched into the kitchen to grab a snack. Since Mom had just stocked the pantry, there was plenty to choose from. I reached for a bag of chocolate cookies and grabbed a handful for my plate. Pouring a frosty glass of milk, I sat down at the kitchen table and stared at my food. I was hungry, but suddenly didn't feel like eating.

The gravity of my situation was taking its toll on me, and it was manifesting physically. My arms felt too heavy to pick up a cookie and dunk it. My head was spinning, and my thoughts were shining a spotlight on every shortcoming I could imagine about myself. I was a friendless nerd who suffered from disturbing dreams that predicted the future. And now I had the impossible task of bending that future by preventing someone's death. Somebody's life was depending on me and my choices. Who was *I* to swoop in and save the day? I wasn't a superhero. I didn't even have my driver's license yet. As I thumbed the blue stone dangling from the chain around my neck, Mom walked in, so I quickly tucked it under my shirt collar. There was no good way for me to explain where it came from, so I figured I'd avoid the conversation all together.

"Hi, honey. How was school?" she asked as she walked around the kitchen counter and emptied the dishwasher.

"It was OK," I lied. I didn't want to get into what happened with Jessica and her friends, either.

"Did you see Dr. Charlotte today? Get your forms in? Did she say anything about your progress?" Mom asked.

"Yeah, I gave her the forms. I only saw her the one time, Mom. There is no progress."

"Is that what she said?"

"Well, no, but -"

"So, you don't know what she's seen." Mom said with an air of victory, having won the conversation - if conversations were things that could be won. I placed my head in my hands and stared down at my plate of cookies, the smell of the chocolate and sugary cream filling wafting up my nose and making me feel ill. "The reason I ask is that you haven't mentioned the shadows and nightmares in a while. I figured whatever she said to you in your first session might be working," Mom said. I'm glad she couldn't see the anger and disappointment on my face. She really didn't know what I was going through. I couldn't talk to her about the shadow dreams, or Isra, or the bank. *Then again, maybe I could trick her into helping me figure out what to do about the bank.* I had an idea.

"Yeah, maybe," I said, closing the subject on therapy. "Hey, I'm working on a riddle, but I can't seem to solve it. Do you want to hear it?"

"Sure. What is it?" she asked, leaning over the counter and giving me her full attention.

"Ok. So here is the scenario. You're you, living in this house, in this neighborhood, in this town. You find out from an anonymous source that on a specific date, let's say the seventh, at a specific place, let's say the bank on Jefferson, someone would die a violent death and *you* need to figure out how to stop it. What would you do?" I watched her puzzled face as she silently reviewed what I said.

"Do I know the person?"

"No. Maybe. I don't know. It doesn't matter."

"Why would I be able to stop it? When it's your time, it's your time."

"It's a riddle, Mom. In this scenario, you can stop it. What would you do?" I pressed, already regretting that I even asked her.

"Well, it's a dumb riddle. If I thought someone was going to die, I'd just call 9-1-1 and send the police over to the address. It's an emergency, right? Problem solved." She looked at me and shrugged her shoulders as she pushed herself away from the counter and prepared for dinner.

"You can't just call the cops, though," I protested.

"Why not?"

"Because..." I had no answer and the more I thought about it, the more logical it was. Why couldn't I go to the cops? Isra said nothing about getting help from others. "... well ... I guess you *could* call the cops. You're right, it's a dumb riddle. Just forget about it," I said, subconsciously popping a cookie into my mouth as I mulled over Mom's solution. "How long until dinner is ready?" I asked.

"You've got about two hours. I'm making roasted chicken with mashed potatoes and carrots," she beamed.

"Perfect. I'm taking my bike out for a little while, but I'll be back soon," I said before chugging my glass of milk and placing the remaining cookies into a napkin, which I shoved into my jacket pocket. My appetite was back, and I'd munch on those on my way to the Morson county police station.

It didn't take me five minutes to get to the police station, and though I'd passed that building a thousand times while walking around town, I'd never been inside. As I got off my bike and propped it up against the plain brick wall by the front entrance, my heart raced. I hadn't thought through what to say.

When I walked in, the building immediately reminded me of my school. Bright florescent tube lights ran across fissured ceiling tiles with ugly brown water damage stains blooming from the ones in the corners. A lady who looked far too old to have a job sat at a linoleum desk near the front, and was filing her nails. I thought people only got away with that kind of thing in the movies. Taking a few steps closer to her desk, I hoped she would direct me, but she never looked up. I tried clearing my throat to get her attention. Still nothing.

"Excuse me. Hi," I piped up; hands clasped together in front of me. The woman looked up with a start.

"Oh, goodness. I didn't see you there, darlin'. The woman said, putting a freshly manicured hand up to her heart. I covered my mouth with my hands.

"I'm so sorry. I didn't mean to scare you."

"No, you're fine. How can I help you, Miss?" She waved off the minor incident and stared at me, wanting to get right back to business.

"Um. I have some information on something bad that's going to happen that I think you guys should know about, and I was wondering how to report it. Do I just tell you or ...?" I trailed off and looked around. The three desks behind her were all vacant, though one of them had a laptop and some papers scattered around like someone had been working there. A uniformed officer walked in from a room in the back. He was holding a steaming cup of coffee and took a sip out of it as he stood in the doorway to what I assumed was a break room.

"Shit!" he muttered as he sucked at his lips to sooth them from the scalding liquid in his mug.

"That's Officer Caitiff. He'll be able to take your statement," the old woman at the desk said. She rolled her eyes, knowing I was the only one who could see her face since Officer Caitiff was behind her. The officer looked up at me and waved for me to come over, which I did.

"Hi. Um. I don't know where to start." I knitted my brows and fidgeted with my fingers.

"Why don't we take a seat." He gestured to the cheap metal guest chair sitting next to his own cheap office chair. "Let's start with something easy. Why don't you tell me your name?"

"My name is Ophelia Clark." I spoke so softly he had to lean in to hear me.

"That's a pretty name. A pretty name for a pretty girl." He gave me a condescending smile, and I shifted in my seat. "What brings you to see me, Ophelia?" he asked.

"Well, um. I have information about something." I looked up at him, but felt awkward, and quickly returned my gaze to my hands.

"Go on. Did you see something happen?" he asked.

"Yes - in a way." I took in a deep breath and chose my next words carefully. "I saw something that *will* happen."

"So... you saw someone planning something?" He picked up his notepad and pen.

"No. I know how this will sound, but you'll need to trust that what I'm about to tell you is true." My face and ears flushed bright red, and I struggled to find the right words.

"Did someone do something to you?" he asked.

"No, nothing like that. I, um, got a tip, but it's from a source I can't talk to you about," I said, not wanting to tell him that my source was a psychic dream. My throat tightened out of nervousness, making it difficult to get the words out.

"You got a tip, but you can't tell me where from? Well, *this* should be good." He put his pad and pen down on the desk and leaned back in his chair. I tried to gain my composure, looking from the notepad to his face and back to the notepad. *He's not taking me seriously.* "Listen, kid-"

"No, wait. It's not like that. I'm not some silly girl looking for attention." My eyes grew wide as I scrambled to figure out what to say next. "Something terrible will happen, and *you* can stop it."

"OK. And are you going to tell me what it is?" he asked, clearly disinterested.

"Someone will be killed at the bank on Jefferson Street on November seventh," I said.

"Killed?" Officer Caitiff bobbed his head, mulling it over. "And how exactly does *that* happen?"

"I'm not a hundred percent sure, but I think maybe it could be a shooting."

"A shooting at the bank? In a small town like Monroe?" His eyebrows raised in disbelief. "That's some really serious stuff. I'll need more information than that. Who told you this? Who is the shooter?"

"My source is anonymous, and I don't know who the shooter is. But, believe me - it *will* happen," I pleaded, though I could tell the officer was considering it.

"I'll tell you what," he said as he tapped his pen on his paper pad. "I've made a note of it right here. I'll give that place on Jefferson some special attention. It was the seventh, right? How does that sound?"

I cast my eyes down, and a slip of paper on the corner of his desk caught my attention. It looked like something he had ripped out of his notepad and had a name and address scribbled down, which read: Isra Kawn 1366 Meadow Creek Dr. *That's odd. What could he want with Isra? Should I ask him?* Deciding I had already gotten what I came for, I answered:

"Yes, sir, I mean officer. Sounds great. Thank you so much."

I left the police station feeling like a new person. The tension and anxiety I'd been feeling had melted away, and as I rode my bike home, I felt weightless and free. The wheels were in motion to bend the future. Fate was no match for me. *I* made the rules around here.

32 BLAKE JONES

October 27

The three of us cruised along I-20 in the Firebird with the windows down. The wind mussed up our hair while the vibrations from the stereo rattled our bones. I sat behind Jay so I could steal glances at Paul in the front passenger seat without him noticing. Leaning back to let the small ray of sunshine peeping into the back seat warm my face, I did my best to look relaxed. I had a job. I had a plan. And now I was rolling with these guys. Life was good.

"Hey, B.J." Paul twisted in his seat to face me. No one called me B.J., but I loved it coming from him. "Wanna see something cool?" he asked with a devilish twinkle in his eye. It took all of my self-control to minimize my level of interest from about-to-jump-out-of-my-seat to a cool nod. Paul reached into the back of his waistband, and before I could get too curious about what he was doing, he pulled out a Glock G29 and pointed it at me. I flinched and stupidly threw my hands up in front of my face. "Whoa, whoa. It's not loaded, man. Here, check it out." Paul handed the gun to me, handle-side first. Still a bit shaken, I carefully took it. Paul's hand accidentally brushed mine in the exchange and a rush of goosebumps shot up my arms and the back of my neck. I tried to focus on the Glock, but I could feel Paul's eyes on me, sizing me up, figuring me out. I pretended not to notice and hoped he didn't realize I was into him.

I'd held guns before. Mostly hunting rifles. My dad took me with him a bunch of times when I was younger, and Gary had a few rifles at home, too. The Glock was comfortable to hold. The black steel was warm from being tucked into Paul's pants for who knows how long. *Quick, think of something manly to say.*

"Can we go someplace to shoot it?" I asked. Jay and Paul looked at each other and, as if communicating through telepathy, shrugged and nodded at the same time.

"We gotta stop to grab some ammo, but sure. I know a place we can go." Jay smiled.

Covington Guns & Ammo was right off the highway. I was hoping Jay would go inside so I could hang out with Paul, but since it was his gun, it was Paul who left the two of us behind. Jay turned off the engine, but kept the tunes playing. We leaned back in our seats and let the music wash over us. Jay only broke the silence when "Doin' Time" by Lana Del Rey came on.

"This chick is so hot," he said, flicking his eyes to look at me through the rear-view mirror. "What I wouldn't give to have some 'one-on-one' time with *her*," he grinned and winked.

I didn't know what to say, so I blurted out something like "Yeah", and stared out the window, hoping that he'd change the subject. Luckily, Paul was already on his way back. He hopped into the car with the ammo in a plastic bag.

"Let's hit it!" he said, sounding giddy. Jay revved the engine, and we peeled out of the parking lot, leaving the smell of burnt rubber behind us.

Twenty minutes must have passed before I poked my head between the two front seats and asked where we were going.

"Ha. We're here, man," Jay said, as he turned onto a dusty dirt road. There was nothing to see but farmland on either side. About a minute later, Jay pointed out a dilapidated barn that started falling over, but seemed to have given up halfway down.

"Awesome. It's still here." Jay pulled his car over to the North side of the crooked barn, out of view from the road. We got out and circled the building as Jay and Paul scavenged for empty liquor bottles, which they found easily. Apparently, this was the perfect hide-away spot for underage drinkers.

"We're losing light," Paul said as we quickly made our way to the West side, squinting into the setting sun on the horizon. Jay stopped a few yards away from the barn to line up three empty bottles on a tree stump while Paul and I put some distance between ourselves and the newly set up target. Jay jogged over to join us once he finished.

"This is where Skeet taught me how to shoot," Jay told me. I smiled and nodded. It had been ages since I'd seen my cousin Skeeter, Jay's older brother. I liked Skeet, but didn't know him very well. There was just too much of an age difference for us to relate to each other when we were kids. Jay was the one I looked up to. Jay was young enough to be interested in me, but ahead by enough years to make him the cool, older cousin.

Paul plucked a hand full of bullets from their box and loaded the gun as casually as he would run his hand through his hair. He snorted and spat out a hunk of phlegm before taking aim at the empty bottle of Jameson Whiskey. Repulsed, but still excited, I held my breath so I wouldn't make a sound.

"C'mon, Paul. Take the damn shot," Jay taunted. Paul whipped around and turned the gun on Jay. Though Paul's face was calm, I could see a raging fire burning behind his eyes. Jay's face went white as he held his hands in the air. "Dude, I'm sorry. I was only kidding. I'll shut up," Jay said, lowering his eyes to the ground. I had never seen my cousin look so afraid and defenseless. Sure, someone was pointing a loaded gun at him, but that was the first time I'd ever witnessed Jay back down. Something in Jay's face told me he knew something about Paul that I didn't. Something dark and hidden, but never too far from the surface. I watched the corners of Paul's mouth raise ever so slightly. His face transitioned from something beautiful to something insane. Fear paralyzed my limbs.

"Damn right you'll shut up! First rule of gun safety, B.J.:" Paul kept the gun pointed at Jay, but turned his head to me. "Don't piss off the guy holding the gun!"

I nodded my understanding but didn't say a word. I didn't want to give him a reason to continue building on that negative note. If living with Gary taught me anything, that was it. Paul turned back to Jay. "See? He gets it."

Jay nodded and slowly lowered his hands. Paul smirked, satisfied he made his point, and then turned around to face the bottles. He lined up his shot and pulled the trigger. The sound of the gunshot was still ringing in our ears after the bottle shattered and fell. Paul looked at us, eyes wide with excitement.

"Nice shooting, man," Jay said, slightly despondent.

"Yeah. That was amazing," I added, trying to bring us back to the vibe we were in just five minutes ago when everyone was having a good time.

"Thanks! See why you never rush a shot? Haha," Paul said as he clapped Jay on the back and handed him the gun. Jay accepted it and I wondered if he was going to turn the gun on Paul to even the score, but he didn't. He wasted no time aiming at the targets, and I breathed a sigh of relief. I realized then that Paul was the one in charge. Jay held the gun with his right hand and closed his left eye. He squeezed the trigger, and the shot rang out, but the two bottles stood proudly in place.

"You can't hit the broad side of a barn!" Paul heckled. Jay's face hardened, and I could see that he wanted to snap back. I broke the tension the only way I knew how.

"That's not true, Paul. I'm pretty sure he literally *only* hit the side of the barn." I pointed to the decomposing structure beyond the bottles. Paul erupted into laughter, and though Jay gave me a dirty look, he couldn't help but let out a few chuckles himself.

"Oh, yeah. Well, watch this." Jay took aim again and squeezed the trigger. The brown beer bottle shattered and vanished off the edge of the stump. "Damn straight!" Jay nodded in approval of himself. "You're up, buttercup." He held the gun out to me.

I took it and tried to hide my nerves while my insides wriggled like a bag of bait worms. Not that I was afraid to shoot a glass bottle. I just didn't want to look stupid in front of the guys. I mimicked the same stance Paul took. Arms out front. Legs slightly spread apart. Paul came over and corrected my posture, but only a little.

"Thanks." I blushed, confused about my feelings for him. I tried to shake it off and return my focus back to the empty bottle ahead. With the sun on my back, I took in a deep breath and exhaled as I squeezed the trigger. The gun fired with a loud, echoing crack, and the kickback sent my arms upward. The bottle remained untouched on the stump. "Shit!"

"It's alright, man. Try again," Paul encouraged as he once again corrected my stance. "But if you don't get it this time, I'll fire you." He winked as he backed away to give me space to shoot.

I licked at my lips. After what I saw today, I wasn't sure if Paul was kidding about firing me and there was a part of me that was terrified of disappointing him. *Will he get frustrated and lose his temper? I don't want to find out.* I aimed the handgun slightly lower than before and squeezed the trigger. The gunshot boomed across the field. My arms went up again from the force, but I anticipated it much better this time. The bullet hit the neck of the bottle and it fell over. All three of us cheered.

"Set up the next round," Paul instructed Jay, who obeyed without complaint.

By the end of the night, I probably shot off about twenty rounds. I missed half of them, but it was still bad ass. Holding that gun made me feel like I could do anything. We hung out until we couldn't see past our hands in the dark, and Jay said it was time to leave. He'd had enough. I sat in the back seat of the Firebird, quietly replaying the events of the day. The guys in the front didn't feel the need to speak either, so we just listened to the tunes on the stereo - the whir of the tires on the road playing in the background of each song. Nothing could have ruined that moment. Or so I thought.

The flashing red and blue lights flickering on the inside of the car from the back wind shield put everyone on edge and spoiled the vibe again.

"Shit. Everyone stay quiet and be cool," Jay said. We barreled down the road, all of us sitting up a little straighter.

33 CAMERON CAITIFF

October 27

It was early evening and already dark out when I left the gas station's convenience store off of I-20 with some Slim Jims and a Gatorade. As I got to my truck, I saw a Firebird doing at least 95 mph blow past me. Flinging the bag onto the passenger side, I leapt into my seat, turned on the flashers and siren, and took off after the son-of-a-bitch.

"Yeah! Come on, now!" I said to no one, grinning from ear to ear as I stomped the gas pedal of my F150 to the floor. "That's right, man. I'm coming for ya!" I locked my eyes on the glowing red taillights ahead. Chasing someone always got my blood pumping. It wasn't just about driving fast. No. It was more than that, something primal, something powerful. I was a hunter, and they were the prey. The cars up ahead took notice of the siren and flashing lights and parted for me like the sea parted for Moses. It only took a few minutes to catch up with the Firebird.

The driver gave no sign of slowing down. I reached for my radio and was about to call it in as a high-speed pursuit, but I changed my mind. I didn't want the station to send another car. Maybe it was stupid of me; probably even dangerous, but I wasn't sharing this with anyone. I turned my siren off and talked into the loudspeaker.

"This is Officer Caitiff of the Morson County Police Department. Pull over." As the light from my flashers flickered into the Firebird, I could see there were three people in the vehicle. Two in the front and one in the back. These guys were mine, and I was going to take them down.

"These aren't the flashing lights of Vegas behind you. This is the law. Pull over. Right. Now," I continued into the speaker. The Firebird slowed down, and the driver signaled he was pulling over to the right shoulder. I followed procedure and pulled up behind them. When we were both stopped, I ran the plates through my computer system. I was sure the car would come up stolen, but I was wrong. The thing was clean. No unpaid parking tickets. No history of speeding. Nothing. I stepped out of my truck and slowly approached the driver's side, keeping my right hand on my holstered gun the whole time. I stood next to the driver's window, which he quickly rolled down.

"License and registration," I said flatly.

"Yes, sir." The young man handed over the required documents and swallowed hard. The other two passengers stayed perfectly quiet.

I took the information to my truck and ran the identification through the computer system. It came up clean too. I didn't know if I was disappointed or relieved. I walked back to the Firebird. "Do you know why I pulled you over, Mr. Garrett?" I leaned into the car's window and got into the driver's personal space. No odor of alcohol or marijuana.

"Mr. Garret was my daddy. May he rest in peace. Please, call me Jay. I think I might have been speeding a little."

"That would be an understatement. I got you doing 100 in a 70," I said, still leaning into the car, looking for anything out of the ordinary. I shone my flashlight on the kid in the back seat. He stayed silent but looked frightened out of his wits. There was something about his eyes that felt familiar.

"Oh, man. I'm sorry, officer. I was trying to get my cousin home before his curfew." The driver tilted his head toward the backseat. "His dad, sorry, his step-dad, is kind of an asshole. I wanted to keep him out of trouble, but it looks like I found some for myself instead. We're really close to his momma's place."

That's when I realized the youngest one with the sad, scared eyes was the Jones boy. I wondered how many times his stepfather put hands on him and thought back to my own teen years. I was so much bigger, playing football, girls all around. My dad wouldn't have dared to raise a hand to me. We all can't come out winners, I guess.

"That's right, boys. You found some trouble. You know I could haul all your asses to the county jail for eluding an officer? Y'all could serve six months. That's not including the massive three-hundred-dollar ticket for speeding," I barked. The three of them hung their heads. The Jones boy held his face in his hands like he was about to cry. Their future was literally mine to decide. *What a rush.* "But I won't do that." They looked up at me, their eyes wide and hopeful. "You boys remind me of myself when I was your age. Sweet ride. Driving around. Having adventures with my friends." The guys smiled at each other, but I didn't want them to get too comfortable. "Don't screw it up! You drive this thing straight home and do the speed limit the entire time. If I catch you flying this bird again, I promise I will not hesitate to bring you down to the fullest extent of the law. Do you understand me?"

"Yes, sir!" they all said in unison. Relief was radiating from their faces. I handed the driver his papers and patted my hand on the roof of their car. "Get on now." I strolled away, satisfied with the way I handled the situation. They were just boys and I know I was doing way worse things than speeding around at that age. And besides, it was good to give folks a reminder that us cops were the good guys.

34 CHARLOTTE MILLER

October 29

Ophelia fidgeted on the gray love-seat in my office. She stared at her hands as she spoke about the vividness of her latest dream. Her ragged school bag sat by her feet, contributing to the picture of misery I saw before me. I sat across from her in the dimly lit room, scrawling notes as she went over the details of her nightmare.

"And how did you feel when you woke up?" I asked, hiding my boredom from listening to the nonsensical dream sequence of a teenage girl.

"Every time I dream it, it feels like I am actually there. My heart beats hard and fast, my chest hurts, and the smell of blood is in my nostrils.

The sound of someone screaming rings in my ears long after I'm awake. It feels like I'm dying," Ophelia said. *Don't slap her. Don't slap her. Yes, she's being dramatic over a nightmare, but I need to keep it together. Gosh, I never used to get so irritated with my patients. What has gotten into me?* I shook it off.

"That sounds terrifying. Sometimes dreams can feel real, even when we know they are just our imagination acting out a random scenario. What did you do when you felt this way?" I asked, though I struggled to feign interest in the answer.

"Umm. See, this is what I've been trying to explain to you. These dreams, the ones where the shadow-woman appears, are not my imagination. They show me real things that will happen in the future. You want to know what I did when I woke up? I gasped for air and cried," she said, visibly upset and shifting in her seat.

"Tell me more." I really didn't want to hear more. *Just an attention-seeking brat and nothing more. Oh, my. I really just need to focus.* "What were you feeling when you were gasping and crying?"

"I was feeling upset. Confused. Frustrated. Someone was seriously going to die if I didn't do something to stop it."

"Do you think it is up to you to prevent bad things from happening?" I stifled an eye roll. *Check out the hero complex on this one.*

"When it comes to my shadow dreams, yes."

I could tell she was getting annoyed with the questions, but it was all part of the process.

"You know, Ophelia, I think you are a high achiever. Often, high achievers can place a tremendous amount of pressure on themselves to not only get their lives in order but also to look after others. This can be incredibly stressful, especially for someone your age. What are some things you do to relieve stress?"

Ophelia considered the question while I tried to focus on our session. *Maybe I should open a window to get some fresh air in here.*

"I don't know. I work at solving the problem until I figure it out, I guess. Like, I'm pretty sure I figured out this last dream and I've made sure no one'll be killed at the bank on the date it showed me."

"Oh? Let's talk a bit about that. What have you done?" *Now this is getting interesting.*

"I reported it to the police. The officer who took my statement promised me he would go there on the seventh and keep watch. I didn't see any cops in my dream. If Officer Caitiff does what he says, his presence will change the entire scene, and no one will get hurt," she said.

"Ophelia..." I started, unsure of what my next words were going to be. I was stunned. *This teenage girl is so delusional and so bold that she actually got law enforcement involved in her psy-*

chosis. "... do you feel you might have crossed a line here?"

"What do you mean?"

"Well, it's one thing to come and talk to a therapist like me about a dream you had, but it's an entirely different thing to make false reports into the police," I said, watching Ophelia's face flush with anger.

"False reports? I thought you understood me. You said that you were here to help, but now you're accusing me of... of... of I don't know what, but I'm telling the truth." She stood up, heaving her heavy backpack onto her shoulder. "I'm glad that I went to the cops, and I think I'll be sleeping just fine from now on." The girl reached into her pocket and pulled out the cash her mother had given her to pay for the session. She placed the bills on the couch and walked out.

"Ophelia, wait!" I called after her, but it was no use. I needed to let her go.

Later that evening, I got a call from Ophelia's mother saying her daughter would no longer be continuing with treatment. She was polite about it, but as I listened to her rattle off a list of reasons she didn't feel therapy was right for her, I remembered having a near identical conversation with Mrs. Larson about her son. Ultimately, Daniel's mother regretted her decision, but it was too late for him now. It was too late for all of us, and I carried what happened to him on my conscience to this day. I knew I couldn't go through it again and needed to act now.

Yesssss. Call him. Call that handsome man. My thoughts whispered in my ear, though the words sounded like someone else's voice.

"That's not a bad idea," I said to an empty kitchen.

Walking up to my fridge, I searched the array of paper scraps being held up by a collection of colorful magnets until I found the business card Officer Caitiff left for me the day he came by. I held it between my fingers and stared at it for a while before working up the nerve to pick up the phone and dial the hand-written phone number on the back. My whole body flushed with excitement. A man's voice answered after three rings.

"Hello?"

"Officer Caitiff? Hi, this is Charlotte Miller. Did I catch you at a good time?"

35 BLAKE JONES

October 30

The bell rang at 3:45 PM, marking the end of the school day. As students scrambled out of the building from every exit, parents were lining up their cars in the drop-off/pickup lanes near the front entrance. It was time for me to go to work. I walked along the row of vehicles until I spotted the minivan with Paul in the driver's seat. The thrill of having a moment alone with him rippled through my body as I contemplated whether I felt giddy because of his looks or guarded because of his temper. I opened the door and slipped into the back.

"B.J., how's it going?" he greeted, twisting around to see me.

"Hi." I blushed at the sight of his eyes and averted my gaze to the floor.

"You know, you look at me the way my girl does." His eyes were peering into my soul, and as he looked me over from head to toe, I panicked. *Deny it. Deny everything.*

"What? Nah, man." I scrunched up my face and acted confused. My nerves took control of my body, and I couldn't bring myself to look at Paul again. I looked around the back of the van, out the window, and stared at my hands, trying to focus on anything but him. I didn't trust my face to hide the truth. *Oh, shit. What if I just pissed him off? What if he loses his temper on me in here?* Sweat rushed out of my underarms, and my palms got cold and clammy. I swallowed hard.

"Uh huh. Are you out?" he asked, still sizing me up.

"Out?" I played dumb. "I don't know what you're talking about." My leg started shaking. He must've noticed.

"Alright, guy. My mistake." He smiled his brilliant smile, knowing that he was right and not believing a word I said. "Here you go, then." He handed me a canvas backpack full of 'special deliveries'.

"Thanks. Uh. Bye." I slung the bag over my shoulder and hopped out from the opposite door. Relieved to be out of there, I drew in a deep breath and headed over to the bike rack on the side of the building to pick up my ride. *What would he have done if I admitted it?* As I knelt down to unlock my bike, I felt a hand on my shoulder and flinched.

"You like to creep on girls, huh?" A tall jock wearing a varsity jacket from another high school cast a shadow over me.

"What?" *Who the hell is this guy?* I scrambled to get to my feet.

"You heard me, you greasy piece of shit!" The jock was posturing for a fight. I didn't understand what was going on until the answer finally appeared on the sidewalk across the street. The four mean girls that were picking on that loner in the hallway were all standing there, pointing and staring daggers at me.

"Look, man. Whatever they said to you, it-" I started. The jock didn't hesitate. He threw his fist straight at my face. I don't remember hitting the ground, but I woke up on the worn-down grass with a crowd standing around me. I stood up, touching the back of my hand to my mouth to check for blood. It came up clean, but my jaw was throbbing. I struggled to get my eyes to focus, like I was sitting in the middle of a carousel that was decorated with students instead of horses. They seemed to move around and around, watching me and whispering to each other.

"Why don't you all go to hell!" I yelled at everyone within earshot. I was swaying so badly I must've looked like a drunk who'd been tossed out of the bar.

"Make way. Move. Move, please." Mr. Everets pushed his way through the crowd. "Are you alright? I saw the whole thing." He inspected my face, cupping his hand around the back of my neck. I wished people would stop touching me. "Let me see you. Are you dizzy? Did you hit your head? The police are on their way."

"Oh, no. That's OK. I'm alright. I just need to get home."

"I'm sorry, Blake, but whenever there is violence on school property, we have to call it in to the authorities and write our own report. It's protocol."

My head was pounding. The adrenaline was already wearing off, and the pain was zinging through one nerve ending at a time. My bike lay on the ground by my feet, but the canvas bag Paul had just given me was nowhere to be found. *Oh, no. Oh, no! Where is it? This can't be happening.*

"I hope you didn't have your wallet or your house keys in your bag," Mr. Everets said. "I saw the guy that hit you take it when you fell."

"Uhh. No, sir. I have my backpack right here. It must have been someone else's." I stood my bike up, but lost my balance. Mr. Everets grabbed me by the elbow to keep me steady. I winced.

"Let's get you seated for a few more minutes." My teacher led me to a nearby bench and sat next to me. A few moments later, a police car pulled up. Mr. Everets waved the officer over and as he approached, I wondered if my teacher noticed the look of recognition on either mine or the cop's face. Of course, it was the same cop who showed up at my door and who pulled us over in Jay's car the other night. This guy was everywhere. *Are there seriously no other police officers in this town?*

"Hello, I'm officer Caitiff. Are you hurt? Do you need an ambulance?" he asked, looking me straight in the eye.

"Hi. No, I'm OK. I really need to get going, though," I said. He gave me a long stare, but I said nothing. This was the first time I was seeing him up close and in the daylight. He was a lot more chiseled and built up than I remembered. *Really? That's what I'm thinking about right now? I'm completely screwed if I don't find that bag. Why am I like this?*

"Alright. Well, I'll need to ask you a few questions. Let's start with your name," Officer Caitiff began, though I was sure he knew who I was. He played it cool in front of my teacher and the few kids who had nothing better to do than to hang out and watch me give my statement. I told him I didn't know who hit me (which was true), but that the backpack the guy ran off with wasn't mine. It was too risky. I asked him a bunch of times if I could go home, but he kept asking me the same questions over and over, differently each time. I think I did alright. He told me to wait while he took down Mr. Everets' statement and insisted on driving me home when it was all done.

Officer Caitiff loaded my bike into his truck and let me sit in the passenger side so I wouldn't feel like a criminal. It was a short and quiet drive home. My face throbbed, but the major pain was in my chest. I didn't know what I just lost in the bag Paul gave me, but I knew I stood to lose much more. *How mad would Paul be? Mad enough to pull a gun on me? Mad enough to use it?*

When mom saw the black and white truck pull up to the house, she went ballistic. She came out in her gross neon yoga outfit, yelling and screaming.

"What did he do?" Mom shrieked as she flung the screen door open and ran down the front steps.

"It's alright, Mrs. Jones. Your son is fine. There was a minor incident at the school, and I wanted to make sure he got home safely," Officer Caitiff explained.

"Well..." she turned her attention back to me. "... what happened then?"

I ignored her and marched straight into the house. Officer Caitiff got her all caught up. I could hear them talking through my bedroom window, including her thanking the officer in her most polite voice. When Mom came back inside, she slammed the door behind her and stomped up to my room.

"Don't you ever scare me like that again!" she yelled as she pounded her fist against my closed door to emphasize the words "ever" and "again".

I spent the rest of the night in my room. I couldn't eat dinner. And since I didn't have time to put ice on my face, I knew it would look like hell in the morning. Not that I cared right then. Maybe Jay and Paul would see it and they'd feel bad enough to not kick my ass. *What was that jock doing with the bag? Did he find what was inside? Those awful bitches know who I am. Will they rat me out if they discover what's in there? No one could prove that it's mine.* I lay on my bed, trying to come up with the best way to explain what happened to the guys. There was no doubt about it. I was in some deep, deep shit.

36 OPHELIA CLARK

October 30

I took my time grabbing my things at my locker. It was best to let the mad rush die down before heading out myself. I walked through the front exit and shielded my eyes from the glare of natural light. As they adjusted, the cool fall air carrying the scent of pine needles and dry leaves filled my lungs. This was my favorite season, and I couldn't wait to hop onto my bike and soak it all in on the way home. As I walked toward the bike racks, I had the strangest feeling. The best way I could describe it was like having déjà vu, but more intense. Something was pulling me in that direction as my memory struggled to recall why this spot in this moment felt so familiar. Though I let the feeling guide me, I put some distance between myself and the school building, giving it a wide birth. Finally, the North side of the building became visible and the pulling sensation stopped. Cupping my hand around the covellite stone that dangled from my necklace, I cleared my mind. *What do you want to show me?*

"... piece of shit!" A deep voice cut through the buzzing noise of teenagers chatting and messing around. I honed in on where the voice was coming from and saw a familiar scene. There was a guy wearing a varsity jacket. Just like in my vision, his back was to me, and Blake was standing in front of him with a look of panic and confusion on his face. I noticed Blake cock his head to the side. He looked in my direction. I hesitated, but raised my hand in a half-wave when I realized he wasn't looking at me at all. He was staring at Jessica and her friends, who were a few feet away. They were watching the scene too, but they were too busy giggling and pointing at Blake to notice me. Before I knew it, the guy in the jacket took a swing at him. I winced and covered my mouth as I watched Blake fall to the ground. The girls erupted with laughter, but kept their eyes on the jock, who was now jogging toward them, a canvas backpack slung over one shoulder. He wore a smug smile, like he was proud of what he'd done.

"Thanks, babe!" Jessica called out to him as he got closer to the group. He wrapped his arms around her and lifted her up as she squealed and giggled with delight, running her fingers through her boyfriend's short, blond hair. Her friends watched and smiled, tilting their heads and pretending not to be jealous of the couple. *Did Jessica ask her boyfriend to attack Blake for helping me the other day?* I had to get out of sight, so I started heading back the way I came.

"Hey!" one girl yelled from behind me. *Oh, no. They're coming after me.* I kept my head down and walked faster. When no one attacked, I sneaked a peek back and saw the group of them goofing off and laughing again. They hadn't noticed me, but I got a good look at all of them. The clothes they were wearing were all the same clothes from the last waking vision I saw when I touched Blake. It all made sense now. The girls who were with the guy in the varsity jacket at the lake were Jessica and her group of friends. As they piled into his car, I was sure they would go there next. Relief washed over me. They wouldn't cause any more trouble.

I turned my attention back to Blake and noticed that Mr. Everets was sitting on a bench with him. Blake's face looked pretty swollen already, even at a distance. And though it wasn't uncommon to see him roughed up that way, I couldn't help but feel bad. I wanted to go to him. I didn't know what I would say or what I could do to comfort him, but just being there seemed like the right thing. *That's what a friend would do. Did I actually have a friend?* I blushed at the prospect of having a friend who was also a boy and waited for Mr. Everets to leave so that I could approach him. Things were awkward enough without teachers around. As I waited, I tried to act natural, but after five minutes of pretending to look for some long-lost item in my backpack, I realized that our teacher wasn't going anywhere and aborted my mission. I'd have to check in on Blake tomorrow. As I picked my bag up off the ground and turned to head home, my body slammed into someone, and I fell straight down onto my butt with a thud. I looked up and recognized who I hit immediately.

"Woah. Are you alright?" he asked, looking embarrassed.

"Um. Yeah. I think so," I said, rubbing at my leg. "It's Officer Caitiff, right?"

"Yes, I remember you. Here, let me help you." He leaned over and pulled me up with both hands. The second we touched, all I saw was: flash, flash, flash. Of all the waking visions I'd seen, these were the only ones that gave me chills.

I needed to talk to Isra and, thanks to Officer Caitiff, I knew exactly where to find her.

37 CAMERON CAITIFF

October 30

It was just past lunchtime when I got in my truck and headed over to Meadow Creek Drive. The crumpled piece of paper with the address scribbled on it sat haphazardly on top of the dashboard. I picked it up and stared at the name written across the top: Isra Kawn. I swallowed hard and gnawed at my ragged thumbnail. When I told Charlotte I'd pay the strange lady a visit, I never intended on doing it, but when she called me last night to tell me Ophelia Clark's police report was bunk, she asked me if I'd been out to see Ms. Kawn. A little tit for tat, I guess. I must admit; I thought it was sexy of the doctor to take charge like that, but now that I was actually out here, my stomach was in knots.

It wasn't uncommon for visitors of Monroe to stay at Meadow Creek. The entire street was full of quaint country homes for rent. Something about wrap-around porches with white rocking chairs and ferns, and gingerbreading on gabled roofs, had tourists flocking in droves.

The sun was shining brightly when I arrived. The bungalow looked like something out of a storybook, sitting on a neatly manicured lawn with colorful flower beds all around. Everything was still except for the ceiling fan under the covered porch. I took a deep breath, knocked on the metal screen door, and spit out a piece of thumbnail I'd been chewing on.

Ms. Kawn came shuffling to the door. She wore nothing but a green, serpentine silk robe. It fluttered and threatened to open with her movement and (to my relief) she clutched at it in the front to keep it from revealing the ancient horrors underneath.

"Hello, officer," she said from behind the screen. "To what do I owe this visit?"

"Yes, ahem. Good afternoon, Ms. Kawn. My name is Officer Caitiff. I don't know if you remember me, but we spoke in the park the other day." I scratched nervously at my hair, lifting my hat up to get at the itch.

"I remember." She continued to stare at me, cocking her head to one side and waiting for me to continue.

"Uh, I'm here to follow up on a complaint from one of our residents on Old Post Road. The lady that lives there sustained some damage to her property and claims to have seen you trespassing several times. Can I come inside to discuss it with you?"

"I'm sorry, Officer Caitiff, you may not. As you can see, I am not dressed to receive visitors, and I also have nothing to say about that old Victorian house. Do you seriously think a woman my age moonlights as a vandal?" Her gray eyes radiated ridicule and disdain for me. My face flushed as I worked to hold myself together.

"The resident also claims the two of you spoke and that you said some disturbing things to her to coerce her into selling her home to you. Is it possible the damage to her property was intended to scare her into being more agreeable to sell? Do you remember that?" I asked.

"I offered to purchase her house, yes. As for coercion, there was nothing of the sort. She declined my offer, and I left. End of story."

"Did you tell her that her house was poison?" I pressed.

"I told her the house had a *history*. Every old house does. Any fool knows that. Will that be all?" She tapped her foot impatiently. The sound of her slipper hitting the floor chipped away at my nerves.

"Ms. Kawn, how long are you planning to stay in town?" I asked. As soon as the words were out of my mouth, my stomach turned. Something I ate must have disagreed with me, and I would need a bathroom soon. Ms. Kawn smiled at me as if she relished in my discomfort, though it would be hard to believe she knew I was in pain.

"Officer Caitiff, you know what they say, don't you? We make plans and the universe laughs." Her gray eyes sparkled. "I have this place rented out for a while longer. When you get to be my age, the future is measured day by day."

"Well, maybe the future will take you some place else. Expeditiously." I tried to straighten my posture, but a queasy feeling had me leaning against the exterior wall with one arm and supporting my gut with the other.

"If I didn't know any better, I might take that as a threat." The glint in Ms. Kawn's eyes went out in an instant and was replaced by something terrifying. What I saw next defied all logic.

The woman's irises darkened and grew and grew until each of her eyeballs looked like shiny black marbles. I rubbed at my own eyes and hoped the terrible sight of her would clear away, but things only got worse. Through the obscurity of the screen door, her smile took on a life of its own as it grew and spread across her face until it became a hideous gaping hole. A row of graying teeth with exposed roots along the gum line bordered the distorted shape, and as she threw her head back in laughter, a thunderous sound boomed from somewhere deep within her body. *This can't be happening. I need to get a hold of myself.* A blustery wind kicked up all around me, and dark clouds rolled in within seconds to block out the sun. Shaken to my core, I stumbled back, my arm still wrapped around my stomach. I placed my free hand on the handle of my holstered gun, but another wave of nausea brought me to my knees.

"Oh, Cameron," Ms. Kawn said. Terrified, I peered up at her and saw the old woman's appearance had returned to normal. The wind died down, and sunlight pierced through the gaps in the cloud cover. I forced myself back onto my feet, still confused and very much in pain. Thick saliva pooled around my mouth, and I staggered back a little further from the door so I could support myself against the white spindled railing along the porch. Breathing heavily, I knew what was about to happen, and there was no way to stop it. "You don't seem to have the stomach for this job, dear boy. We are done here," Ms. Kawn said as she closed the inner door to the home. The moment the lock hit the latch, I tilted my head over the rail and puked my lunch onto a bed of purple and white petunias.

It took all my energy to stumble away from the house and get back into my truck. Though I started feeling better the moment I was in my seat, I was furious. *How dare she call me 'boy'? I am an officer of the law and I command respect, damn it!*

38 CHARLOTTE MILLER

October 30

Sitting on my heels, I leaned over the flower bed in front of the old Victorian house. I had pulled my hair into a messy bun and could feel the sun on the back of my neck, though the crisp fall air was cool enough to send shivers down my spine. *Should I run in and grab a sweater? Nah, this won't take long.*

Pulling on my gloves, I reached for the spade and the pallet of violas I bought at the nursery this morning. Perhaps some gardening would help me de-stress. I hadn't felt like myself in a while, and I thought some fresh air might take the edge off.

As I dug into the soil, I scooped the earth and placed it to the side. The dark granules clung to my gloves, obscuring their colorful daisy print, but I was unbothered. I closed my eyes and drew in several deep breaths. The smell of petrichor and flowers filled my nostrils while a sense of peace washed over me. As I worked, I cleared my mind, and it wasn't long before my body fell into a comfortable rhythm. I had slipped into a meditative, trance-like state. *Dig a hole. Remove the flower from its pot. Plant the root. Fill with dirt. Start again. Good. And again. Yes. And again.* The only trouble was, when I snapped out of it, I didn't remember a thing.

I gasped as my consciousness returned to me all at once. Judging by the sun, it appeared as though I had been out here for several hours. I was freezing cold. Standing over a sizable hole in the garden, I looked around for more flowers to be planted and saw I had finished them all. *Why on earth would I have dug this?* I surveyed the pile of dirt that lay next to it and, as I brought my hand up to scratch my temple, I realized there was something caught in my grasp. My stomach turned as I stared in horror, too shocked to move.

Laced between my fingers was a long and fluffy tail. A gray and black striped cat swung upside down from my tightly clenched fist. Blood dripped from its mouth as it peered out with milky, unblinking eyes. I screamed, and when I forced my trembling hand to open, the poor creature dropped straight to the ground with an unceremonious thud and lay there in a crumpled heap. *Wait a minute. What is going on? Did I just dig up a dead cat? No. The cat's hair isn't even dirty. Not with soil, at least. Then what happened?* I looked at the garden spade by my feet. A rust-colored liquid stained its tip. I picked it up, and when I smudged it with my thumb, I was certain I knew what it was. Blood. *Oh no. What have I done?*

I paced the lawn, searching for someone who might have witnessed something. The street was deserted. Though I couldn't make sense of what had happened, I was sure that, if I *had* caused the cat's demise, it was entirely accidental. *This is awful. I should try to find its owner.* I looked back at the furry pile. *No collar. What am I supposed to do? Put it in a bag and store it in my freezer until I find someone hanging posters of their missing cat?* I directed my attention back to the large hole. *No one saw. No one needs to know.*

39 GLORY WALKER

October 31

I sat at my kitchen table with my coffee and a stack of bills I had sorted into three piles: Due, Past Due, and Final Notice. Checkin' the balance of my bank account from my phone app; my chest tightened. I picked up the 'Due in 30 days' pile and tossed them into the trash. I thumbed through the 'Final Notice' pile and stared at them for a while, plannin' my next move. If there was another option instead of doin' what I was about to, I couldn't find it. Still holdin' my phone, I tapped at my contacts list until I found the number I needed. I took one more gulp of coffee and choked it down. The stuff was cold and weak, but the real dread came once I heard the phone ringin'.

"Hey, Momma." I did my best to sound upbeat and pleasant, though I hadn't spoken with her in months. We had a strained relationship ever since I married Cooper. Not that my folks disliked him as a person, but they didn't much like me marryin' a military man. They thought it would be too hard for me and said I lacked the strength and skills to live on my own. The biggest blow came with Trenton's autism diagnosis when he was two years old. I didn't know what to do and cried for days. It was around that time that Momma and Daddy decided they would leave Georgia and the house they lived in for 35 years and retire in Minnesota. From that point, I was on my own.

"Oh, Glory!" Momma said. The surprise in her voice was a little over the top. "Donald, it's Glory." She yelled over to Daddy, who must've been in another room. "I'm sorry it took so long for me to pick up the phone. I didn't hear it ringin' because I was in the kitchen makin' meatballs. Your daddy picked up this Italian cookbook and wants to try out all the recipes-"

"That sounds great, Momma," I interrupted. If I hadn't cut her off, I'd be listenin' to a story that went nowhere for at least 45 minutes before she'd say she had to go.

"Yes. Right. How are you?" She said stiffly.

"I'm doin' fine. We got some amazin' news from Coop the other day." I hadn't planned on sharin' this with her, but I needed somethin' to break the ice. "His unit got confirmation that their mission is endin' early and he said there's a good chance he'll be home by Christmas." It was the first time I spoke those words out loud to anyone. Two weeks ago, I couldn't remember what it was like to hug my husband, but now I knew *exactly* how it felt. I could picture him comin' through the door, and me throwin' my arms around his neck, his powerful hands pullin' me close. I remembered how he smelled when I buried my face into his chest and the feelin' of his 5 o'clock shadow scratchin' my forehead.

"Well, it's about time you got some help over there. My poor girl is raisin' a child all on her own."

"Momma..." I interrupted again, tryin' to prevent another lecture.

"How *is* my grandson, anyway?" she asked. *Here we go. It's now or never.*

"Trent's doin' good. Real good. Actually, he's the reason I called." I hated lyin', but I didn't need another scoldin' about money management.

"Oh? That's good to hear. What's he up to?"

"Well, there's this after-school program I think he would love. It's made for kids just like him. The instructors take the kids to the playground and bowlin' and swimmin' and stuff. It starts in January, but registration starts now and closes at the end of November."

"Uh huh."

"The only thing is that it costs five-hundred dollars and with Coop away, I just can't afford to send him. I was hopin' this could be a Christmas gift from his Nanna and Pappy." I waited in silence for a while before I asked, "What do you think?"

"It sounds like a great program. It's just a little on the pricey side, don't you think?" I had really hoped she wouldn't make things this hard.

"It is, but they need to have a lot of facilitators on staff, so it makes sense," I answered. *This was a mistake. I'll never get the money.*

"OK. I'll have to talk it over with your daddy and get back to you," Momma said. "But you know what, honey? I've got to let you go. He just put a movie on the Netflix. Give my grandson a big old hug from me."

"I will. Thanks, Momma. You say hi to Daddy."

"I'll tell him. Have a happy Halloween." Momma hung up.

Halloween? Trenton had been tellin' me we needed to get a costume, but I completely lost track of *my days.*

Damn it!

40 OPHELIA CLARK

October 31

I stood outside and stared at the doorbell. I hadn't prepared for what I would say, but I knew I would burst if I didn't talk to her. The outdoor lights were on, and I could see the flickering glow of candles through the window. An uncarved pumpkin sat on the porch. Aside from that, there were no holiday decorations even though Halloween was in full swing. The sun had gone down and all of Monroe's little ghosts, fairy princesses, and superheroes were knocking on doors to collect candy. A small group of kids walked up Isra's porch steps. As anxious as I was, I couldn't help but smile at their outfits.

"What's your costume?" a boy (aged around seven and dressed as a dairy cow) asked me.

"Um. Well, I guess I'm dressed as a teenager," I said, smoothing out my jean jacket.

"That's lame!" a girl dressed as a scarecrow (presumably the cow's sister) said as she stepped around me and pounded on the door.

The other children pushed to get in front of me while I waited for Isra to come to the door.

"Trick or treat," the children sang in unison.

"Well, don't you all look fantastic!" she said, dropping fists full of lollipops and mini chocolate bars into the bags they held out. "Here you go, mister cow, missus scarecrow. Some for you too, princess," she winked. She hadn't noticed me until all the children started walking away. "You're not here for candy, are you?" she asked.

"No, ma'am. And I'm really sorry for just showing up like this. I know I'm not supposed to be here, but I really need to talk to someone who understands what I'm going through," I said, my heart pounding in my ears. *She's going to turn me away, I just know it.* Isra contemplated; her eyes moving from the stone on my necklace to my face. *Busted.* To my surprise, she said:

"I see. Come on in then. I've got the kettle on." She held the door open and motioned for me to enter.

Though dim, the house felt cozy and smelled like sage. Isra had pillar candles lit in nearly every room and, as far as I could tell, they were the only source of light inside. Everything was quiet except for the faint sounds of giggling and rustling coming from the trick-or-treaters outside.

We walked through a contemporary family room at the front of the house to a fifties-style kitchen that desperately needed an update. There were three pillar candles on a dish at the center of the table and more spread around the kitchen, as needed for Isra to find her way around. When the kettle whistled, Isra reached into the cupboard and pulled out a second cup.

"Have a seat, child," she said, as she prepared the tea.

"Thanks." I pulled out the vinyl banana-yellow chair and tried to get comfortable. "So... what's the deal with the candles? Did someone forget to pay the electric bill or something?"

Isra shot me a look from over her shoulder, and I immediately regretted my attempt at humor. "I'm sorry. I didn't mean it like that."

"Indeed. The lights are working just fine. The candles are for me. As you might have noticed, tonight is All Hallows Eve, the night when the veil between the living and the dead is at its thinnest. The flames help me meditate and receive messages from the spirit world. I was just lighting the last few when you arrived." Isra sipped her tea and studied me. *Could she see how much stronger I had become?*

"I'm sorry if I'm keeping you from your... um... practice?" I grasped for the right word, desperate not to offend the only woman who could give me guidance. At least, not again.

"You're not keeping me from anything. The children will ring my bell for at least another thirty minutes. Why don't you start by telling me why you've come?" Isra brought the cup back to her lips and took another deep drink. The tea was still much too hot for me.

"I don't know how to say this or if this is even a real thing, but I've started having visions while I'm awake."

"Hm. Interesting. Go on," Isra said, mostly preoccupied with her drink.

"It happens when I touch people. Well, not all people and not always. Definitely sometimes. Like, I had these flashes about some girls I go to school with. Each of them was doing something I hadn't seen before, though the way it popped into my head was like I was remembering something from a movie. And then I touched Blake's hand. He's from my school, too. I saw a bunch of terrible things, and one vision came true a couple of days later. It was crazy déjà vu. Is this making any sense?" I paused, searching her expression for any sign of validation. I got none.

"Let's try something," she said. She held her hand out from across the table. "Give me your hand."

I wasn't expecting that. Did she really want me to see flashes of her? I timidly reached for her hand and closed my eyes, trying not to think about how her skin felt like crepe paper. I concentrated as hard as I could, but the only thing that came to mind was that Isra needed to moisturize. No visions. No vibrations. Nothing. I failed.

"I'm sorry. I'm not getting anything from you."

"That's quite alright, child." Her mouth curled to one side. "I was blocking my thoughts, but I can tell that your light is getting brighter every day." She patted the top of my hand and let go, never taking her eyes off me. "It takes many years of practice to use your abilities on command. That your vision was clear enough for you to recognize it when it came to fruition is a big step in the right direction."

"Really? But the most recent vision I had was a random, confusing jumble," I admitted.

"Tell me, child."

"Before I get into that, you should know I figured out the date and location of the death that I've been dreaming about. It will happen on the seventh at one of our banks in town. From what I can tell, someone gets shot, so I reported it to the police. I went to the station and met a cop named Officer Caitiff. Actually, that's how I found out where you lived. The cop had your name and address on a slip of paper on his desk. Do you know him?"

"We are acquainted," Isra said. "Go on."

"He told me he would pay extra attention to the bank on the seventh, and I thought he was going to do it, but after what happened *yesterday* I'm not so sure." I described Blake's fight, and that a cop came to the school. "Just as I was leaving, I walked straight into Officer Caitiff and fell. When he helped me up, images started rushing to my mind. It all happened quickly, but these flashes were different from the others. They were dark and abstract."

"What did you see?" Isra put her teacup down and leaned in. I had her full attention.

"The first thing I saw was Officer Caitiff sitting in the police station. It was evening, and he was holding his desk phone receiver up to his ear. In a flash, my vision followed the path of the phone cord from the receiver to the cradle and then down through the wall-jack, into the wall and out the other side to where the cable was buried into the ground. Like some kind of subterranean creature, I burrowed through a path right across town. I sped through clumps of dirt, rocks, worms, and beetles. I even saw some plant roots wrapped around a small pile of bones. At that point, I followed the cable up out of the ground, through the wall of a house and into Dr. Charlotte's phone, which she held up to her ear.

In the next flash, I saw the officer again, only this time he was at his desk during the day. He was slouching in his chair, scrolling through some fantasy football website on his computer.

The bottom right corner of his screen showed the time and date. It was 4:30 PM on November seventh. Things only got crazier and more confusing from there," I continued. "The next flash was an image of a dim room. Small, round white things started appearing like stars across a velvet sky and I realized they were eyeballs and they were all staring at me. Then there was a sudden burst of camera flashes, and everything turned black. Finally, the last vision came - a pair of bloody hands with the fingernails chewed off. Then, I heard laughing and everything went dark again.

When it was all over and I snapped back into reality, I was in the parking lot and standing in front of him with a dumb look on my face," I said, touching the covellite stone hanging around my neck. "I thought this thing was going to help me see more clearly."

"It sounds like it is working wonders," Isra said.

"But I don't get it. Is Officer Caitiff going to do something or not? What am I supposed to do with images of eyeballs and flashing cameras? None of it makes any sense!" I protested. Isra stood up.

"Ophelia, this is *your* journey. I cannot interfere with your challenge." She looked up at the clock on her wall. "It is getting late. You should get home before the *real* ghosts come out."

"Please. I want to learn how to see what you see." I got up from my chair. Isra pressed her lips together and stared a long time before saying:

"I will come for you, if ever you are ready. Until then, I cannot help you." There was a hint of sadness in her voice. Placing a gentle hand on my shoulder, she escorted me to the front door. "Good luck, Ophelia."

41 BLAKE JONES

November 1

I spent the better part of the last two days looking for the backpack that asshole jock stole from me. Talking to Jessica (or her friends) wasn't a realistic option. The last thing I needed was another visit from her boyfriend. I ditched class yesterday and rode my bike to all the popular spots kids with cars hung out in town: the Walmart parking lot, the coffee shop parking lot, the pizza joint parking lot, etcetera. I checked every trashcan and alleyway and even climbed into a few dumpsters. Aside from a wound I got from cutting my hand on a piece of glass that was poking out of a garbage bag, I came home with nothing. There was only one more place I could check, but it would be useless to go there in the dark. I'd need to wait until morning.

The next day, I woke up and headed straight for Armitage Park. The place was massive, with over a dozen sports fields, multiple picnic areas, a playground, and a few hiking paths. I had *a lot* of ground to cover, but if I wanted to keep my job and stay on Paul's good side, I needed to find that bag.

Armitage was empty when I got there. Everyone was at school. And while they were nose-deep in their textbooks, I was riding my bike through every square inch of the park, only getting off to check the public restrooms. Morning turned into afternoon, but the bag was nowhere to be found.

My stomach was in knots as I pedaled through the wooded trails. *I'm so screwed.* This was the last place I could think of, and if it wasn't here, it wasn't anywhere. The sun poked through the canopy of leaves and made it hard to see where I was going. The massive tree roots sticking out of the packed earth threatened to throw me from my ride at any moment.

As I slowed down to take a turn, I saw something hanging from a tree branch near the clearing by the pond. *The bag!* I sped toward it, a shot of adrenaline coursing through my veins. *Please let it be full. Please, please, please.* My heart pounded with excitement. I hopped off my bike and ran toward it, but as I got closer, all hope vanished. It wasn't a bag. Someone had tied a dark-colored sweater to a branch and left it here. I ripped it down and flung it to the ground.

"Shit!" I screamed into the woods, picking up a fist-full of pebbles and whipping them into the water.

"Blake? Are you ok?" a girl's voice said. Startled, I spun around to see where the sound came from. Beyond a mess of tall grass, the weird girl from my class was sitting on a park bench in front of the pond.

"Uh. Yeah. I'm fine. Shouldn't you be in class or something?" I ran my hands through my hair and continued pacing as I tried to calm myself down.

"School is out. It's 3:30."

"Oh." I glanced at my wrist, though I wasn't wearing a watch. *Idiot.*

"I'm sorry if I scared you. I was just sitting here trying to clear my head," the girl said as she awkwardly fidgeted with the blue stone on her necklace.

"You didn't scare me. I'm looking for something."

"Is it a backpack?" she asked, cringing. My head shot up to look at her.

"Oh my God, YES! Have you seen it?"

"I've seen it. Sort of." She hesitated before turning her back to me and pointed toward the water. "It's in there," she spoke softly and hung her head.

"What?" I ran toward the pond, pushing past her and through the brush. Stepping up to the edge, my shoes sunk into the mud as I looked into the water for any sign of the bag. All I could make out in the murky pond was my own pathetic reflection. If this girl was right, it was game over for me. "Are you sure? How do you know it's in there?" I asked, clinging on to one last shred of denial.

"I'm pretty sure. After those jerks left the school, I saw them take your bag with them and they ended up here. The guy flung it into the water. I think all your books were still in it. It made a pretty big splash," she said. Her voice was sympathetic, but something wasn't adding up.

"You were *here*? With *them*?" I watched her eyes go wide.

"No, no, of course not. I was avoiding those assholes at all costs. I wasn't with them, but I saw them. That's all I can tell you, but I swear it's the truth," she said. Her kind, but worried, eyes looked me up and down before she furrowed her brows. "Oh, no. Your hand - it's bleeding." She pointed.

As I inspected my hand, I saw the red stain spreading on the white gauze wrapped around it from yesterday's dumpster dive. I must have reopened the wound during my small meltdown before I noticed the girl sitting there. I didn't feel it happen, but now that I was looking at it, it was pulsating.

"Here, let me help you." The girl took a few quick steps toward me and reached for my bloody, filthy hand. I pulled away, not wanting to repeat that awkward moment we shared in the hallway.

"No, that's OK. It's fine," I said, wasting no time getting back on my bike. The girl looked a little sad as she stood by to see me off. I think I hurt her feelings. "Hey, I know I should know this already, but what's your name again?" I felt like an ass for asking.

"It's Ophelia."

"It probably doesn't mean a lot coming from me, Ophelia, but you're pretty cool." A shy smile spread across her face.

"Thanks. This probably doesn't mean a lot coming from *me*, but I think you're pretty cool too," she winked. "See you around."

"Yup. See ya," I said right before taking off back down the trail.

I had just gotten home from the park when Jay called me. He sounded really pissed off. It didn't take long for Paul's clients to call to complain that they didn't get their packages. I explained the whole thing about me helping Ophelia, and how Jessica got that meathead to sucker punch me and steal the bag.

"I can't believe you didn't call us right away, man," Jay said. I could hear him pacing back and forth.

"I'm so, so, sorry. I didn't want you to worry about me." The moment the words left my mouth, I knew they were wrong.

"Worry about YOU? Are you insane? Do you have any idea how much that bag you let some asshole toss into a frick'n pond was worth? Do you have any clue who our customers are?" Jay asked.

"Actually, *no*, Jay. I *don't* know. I don't have a clue who they are. I don't know what's inside the packages. And I don't know what the bag was worth. But I'll pay it back. Every cent. Just please don't fire me, Jay. I'll do anything you want. I've got the money Paul gave me for my first week-"

"Just stop." Jay shut me down. I had used up all his patience and now he realized I was only a young, dumb punk. "I gotta make some calls and let the bosses know what happened. Stay glued to your phone. I'll call you right back."

"OK, will d-" Jay had already hung up before I could finish.

Gary and mom were yelling at each other in their bedroom, so I put on my headphones to drown out the noise. Laying on my back and resting my head on my pillow, 'Cry Little Sister' was the first song that came on and it instantly reminded me of the day I spent with the guys. I let out a long sigh. *They'll never forgive me.* Ten minutes later, my phone was ringing.

"Jay, I'm really..."

"Never mind that, listen up," Jay said. "I talked to my boss, and he's agreed to give Paul another bag to deliver to the clients. I told him it was my fault for vouching for an inexperienced kid and that I've already taken care of things with you." My heart sank. "He's giving us a few days to come up with the money to replace what was stolen."

"Absolutely. I'll give it all back."

"I DON'T THINK YOU GET IT, BUD. Your couple hundred bucks won't cut it. That bag was full of top-grade shit. We need fifty-thousand dollars. Do ya got FIFTY-THOUSAND DOL-LARS somewhere?" Jay was yelling now.

"Of course not, Jay. Tell me what to do and I'll do it. I'll work it off until I pay you and Paul back. I'll do more. Just tell me." I felt like I was drowning, grasping at anything that might help me stay afloat.

"We don't got that kind of time. What about Joleen and Gary? Can you get it from them?"

"What? C'mon, Jay. You know mom and Gary have nothing."

"Do you have any friends you can borrow from?" Jay asked.

"No. Can I borrow the money from *you*? I'll pay you back, I swear!"

"Dude, I don't have that kind of cash lying around. And as pretty as your mouth is, there's no way I can turn you out and earn what we need in time. They're gonna *kill* us, man," Jay snapped, and I swallowed hard. I hoped he was joking, but when he got quiet, I knew that this was for real.

"Name it, Jay. Tell me what happens next and I'm in," I said. Jay was silent for a while.

"Alright. I need more time to think. In the meantime, Paul is going to bring you another bag tomorrow. You're going to do your delivery route immediately. Do you understand me?"

"Absolutely. One hundred percent. Consider it done."

"Oh, and in case you haven't figured it out yet, Paul is kind of nuts, so *don't* piss him off!"

"I won't," I assured, but the line was already dead.

42 GLORY WALKER

November 2

Momma made me wait two days before she called and told me she and Daddy were goin' to give me the money. I was so relieved I let her keep me on the line while she rattled off every detail of every single thing she did that day. Three hours later (and right before my head exploded) she told me she had to let me go so she could get dinner started. It was only 4 PM, but I wasn't about to argue. The money transfer would arrive in a few days and I'd finally be able to get the gas company off of my back. I hung up the phone and let out a long sigh, but the feelin' of relief didn't last.

Somethin' was wrong. The house was quiet. Much, much too quiet.

"TREN-TON?" I yelled down from the hallway on the second floor. Usually, Trent would watch T.V. in the livin' room, but I couldn't hear anything. Not the T.V., not Trent's hummin'. Nothin'. "Trent?" I called again, but he didn't answer.

I hustled down the stairs as quickly as I could. As soon as I reached the livin' room, my heart sank, and I felt like someone had kicked me in the stomach. One of the knittin' needles was lyin' on the carpet, completely bare of yarn. Panic set in. I took another step inside, and that's when I saw him. Trenton was sittin' on the floor with a pile of unraveled yarn all around him. It looked as though he'd emptied a can of silly string all over himself. All of nanna's stitches - gone.

I stood there with my mouth open, tryin' to tell myself that it would be OK. As if on cue, Trent looked up at me and smiled, his mouth wet and his eyes wild with satisfaction. When I looked into my boy's face, somethin' broke inside me. I was lookin' into the face of pure evil. At that moment, Trent was not my innocent little boy. He was somethin' vile and destructive.

In a blind rage, I picked up the knittin' needles and yanked him up to his feet. He was light as air. I whipped his backside with the plastic rods as he struggled and screamed. All my anger, all my stress, all my sadness, and all my grief poured through my descendin' arm. Relief came with each strike to the beast in my gripped hand. Trent squirmed and squealed, but I held onto him tight.

"Mama!" he cried.

When I heard Trent's voice, I realized what I was doin' and threw the knittin' needles to the ground. Still in shock, I loosened my grip on his arm and half carried, half dragged him up the stairs. I locked my sobbin' boy in his bedroom and sat behind the other side of his door, shakin' and wipin' tears from my eyes. When I was sure he'd fallen asleep, I went back down to the livin' room to clean up the mess. I collected the loose pile of yarn and brought it up to my face. Instead of smellin' like White Diamonds, it smelled like the peanut butter sandwich Trent ate earlier that afternoon. For as long as we both shall live, I don't think either of us will ever forgive the other for what happened tonight.

43 BLAKE JONES

November 2

“Well, if it isn't Captain Do-good, saving damsels in distress when he should lie low and mind his own business,” Paul said the moment I got into his van at the school pickup area. He was upset, but I couldn't tell how much, so I kept my head down and my mouth shut. “Jay told me everything. You see what happens when you stick your nose where it doesn't belong? You end up getting screwed and taking your friends and business partners down with you.” As much as I tried to fight it, my entire body trembled in the back seat. *What would he do to me?* “And this little girlfriend of yours. Where is she now? Is she going to get you out of this mess?" Paul's stunning eyes stared emerald-encrusted daggers at me as he waited for an answer.

"Paul, I... I'm really sorry. I told Jay, I take full responsibility-"

"I asked you a question," he snapped.

"No. No, she can't get me out of this mess," I answered, humiliated.

"That's right. You did a stupid thing, man."

"I know. And I'm-"

"Yeah, you're sorry. I heard you the first time. Now the real question is..." Paul relaxed his face and twisted around in his seat. As he raised his arm, I flinched and covered my face, thinking he would hit me, but he put his hand on my knee instead. A tingling sensation rushed through my body, radiating from the heat of Paul's hand. Confused, I let my hands fall away and waited patiently for him to talk again, my mind running wild with ideas of what he might ask me to do for him. "... what would you be willing to do to fix it?" Paul flashed his brilliant smile, and my thoughts got lost in his dimples.

"I would do anything. Whatever you want," I blurted, licking my dry lips out of habit. *Ugh, I hope that didn't look gross.*

"I'm glad to hear you say that, man." Paul gave my knee a little squeeze, but didn't take his hand away. "'Cause Jay and I - we had a long chat last night, and we figured it out," he said as he stared directly into my soul. *Oh, no. Would they really turn me into a prostitute?* "We still have a few details to nail down, but we're going to run something out of one of my old playbooks from a few years back. It's risky, but nine times out of ten, no one gets hurt." Paul gave my knee another gentle pat. I was so excited, I thought my spirit would leave my body. "Now, your cousin is really sticking his neck out for you. As for me, I've got to save face and do some damage control on the reputation of this fine enterprise. Jay wanted to keep you out of it, but I thought you'd want a chance to make this right. Am I correct in that statement?"

"Yes! Of course," I stammered.

"Can I count on you to do what you're told? No questions asked?" He raised one eyebrow and lifted his chin. I melted.

"Absolutely. I'm your guy."

"I knew it!" Paul slapped my thigh hard and laughed. "So here's the deal. You grab that new bag back there and make your deliveries today. *Don't* screw it up. Then, in 6 days' time, me and Jay will come pick you up from school. We'll be in a different van and parked down the street. You'll take your bike and meet us on the corner of Armitage Park and Brown Line."

"Ok. Got it. No problem. Then what?" I asked, relieved to be included in a plan that involved the three of us, no matter how sketchy it might be. Paul didn't hate me. I was over the moon.

"That's all I can say for now. Now go out there and do your job."

44 OPHELIA CLARK

November 7

Leaving Isra's house with no answers was devastating. I'd never felt so alone, with no one to talk to. No one to ask for help. Even the covellite stone seemed to be maxed out on its power to clarify my visions. And night after night, the shadow dream continued to play out the same way. If talking to Officer Caitiff made any difference - if I had *actually* bent the future, my dream should have changed. But over and over, the sound of a gunshot rang out. The blood oozed from my chest, and the life drained out of me. Some poor soul would suffer this awful fate today, and I didn't know what to do about it. My stomach was doing back flips as I rested a trembling hand over top of it to settle it down. *Keep it together. Breathe.*

My mind was racing as I sat in class. Time was nearly up. Mr. Everets was giving a lesson on security in technology, but I could barely focus. He was droning on about how to create virtual private networks and how to establish an encrypted internet connection. *I shouldn't be here. I need a new plan, and I need it now.*

"There are companies that pay their employees big bucks to set up and maintain their secure networks. Information is the new currency, and you need to know how to secure it. The last thing any Fortune 500 office needs is to have some cyber-criminal sneak into their network and install a virus that goes off like a bomb, and then poof! Their data is stolen or unusable, and the attacker disappears without a trace. And if you want to get really fancy," Mr. Everets continued, but I was off in my own world.

"Alright, class. We are going to practice setting up our VPN servers. Everybody up and over to the machines. Let's go." Mr. Everets gestured toward the row of old computers that lined the entire perimeter of the classroom.

I slunk to my designated seat in front of the computer and used the rubber tip of my pencil to press the filthy power button to turn the dusty thing on. As I waited for the operating system to load, I propped my chin up with my hands and closed my eyes.

Do something. It doesn't need to be magical, it just needs to be something. Think, O, think! I could go to the bank myself. It would be dangerous, but maybe being there would help me figure it out from the inside. Maybe I could stop people from going in, or maybe I could... Lifting my head, I gasped. *I've got it! Being in Mr. Everets's class today would pay off after all.*

As soon as class ended, I headed straight for Main and East Jefferson Street to watch my handiwork in action. I was glowing with excitement. Peeking around the corner, I could see cars pulling in and out of the parking lot and people coming and going as usual. *Oh, no.* The giddy smile dropped from my face. *Why does everything look so normal? It should have worked by now.*

"What are you doing, child?" Isra's voice came from behind and startled me. Though her shadow appeared in my dream of this day many times over, I hadn't actually expected her to be here. At that moment, rushes of people poured out of the bank as well as the neighboring business units. The flashing lights from police cars were heading our way. My giddiness returned.

"I think I've done it!" I watched the crowd gathering in the lot across the street and made my way over to get a better look.

45 CAMERON CAITIFF

November 7

"Calling all units. Calling all units. Reporting a 10-89 at the Neelan Thomas Bank on East Jefferson."

Marge's voice crackled over the radio as I inched my truck along the drive-through at Dunkin' Donuts.

"This is 0-4-7. Marge, I thought I heard you say there was a 10-89. Is that a bomb threat?" *She must be joking.* No one has ever called that code in Monroe. At least not since I've been with the force.

"It sure is, Cammy," Marge said, a hint of concern in her voice.

"10-4. I'm on my way," I rushed my words into the radio and clicked off. As soon as I returned it to its cradle, I clicked back on and added, "And don't call me Cammy!"

I flipped on the flashers and forced the cars ahead of me to move past the pickup window without grabbing their food. *That's right, folks. Move it along. I'm about to be hailed as a hero all over the five o'clock news. A pretty cool thing to have on a resume. In fact, if I pull this off, the Atlanta police department would practically BEG me to transfer to the big city. Then it's: sayonara, sleep town!*

It was 3:15 PM. Rush hour. My siren and lights were on, but the traffic was extremely slow to pull over to the side. I gnawed at my fingernails, spitting pieces of them out like sunflower seeds.

Pulling into the parking lot, my chest tightened. I arrived within six minutes, but it was too late. I was the third police vehicle to arrive. Two other officers were in command. Whatever happened now, I was not likely to get the lead credit. Not unless I could find an opportunity to do something extraordinary. As I stepped out of the car, the glass front doors of the bank flew open. An officer held the door and ushered a hand-full of patrons and bank employees out.

Was that officer Anderson? That fat old fart? You'd got to be kidding me. The guy who barely did a thing all year, who'd break into a flop sweat every time he'd get up out of his chair; he's the one who ends up being first on scene to a bomb threat at a bank? Well, isn't that just flipping fantastic!

The last civilian shuffled past me as I approached the front entrance. He didn't look like a local. Monroe attracted a lot of tourists in the fall. They came for the colorful show of changing leaves. They also annoyed the hell out of local residents.

"Just stand back there with the others." I motioned toward the group of employees and customers huddled together across the street as they gawked at the building. The tourist glanced at me without making eye contact, but nodded to confirm he had heard me. He walked to his car and left the scene. I tried to conceal my irritation from Anderson and just took down the man's license plate number in the event we needed to question him later. As I tucked my pen and notepad into my vest pocket, something caught my eye in the crowd. I didn't see her at first, but when a cloud of white hair popped up, I knew it was that old bat. And wouldn't you know it, she had a little friend; that girl, Ophelia, who came to the station asking me to monitor this very bank on this very day. Something was up with those two. I was sure of it.

I walked into the bank and Officer Mayberry briefed me on the situation. I had more tolerance for this man than I did for Anderson. Mayberry was in his forties and grew up in this county. He knew the community well and took his job seriously. Sometimes a little too seriously. Now he was instructing how they would search the premises.

"Remember. If you find anything that even remotely resembles an explosive device, do not touch it. Report back to me and we'll call in the bomb unit."

The bank branch was small, and the search in both the interior and exterior surroundings did not take very long. When we finished, we regrouped out front, and paid no attention to the growing number of spectators. None of us had found anything.

"Looks like the call was a hoax," Officer Mayberry said. He sounded relieved.

46 OPHELIA CLARK

November 7

You did this?" Isra walked with me as the crowd outside the bank got bigger and bigger. Everyone was exiting the nearby shops and offices. My adrenaline was pumping, and blood rushed to my cheeks and ears.

"My shadow dreams never showed me who I needed to save or who I needed to stop. I ran out of time, so I figured - if I couldn't prevent the people I dreamed about from going in, then I would have to prevent *everybody* from going in. If everybody is outside, no one can get hurt in the bank, right?" I grinned, looking at Isra for approval.

The noise of the chatting crowd got louder around us. All I could make out were bits and pieces of conversations about "bomb" this and "explosive materials" that. *I freaking did it! My untraceable, encrypted, anonymous message to the Morgan County police station about a bomb being planted in the Neelan Thomas bank WORKED.* Isra turned her attention back to me.

"Please tell me you didn't use your own phone to call in a bomb threat," she whispered.

"Of course not. I used a burner app that uses the Internet and creates another number to dial out from a computer at school. I even blocked my I.P. address -"

"OK, OK." Isra held up her hands in surrender. "That stuff is even more complicated than channeling the spirits and bending fate." She softened her face.

"If anyone was planning a robbery, there is no way they could do it now. Not with three cop cars in the parking lot." I looked at Isra again, smugly awaiting congratulations, but she only stared at the building. "Isra? I passed the challenge, right? What happens next?" I asked, barely able to contain my excitement.

"You did well, child." Isra patted me on the back while her mouth settled into a grimace.

"What's wrong?"

Her silence chipped away at my confidence, though I was certain I saved someone's life today. She didn't answer. Instead, she watched the glass doors of the building. After what seemed like ten minutes, Officer Caitiff came bursting through the exit and approached the evacuees, who were anxiously awaiting word on what had happened. He said something I couldn't quite hear, but ended with:

"... thank you for your patience. It is now safe to return inside and go on about your day." The crowd mumbled to each other and collected themselves to move along.

"What? NO! He can't do that." I turned to Isra, my eyes pleading with her to do something. If those people went back now and the police left, there'd be a bloody body on the floor before sundown.

47 CAMERON CAITIFF

November 7

I'll give the employees the 'all clear'," I volunteered, fixing my eyes on Ms. Kawn and the Clark girl. "Okay, folks. The good news is we didn't find any explosive devices in your building. We believe the phone call was a prank. Thank you for your patience. It is now safe to return inside and go on about your day," I said, watching a look of horror spread like a rash across the teen girl's face.

"Hey, y'all." The heavy-set branch manager called her employees into a team huddle. "Just grab your stuff and head on home now. I'll deal with the closin' activities and lock up for the evenin'. It's nearly closin' time, anyway," she said. The bank staff looked relieved, if not haggard.

"You're closing the bank?" I heard Ophelia ask the branch manager. Her demeanor changed, and she was now smiling from ear to ear.

"Don't worry, honey. You can come back tomorrow. These people are shook up and need to get some rest. We all could've lost our lives today," the manager said. "They wanna go home and hug their kids." She smiled, revealing a sizable gap between her two front teeth. When the last of the employees exited the building, the woman went inside and flipped the sign in the window to "Sorry, we're closed."

The young girl was beaming, though Ms. Kawn appeared stiff and expressionless. She gave her little friend a pat on the back.

"Is everything all right here, ladies?" I asked as I approached them, studying each of their faces.

"Yes, officer," Ms. Kawn answered evenly. "It's just such a shock when something like this happens. Especially in such a charming town as this."

I looked at Ophelia, who was doing her best to reign in her excitement.

"I will ask the two of you a question, and I want you to think long and hard about your answer. Did either of you have anything to do with calling in this bomb threat?"

Ophelia looked at Isra, who answered for them both. "No, sir."

"No, sir," Ophelia parroted. They were lying. These two were up to something.

"You didn't make a prank phone call just to get me out here?" I stared at the girl, unblinking. She opened her mouth to say something, but thought better of it and snapped it shut.

"She did nothing of the sort." Isra put her arm around the girl's shoulders.

"Alright. Just so you know, we'll be checking the bank's phone records to find out where the call came from. You sure you have nothing to say about this?" I monitored the girl's reaction for even a flash of concern, but there was nothing there. "Enjoy the rest of your day, ladies." I tipped the brim of my hat and returned to the other two officers to debrief before wrapping up. Out of the corner of my eye, I watched Ms. Kawn pull Ophelia in for a brief hug before they parted ways on foot.

"Is everything OK, Caitiff?" Officer Anderson asked. When I didn't answer, he added "You look like somebody pissed in your oatmeal."

"Leave him alone, Anderson. It's been a stressful day. If the bomb threat was real, we could have died," Mayberry offered. He was the peacekeeper of peacekeepers, but I wasn't in the mood.

"I'm fine," I answered. "I just don't understand why someone would do this. Why call in a threat that isn't real? Do they think it's funny to watch us come out here and dance around like idiots? What do they get out of it?"

"That's not for us to figure out. There could have been many reasons. A disgruntled employee. A pissed-off customer who didn't get the mortgage rate they wanted. Who knows? Don't take it personally, Caitiff. It's not about us. We should be glad we get to go home safely today," Mayberry said.

"Yeah, I guess. Are y'all okay for me to take off? I have some business to take care of before I wrap up my shift tonight."

"Yup. See you back at the station tomorrow," Mayberry answered.

Maybe I was being paranoid, but it was too much of a coincidence to see Ophelia here with that creepy old woman. I knew they had something to do with this, but I said nothing to the other officers. This was my lead, and if anyone was going to get the credit for bringing whoever did this to justice, it would be me. I needed some answers, and I knew someone that could help.

48 CAMERON CAITIFF

November 7

I pulled my truck into the dirt driveway of the old Victorian house, and though I needed to talk to Charlotte, the young boy in me (the one who would walk on the opposite side of the sidewalk to keep a safe distance from the witch's house) was hesitant. It was early evening, and the windows flickered with the soft glow of a T.V. The lights were on in the kitchen at the back of the house, and I figured Charlotte was fixing her dinner. Everything looked perfectly normal, but being here still made my hair stand on end. I thought about the last time I'd come, and how Charlotte complained about finding Isra Kawn on her lawn. I shuddered. That old crone and this awful house were a match made in hell. *Maybe Charlotte should sell the thing to her. And maybe it would burn down with the old bat inside.* I snapped out of my morbid fantasy and, as I tried to work up the nerve to get out of the truck, I saw something move behind the window on the second floor. I couldn't make it out, but it looked as though a shadowy figure was standing at the glass, holding the curtain to one side and then releasing it so that it closed in the center. My heart jumped up into my throat. I gripped the steering wheel and pulled myself together. *It was just Charlotte*; I told myself, and taking a deep breath, I stepped out of the truck and walked up to the front door, where she greeted me before I could even knock.

"Officer Caitiff!" Charlotte flung the door open and caught me off guard. It was almost like she was waiting for me. "Did I startle you? I'm so sorry."

I forced an unconvincing laugh.

"Nah, that's OK. I, uh... I've been having a strange day, I guess."

"Oh? I hope everything is alright. Is there something I can do for you?" Charlotte's dark hair framed her porcelain face in loose waves and her eyes flickered like distant stars in the night sky. I remembered her being beautiful, but there was something different about her this evening. Something primal in the way she looked at me.

"Actually, there might be. I wanted to ask if there was anything more you could tell me about Isra Kawn or Ophelia Clark. Can we talk?"

"Certainly." She ushered me in. "I will tell you what I can, but understand that with Ophelia, I need to uphold Doctor-Patient privilege - unless breaking confidentiality can be justified in the best interest of the public." She twirled a strand of hair around her finger and flashed a coy smile.

I followed her into the room with the large bay window to the left of the foyer. A white sofa faced a television set which broadcast the five o'clock news. On the coffee table sat a few Home & Garden Magazines, and a short vase with a single white ball of hydrangea. A bottle of red wine and a steaming single-serve frozen dinner sat off to one side. *If Charlotte had been eating down here, then who moved the curtains up-stairs?* I heard a light shuffling from above and placed my hand on the handle of my holstered gun as I stared up at the ceiling. *Maybe it's the ghost of the witch who used to live here. No, that's stupid.*

"Not to worry, officer," Charlotte said, reading my mind and body language. "This old house makes a lot of noise, but I've gotten so accustomed, it doesn't phase me anymore. In fact, I've grown to appreciate it. It's just the two of us here."

"Are you sure?" I asked. She nodded in the affirmative and gestured for me to have a seat on the couch, which I did, though I was cautious not to get too comfortable. "I've interrupted your meal. I apologize. Oh, and please, call me Cameron," I said, still listening for signs of another presence (real or otherworldly).

"On the contrary. I think you've saved me from poisoning myself. It looks dreadful - doesn't it?" She wrinkled her nose at the sad tray of sliced ham, peas, and mashed potatoes before dumping it into the trash bin in the kitchen. "Can I offer you a drink? I have wine, scotch, cola, water..."

I didn't hear Charlotte say anything after "water" as the T.V. now had my undivided attention. A news broadcast showed a female reporter standing in a parking lot with her microphone. She was flanked by two familiar faces, both in uniform. The banner at the bottom of the screen read: "Local News: Live from Jefferson Street in Monroe". I scrambled to find the remote and raised the volume.

"... and we immediately evacuated and combed the area. The search did not result in the discovery of anything that would be potentially dangerous, and there were no explosive devices found. At this time, we'd like to remind the public that making false threats is a federal offense. It can cause distress or injury to the folks that are on the premises and to the first responders. We've got to remember that it costs the taxpayer money when an emergency call is made and, if you are caught making a false call, you can be sentenced to time in jail," Officer Mayberry spoke authoritatively into the reporter's microphone.

"Well, we are so glad that you were here to take control of the situation and make sure everyone at the plaza here on Jefferson was safe. Officer Mayberry, Officer Anderson, thank you. Back to you, Tom," the reporter closed.

I hadn't noticed Charlotte return to the room. I was too busy gnawing on my thumbnail and staring at the T.V. My blood was boiling.

"Is everything alright?" she asked.

"I was just over there. That could have been *me* giving an interview and those two assholes didn't even *mention* me!" I raised my voice and gestured toward the screen.

"Oh, my. What happened?" Charlotte looked at the T.V. and back to me, her upturned eyebrows softening her look.

"Ophelia Clark and that creepy lady Isra Kawn. *They* happened."

"What did they do?" she asked, taking a drink of her wine. She dabbed at the corners of her mouth with her fingers and her glistening red lips nearly made me forget the reason for my visit. I told Charlotte about the incident at the bank this afternoon and how I found Ophelia and Isra watching the whole thing from the parking lot.

"This is exactly why I reached out to warn you last week. I was worried she was losing touch with reality and when she told me she filed a report with you, I ..." Charlotte looked up at me through her long, dark lashes. "... I wanted you to understand that what she believed to be true was simply an overactive imagination. And who knows how that Isra woman is involved." Charlotte shook her head. "To make matters worse, I can't do anything about this anymore. Ophelia's mother let me know she would no longer be seeking treatment. At least not with me," she grimaced.

"So she's not a patient of yours anymore?"

"She is not."

"So, may I see her file?"

"What? I'm sorry, no. I can't just hand over someone's file," Charlotte said.

"Well then, what else can you give me on Ophelia Clark?" I pressed. Charlotte stared at me, contemplating.

"I bet you haven't eaten yet," she said. "How about I order in, and we can have a chat? Do you like Chinese food?" I liked the idea of being with Charlotte a while longer.

"I don't want to impose," I said as I removed my hat and placed it on the table, making myself more comfortable.

"It's no imposition at all," she said as she tapped the food order into her phone and grabbed a second wineglass. Returning to the living room, Charlotte sat next to me. "Now where were we?"

She poured a generous helping of wine into my glass.

"Ophelia. Do you think she would call in a bomb threat? If so, she made fools of all of us out there. It ain't right. There are consequences for messing with the law. We're out here to protect and serve, not for some teenager's personal amusement." I became flush with anger just thinking about it again.

"I'm not sure I can answer that, but if Ophelia called in the threat, I don't believe it was her intention to cause anyone harm or impose mischief. From what I've learned, Ophelia is a very observant girl. She is hyper-intuitive, which can cause people like her to believe they possess psychic abilities. Because of their intellect, they seem to be one step ahead and are often correct in their presumptions, further proving to themselves that they are gifted with this magical talent. In Ophelia's case, she really believes that she sees the future in her dreams. She was convinced that something terrible would happen at the bank today, and sure enough, someone called in a bomb threat. If it *wasn't* her, she probably believes her psychic dream was correct." Charlotte took a deep drink from her glass and leaned in a little closer to me.

I absently gulped at my wine and stared into her eyes. *God, this woman is beautiful. Why am I whining about being played when I could play a game of my own right now?*

"I've seen this kind of thing before," Charlotte continued. "Unfortunately, if it gets out of control, this type of delusion can spiral and become much worse. I used to have a patient like her..."

Charlotte went off on a tangent about a former patient of hers. Truth be told, I could barely focus on a thing she said. There was only one thing I was thinking about, and it wasn't the Clark girl, the old lady, or this creaking hell house. When she finally stopped talking, I said something like:

"Yeah, that must have been tough." (Whenever a woman talked about her past, this was my go-to response). It worked every time.

Charlotte smiled and got so close I could feel the heat of her body. Her lips were just inches away from mine, and I knew it was time. The moment I put my mouth on hers, things escalated quickly. She smelled so good and felt so soft. She seemed to want it as much as I did, clawing and pulling me toward her. We moved from the couch to her bedroom and were resting in her tangled sheets by the time the food came. She threw on a robe and brought it back to the bed, where we ate and drank another bottle of wine. We talked for a bit, but once she got close to me again, there was no question. It was time for round two.

49 CHARLOTTE MILLER

November 7

Last week, I called Officer Caitiff to warn him against Ophelia's fantasies. It was one thing for a patient to talk through their thoughts and feelings during therapy, but it was something else when they incorporated their delusions into real life by anchoring them and convincing strangers (especially authority figures) of their distorted version of reality. Though Ophelia was no longer receiving treatment from me, I couldn't stand by and allow her to drag the officer into her psychosis. Not after he had been so kind the day he came to the house to take my vandalism report and helped me clean up the mess.

After we talked on the phone, I spent most nights thinking about Officer Caitiff. It wasn't like me to fixate on a man, but with every passing day, I longed for his company. I barely knew him, but I missed him tremendously. I thought about Grandma Ruth and how she must have felt, waiting in this grand old house for a man who never returned. Though my heart broke for her, I knew my story would be different. I was ready to put myself out there and go after what I wanted.

I had just pulled a frozen dinner out of the oven when I heard a truck pull into my driveway. A quick peek out of the living room window revealed it was Officer Caitiff, and I panicked. Tossing the tin tray of food onto the coffee table, I rushed to my bathroom to put on some lipstick and mascara. I practiced my smile in the mirror and waited for him to knock, but none came. I opened the door to investigate and found him standing there, looking as sharp as ever.

It wasn't long before the man I was fantasizing about had my stomach full of butterflies. He asked me to call him Cameron, and soon after that, we were on my couch with a glass of wine and Chinese food on the way. Conversation flowed easily, and it surprised me to learn how great a listener he was. For the first time in months, I felt safe with someone and allowed myself to be vulnerable.

"I used to have a patient, just like Ophelia. His name was Daniel," I said. "I remember the day his mother came into my practice. She told me that her son was worse than ever. He had been in therapy for six months, but he was spiraling out of control with his wild and paranoid beliefs that someone was going to kill him. Daniel said he could read people's minds and was making himself sick over the stress of knowing what everyone was thinking all the time. He had trouble sleeping because he imagined he could hear his parents' thoughts about his mental state. Daniel said they considered him a freak and wished he could be more like his older, 'normal' brother. In the end, what happened to that boy made me quit my job in Dallas..."

Daniel Larson's head was pounding when he stepped off the school bus that morning. His lanky body swayed as the other kids pushed past him, eager to greet their friends and get to class. For Daniel, the Sunset High School building was just another monster that could swallow him up and bury him deep within its bowels. He was pale with fear, and he could feel the darkness spreading across his brain like spilled ink on a desk. *I'm going to die today*, he thought.

Swallowing hard, he pulled the hood of his black sweatshirt up and over his head and though he tried to go inside, the muscles in his legs wouldn't allow it. He closed his tired eyes and drew a long breath, but the air that filled his lungs was shallow and unsatisfying. His heart was racing, and his hands were clammy. The school bell rang for first period, but the boy's instincts told him to run. So, he did.

The sounds of rushing traffic fed Daniel's anxiety. His chest tightened with each step, and he knew he couldn't keep his pace for long. Though he was on the sidewalk, his fear of being hit by a car forced him to run up the nearest driveway and climb several fences until he found himself in the middle of a subdivision. With his hands on his knees, he caught his breath, eyes darting wildly, looking for signs of danger. The cold, bony finger of death stroked the back of his neck, sending shivers down his spine.

Everything was a threat. The power lines that were strung along the poles hummed with warning. A gardener brandished a gas-powered trimmer as he marched toward a boxwood hedge. A table-saw screamed to life in a nearby garage, chewing through two-by-fours like they were butter. Daniel needed to find a safe place to hide. To his relief, salvation was within a few hundred feet.

Daniel set his sights on a red brick house with no cars in the driveway and an open window. If he could get inside and sit in a quiet place for a few minutes, maybe he could calm down and come up with a plan to get himself home safely.

When he was sure no one was watching, Daniel crept up the lawn and crawled through the kitchen window, a set of blue linen curtains brushing his shoulders as he passed through and landed on the hardwood floor. The house was silent, but the commotion from outside still rang in Daniel's ears. He scrambled to his feet and, with some force, he slid the window down to a solid close. The cacophony of sounds immediately dampened to a whisper. For the first time all day, Daniel could hear his own thoughts and felt at peace, if only for a moment.

A few seconds later, there was a rustling sound from another room. A rush of words he didn't understand entered his mind. Whatever it was, it sounded like Spanish, and it headed straight for him. Daniel turned to open the window, hoping to slip out the same way he came in, but it wouldn't budge. He peered over his shoulder as footsteps approached from behind him. He saw nothing and tried the window again, pulling at the stubborn wooden frame with all his strength, but it was no use. The last thing he heard was a woman's voice shrieking behind him.

"INTRUSO. INTRUSO! DIOS AYUDAME."

He turned around just in time to see a terrified housekeeper swinging a baseball bat at his head. Daniel didn't hear her thoughts when he came in. He figured she must have been sleeping and woke up when he slammed the window closed.

He supposed if she was napping on the couch, she would have grabbed the nearest object laying about to protect herself from a potential threat. And here he was, a male in a hoodie, standing in the middle of her employer's kitchen.

The bat connected with Daniel's right temple, and he dropped to the floor like a marionette cut from its strings. The housekeeper threw down her weapon and ran out the front door, screaming. Daniel lay there, his eyes dimming as he watched his own blood spread across the kitchen floor. When emergency responders found him, he was dead.

50 OPHELIA CLARK

November 8

I came home from the bank yesterday afternoon feeling incredible. Even though the police officers figured out there weren't any bombs in the building quicker than I thought they would, the manager closed the branch for the rest of the evening, anyway. I even watched the news at 5:00 and at 11:00 as well. There was nothing about anyone getting shot. I did it! I passed the challenge! All I had to do now was wait for Isra to reach out to me with instructions on when I could start my training as a diviner. For the first time in weeks, I went to bed knowing that I could rest easy and that the shadow dreams about the awful murder in Monroe were done and over with.

Ophelia's bare feet were covered in sores and filth. She staggered across the strip mall's parking lot and made her way toward the bank, her once white nightgown now gray and rotted. Her joints were stiff from the cold, her steps awkward and jerky. She looked for the knit blanket she had discovered the last time she was there, but it was nowhere to be found. She must have dropped it along the way.

The dark clouds rolled in as she approached the glass door. The lights were on inside and she could see the tellers standing behind their wickets while people waited in line to see them. Ophelia frowned when she noticed the flip calendar which read "Today is the 7th" sitting on the front desk.

"That can't be-" she said, but before she could finish her thought, three figures in white came up from behind her. She gasped as they entered the building, passing through her body as if she were nothing but air.

"Why is this still happening? The seventh was yesterday!" she shouted, pounding on the door with her fist. No one paid her any attention and within moments, the figures drew their guns, and people were screaming.

Ophelia tried to enter, but lacked the strength to pull the heavy door open. She watched in horror as the people inside were forced to the ground. She crouched down, and as someone approached, the sound of a gunshot soon followed. Ophelia looked down for the crimson bloom to spread across her chest, but none appeared. The young girl cupped her hands around her eyes to peer inside, but a mess of blood had spattered against the window and concealed everything inside.

I woke up screaming - the gunshot from my dream still ringing in my ears.

51 CHARLOTTE MILLER

November 8

For the first time in a long time, I awoke with a genuine sense of happiness. I opened my eyes to find Cameron still laying beside me, his chest rising and falling with his heavy breath. What an amazing night. We connected on so many levels. It was wonderful to be vulnerable with someone who truly saw me for who I was. Beyond the physical aspect, I had this feeling of acceptance that I had never experienced with anyone else. Waking up next to Cameron made this house feel like a home.

As I lay in bed and savored the moment, I wondered what our future together could look like. Would I keep my practice here, in Monroe, and have Cameron move in with me? Could I be the level-headed, practical one and he the passionate, spontaneous one? Would we have a child right away? Perhaps we would have a daughter and she would be the apple of his eye. My heart was fluttering with excitement. The possibilities for us were endless.

Everything changed the minute he woke up, though. The magic of the evening had gone and all I could feel was anger at myself for letting my imagination hijack my emotions. I don't know what happened, but the man who entered my bed was not the same man who left it. All I can say is that I never thought I would spend the morning scrubbing bacon, eggs, and shards of porcelain off my wall.

My professional diagnosis: Cameron Caitiff is a total bastard.

52 CAMERON CAITIFF

November 8

I woke up to the sound of my cell phone vibrating instead of my alarm clock. Groggy, and squinty-eyed, I reached for it on my nightstand, but when I touched nothing but air, my eyes shot wide open. The sun flooded the room with bright light. *Where the hell am I?* My head was pounding, and though it was a feeling I was familiar with (you don't drink as much whiskey as I do without getting a hangover once in a while), I winced at the thought of getting up. I fumbled around the regal-looking room and finally found my phone under the bed.

"Officer Caitiff," I answered with a dry crackle in my voice.

"Oh, thank God. Cammy, are you OK?" Marge let out an exaggerated sigh of relief. "When you didn't show up for work this morning, I got worried. I called your phone a bunch of times and when you didn't answer, I made Mayberry take a drive to your house. He just got back to the station and said you weren't there either."

"Yeah, no. I..." My temples throbbed as I remembered my evening with Charlotte. "... wasn't feeling well, so I spent the night at a friend's house. I'll be there soon." I hung up before Marge could ask any further questions. The home screen on my phone said it was 9:30 AM. I was three hours late for my shift. "Shit," I muttered to myself as I shuffled to the bathroom to wash up.

I had a quick shower and when I turned the water off, I could smell coffee and frying bacon. It made me hungry and nauseated at the same time. I wrapped a white towel around my waist and headed for the kitchen, where Charlotte was cooking breakfast. She wore a white tunic with matching flowing pants.

"Good morning, handsome."

"I didn't mean to spend the night. Why didn't you wake me?"

"You looked so peaceful. I didn't want to disturb you. You know, you have a pretty stressful job. Sometimes the body is telling us something. You fell asleep quickly last night, and obviously needed the rest." She grabbed a plate from the counter and piled a helping of freshly made scrambled eggs, bacon, and pancakes. "And now it's time to feed that body of yours." She blushed and tried to hand it to me. "How do you like your coffee? I'll fix you a cup. Go have a seat at the table." The cheer on her face faded as she read the expression on mine. I wasn't in the mood to play house.

"Where's my uniform? I looked all over, but I can't find it."

"Oh yes! I gave it a quick wash and press this morning. I'm an early riser and figured you would need to go into the station straight from here. I wanted to make sure you had something clean to wear." Charlotte's extended arm trembled with the weight of the plate she still held in her hand. She finally set it down. "Everything is in the laundry room, just around the corner."

I left the kitchen and got dressed. By the time I returned, Charlotte had made up her own plate and brought two cups of black coffee to the table where a tray of milk, cream, sugar, and sweetener was waiting.

"I didn't know how you take it," she said with an awkward shrug. "Come. Have something to eat." She patted the seat next to her. *How the hell did I let this happen?* I needed to get out of there. The reality of being in the old witch's house played in my mind again. I don't know how I got past it last night, but this place was unsettling - even in the daylight.

"I have to go to work. They were expecting me hours ago," I said, avoiding eye contact with her.

"Oh. OK," she said, glancing at the steaming pile of food she made. "Would you like to take this with you? I can wrap it up."

"No, that's OK. I'm not really a breakfast person," I said, watching Charlotte's eyes shift nervously. *Nice work, Cam. You hooked up with a clinger.*

"Call me later?" She sounded desperate. I cringed.

"Uh. Maybe that's not such a good idea. To be honest, I'm not even sure how last night even happened. It was a mistake. I came over here on official business and shouldn't have stayed. I should never have... you know... with you. I'm really sorry."

Charlotte carefully put down her fork and stared at her plate. When she finally looked back up, her smile had gone. She looked tired. Nodding, she said "OK. I understand." She walked out of the kitchen, her billowing pants and graceful steps creating a dramatic exit. I left without saying a word. As I reached my truck, I heard Charlotte yell, followed by a crashing noise. *Did she just smash a plate?* I didn't care to know the answer, so I drove straight to the station.

Marge was at the front desk when I walked through the doors. A smug smile and glint in her eye told me I would hear about it.

"Feeling better, officer?" she asked, laughing through her words. That she even used the word "officer" was a clear sign she was laughing *at* me and not *with* me.

"Ha-ha-ha. I'm just a flipping joke to you, aren't I? Well, there's nothing funny about police business!" I snapped, marching past her as I headed to the station's kitchenette for some coffee.

"Okay, then," Marge said, loud enough for me to hear. She sat back down at her desk and continued whatever she was doing, shaking her head at me. *Ok, so I'll never get the respect I deserve from her, but at least most folks in town still hold us cops in high regard. That's all that really matters, right?*

By 11 AM, the caffeine had kicked in and my headache finally passed, allowing me to trudge along with the same paperwork and same patrol spots I normally covered. It was just another lame day at work. Then all hell broke loose.

53 BLAKE JONES

November 8

The sun was low on the horizon. It was only 4:30, but the days were getting shorter, and it would be dark soon. Though I was excited to meet up with Jay and Paul that afternoon, I had a sinking feeling in the pit of my stomach. I *couldn't* let them down again.

I rode my bike to the meeting point and found the two of them in a dark blue mini van with Florida license plates. Paul popped the trunk, and I tossed my bike in before getting in the back seat, careful not to step on the duffel bag that was slumped on the floor.

"Hi guys!" I said with entirely too much enthusiasm. I could feel both of them wince, though they had their backs to me.

"Hey, kid." Jay twisted around from the passenger seat. He gave me a fist bump, but there was something wrong with the way he was staring at me. Everything in my body told me I should leave, but these guys were about to give me another chance to fix my mistake. Plus, where would I go? Home? With Gary? Forget that. I was staying.

"So now that you're here, it's time to talk about next steps," Jay began. "We're going to get the rest of my boss's money today and it will take very careful coordination from all three of us. We need to work as a team. Things are going to get serious, but Blake, I need to know that you'll be able to follow mine and Paul's instructions *exactly*." Jay paused and, for a moment, there was only silence. "You're looking at me like I just ran over your dog, man. Say yes if you understand me."

"What? No. I mean, yeah. For sure, Jay. Absolutely." I nodded eagerly and tried not to sound like an idiot.

"That's good to hear, bud. Now listen carefully." Jay pivoted in his seat a little further to close the distance between us. "Paul rented this van in Atlanta using one of his fake IDs. He borrowed the Florida plates from another car in a grocery store parking lot. When we're done with what we need to do, we'll all go our separate ways," Jay said. I still didn't know what he was talking about, but I nodded anyway as the knot in my gut squeezed tighter.

"We're gonna wear these over our clothes." Paul reached into the duffel bag and pulled out a wrinkled (though clean) white coverall with a hood. I took it from him and held it up against myself.

"Painter's clothes?" I asked.

"Easily disposable, long pants, long-sleeved shirts with hoodies that make us difficult to describe," Jay answered.

"Ah. Right," I said. *What the hell am I getting into?* "What about our faces?"

"We got that covered too." Paul's eyes glinted as he rummaged through the bag, smirking at Jay. A pang of jealousy of the little secret joke they seemed to share jabbed me in the heart. Paul pulled something out and flung it at me. The guys tried to contain their laughter as they watched me unfold it.

"Pantyhose?"

"The final touch to any ensemble," Paul mocked.

"For sure," I agreed, though I still didn't know what any of this was for.

"Ok, guys. We have to get moving soon. Start getting your gear on." Jay broke off the grins and giggles and brought order back to the van. I did what I was told and slipped into my coveralls. Paul climbed into the back with me so he could do the same. Jay put on his disguise in the passenger seat and continued outlining the plan.

"When we pull up to the building, we'll already be wearing the nylons over our heads. Do *not* remove or lift your nylons for any reason until we have driven away. There are cameras both inside and out."

When Paul finished dressing, he reached back into the duffle bag and pulled out two handguns. He handed one to Jay and one to me.

"You remember how to handle that, don't you?" Paul asked me as he pulled a third gun out for himself. My face went pale. I think I might have opened my mouth, but no sound came out.

"Don't worry. They're not loaded. Nobody will get hurt, B.J." Paul clapped me on the shoulder and winked.

"That's right. If we work together and stick to the plan, no one will get hurt," Jay repeated. "Now, listen up. We'll have our guns drawn when we get out of the van. Paul will instruct everyone to get on the ground and will bring everyone into one central place. I'll be carrying the bag and will get the girls to fill it with the cash. Blake, you have a very important job. You're going to be doing crowd work." He used his fingers to draw air quotes. *Is this happening?* My breath got heavy and ragged, and the bile in my stomach turned and gurgled. The thin jumpsuit over the top of my clothes made me sweaty, and I wanted to burst out of the van to feel the cool air on my face. Instead, I sat as still as I could, listening to my cousin.

"You will grab the nearest lady you find and hold her like a hostage. You'll tell everyone to do what we say, or you'll shoot her. Everybody will be so focused on kissing tile they won't get any brave ideas. Once I get the fifty grand, we'll all back ourselves out of the front door. You'll hold on to your hostage until we are through. At the last minute, you'll shove her to the floor and then we'll all get back into the van. Paul takes us to the Firebird I parked just outside of Monroe. I get in and head back to Atlanta. You get on your bike and go home. Paul takes the rental to his garage, puts the licence plates back on, and returns it to the rental place in the morning. Then the three of us have no contact for a few weeks," Jay finished.

My mind was spinning, and my gut clenched tight. *Oh, no.* I pulled on the door handle and got it open just wide enough for me to stick my head out. The tuna sandwich I ate for lunch painted the curb in pasty chunks. I wretched a few more times.

"Better get the jitters out of your system now," Paul said.

With my head still hanging out of the door, I wiped my mouth on the sleeve of my shirt. "Are we really going to do what I think we're going to do?" I asked. My throat burned from my stomach acid. Jay only grinned at me before turning to face forward as Paul started the engine.

54 GLORY WALKER

November 8

I got a call from Momma this afternoon. She and Daddy had sent the money transfer I'd asked for, and it was sittin' in my account. Unfortunately, the cable company had already disconnected my Internet service a few days ago for defaultin' on the payment for the third month in a row and if I wanted to take care of business today, I'd have to either guess my neighbor's Wi-Fi password so I could pay online or head on over to the bank and have the teller do it. Lord knows I'd already tried enterin' their pets' and kids' names with no success, and since I needed a little cash to keep in my purse, I grabbed my stack of bills, loaded Trent into the truck, and headed over to Jefferson Street. Trent came along quietly, and though I had apologized to him about a thousand times for losin' my temper last week, I still couldn't look at him without feelin' guilty.

The bank's florescent lightin' bounced off the black-and-white checkered tile, which was a bit distractin' for Trent. He amused himself with his reflection on the floor. I had to hook my arm into his so I could keep him beside me as we followed the velvet rope to get to the teller's wicket. We waited in line long enough for me to notice the plants needed waterin' and that the Page-A-Day calendar was still showin' yesterday's date. A young teller at the last wicket waved us over.

"OK, Mrs. Walker. I've submitted these for payment, and they should be received by the billing companies by tomorrow morning. Is there anything else I can help you with today?" The girl asked. Before I could answer, Trent started clappin' his hands and laughin', startlin' me, the woman behind the counter, and about a half-dozen strangers in line. We all turned to look at him and realized that he was focused on the glass doors, where three men, all dressed in white and wearin' pantyhose over their heads, rushed in. I froze.

"Everybody, put your hands in the air. This is a robbery!" the first man screamed as he stood in the center of the room, wavin' his gun. The two men that came in behind him sprang into action and did the same.

"Get down, get DOWN!" the second man screamed. He made his way to the teller's counter, pushin' folks to the ground as he moved past. My mind went blank. All I could think to do was hold Trent close to me with one arm and hold the other one up in surrender.

"Don't move, baby," I whispered to my son, grippin' him tight as I watched the third man pull a woman up off the floor and hold a gun to her head.

"Do as we say, and nobody gets hurt," the third man said. His voice sounded small and unconvincin', but the gun spoke loud and clear. "You! Don't look at me or the girl gets it in the face!" he yelled at a customer who was peerin' up from the floor. They turned their head away from him and now faced me and Trent with panic in their eyes.

"Hurry up! Cash in the bag. Cash in the BAG!" man number two shrieked at the teller, who was frantically grabbin' bundles of cash from the wicket drawers.

I could see that man number three was strugglin' to keep hold of the woman he'd grabbed because she was squirmin' so much. *Dear Lord, please let me get through this.*

"We got it! Go, go, GO." Man number two instructed his partners as he ran back out from behind the counter. His bag barely looked like it had anythin' in it. Man number one ran out the front doors with man number two right behind him. Man number three said somethin' to the woman he was holdin' as he started backin' towards the exit. It looked like he was tryin' to take her with them, and she started strugglin'.

Then there was a bang.

55 CAMERON CAITIFF

November 8

“Calling all units. Calling all units. There’s a 10-17 in progress at the Neelan Thomas Bank,” Marge announced over the radio. *First a bomb threat and now armed robbery?* I didn’t believe it, but I was less than two minutes away.

“O-four-seven responding,” I radioed back. I turned on the sirens and flashing lights. There was no way anyone would beat me to the scene this time. And if I see Ophelia Clark or Isra Kawn anywhere *near* the bank, I’ll have them in handcuffs before they know what hit them.

“Cam, there are three armed suspects. Someone’s been shot. The suspects are reported to have just left the scene. Backup is on its way. An ambulance is heading over there as well," Marge called back.

I hadn't heard fear or worry in Marge's voice until just then. I did my best to shake it off. This was my big chance to command a scene. A career-defining moment. My adrenaline was pumping when I pulled my truck into the parking lot.

First on scene. YES! A wave of giddiness washed over me, and I took a few seconds to compose myself.

"Marge, this is O-four-seven. I'm on scene and proceeding to clear the area for the paramedics."

"Cam, wait for back-"

I got out of my truck and withdrew my weapon.

56 GLORY WALKER

November 8

The sound of the shot was still ringin' in my ears when my boy hit the ground. Without thinkin', I dropped to my knees and scooped Trent into my arms. The entire world went dark and silent around us.

"No, baby. No." I searched his face for answers and was stunned. I know no one will believe this (I don't think I'd believe it if it didn't happen to me), but at that moment his face transformed. The Lord knows I couldn't pay my boy a million dollars to look me straight in the eye, but for a second, I saw the face of a handsome young man lookin' right into my soul. That face, those eyes, knew me for the weak person I was. He saw through all my anger and pain. He saw me for all of my faults. And he *smiled* at me. It was a kind and gentle smile. *He forgave me. Thank God, he forgave me.*

Before I could understand what was happenin', the face I was lookin' at melted away and I found myself holdin' a dyin' boy that looked just like Trent. He coughed only once. A glob of blood spattered out of his mouth and ran down his cheek. His gaze drifted up to the ceilin', and he looked confused. A burst of blood had spread out on the front of his shirt. I pressed down on it with my hand, and I could feel somethin' warm and wet on my legs. I didn't realize until later that I was sittin' in a pool of his blood. Without makin' a sound, Trent's head rolled to the side, and he was gone. My boy's life drained out onto the floor like a broken bottle of molasses, and all I could do was scream.

57 CAMERON CAITIFF

November 8

As I walked up to the glass doors, a terrified teller approached from the inside. She slid the lock to let me in, but I motioned for her to stay quiet and wait there. She nodded, re-locked the door, and took a few steps back.

My training kicked in and I was operating on autopilot. It was like a higher power had taken control of my body, and I knew exactly what to do. I assessed the area, tucking around corners, surveying the shrubs and garbage bins that lined the perimeter in search of hiding suspects. The area was clear. I could hear sirens approaching

from the distance, and if I wanted to make head-
lines, I needed to act fast.

When I returned, the same girl was waiting.
As soon as she opened the doors, the smell of
gunfire and something metallic hit me, but it was
the crowd of people yelling and crying that
pulled my focus toward the back of the room.
They had formed a circle around something.

"Paramedics and more officers are on their
way. Wait for them right here," I instructed the
teller before heading to the back. "My name is
Officer Caitiff. I'm here to help. Please move
away. Move away!" I wedged a path through the
small crowd. As I pushed through and got closer,
everything seemed to move in slow motion. I had
time to think, to assess, and to notice that the
sound my shoes were making on the tiled floor
had changed from a 'clack' to a 'splash'. The metallic smell was stronger here and when I realized
what it was, I could barely bring myself to look
down.

My adrenaline was waning, and I realized I
was standing in a pool of blood. I stood there,
paralyzed, staring at my shoes in the center of a
coagulated crimson puddle. The sound of the
door bursting open and paramedics rushing
through broke my trance, and I sprang back into
action.

"Everybody, get back!" I cleared an opening
for the emergency responders. The crowd parted
and revealed the horror that was laying in the

middle. All that blood - it was coming from a little boy. He couldn't have been over ten years old. His face was as white as a sheet. His bloodied mouth gaped open, and his brown eyes stared up at me, frozen and unchanging. The boy's cheeks and forehead were covered with bloody fingerprints from his mother, who was still holding him and rocking him back and forth. He was wearing a striped t-shirt that was completely soaked in his blood and there was a small hole in the left side of his chest.

The paramedics were on top of him within seconds. One of them immediately cut his shirt away and applied some sterile tape to three sides of the bullet hole. Another confirmed that he wasn't breathing and secured an oxygen mask to his face. They lifted him onto the gurney and began chest compressions with ventilation as they wheeled him toward the exit. His mother stumbled over herself, but followed. She was hysterical and kept repeating the words "I'm sorry." It gave me the chills. Though the paramedics followed protocol, deep down I knew that kid had choked to death on his own blood and was never coming back. The room started spinning.

A second and third squad car pulled up. It was Anderson and Mayberry arriving just in time to hold the double doors open for the paramedics. I began walking toward them, but the floor felt like quicksand, and I became unsteady. As the two other officers approached, Anderson noticed my face didn't look right and cocked an eyebrow at me. Mayberry said something to him, but I couldn't make it out. It sounded like everyone was under water. I needed some air. The smell, the blood, the people staring at me and waiting for direction - it was more than what I prepared for. I should have briefed the other officers, but I had to get out of there. Just for a minute.

I felt my stomach wretch, and I bolted for the exit. The moment I was outside, the bile erupted from my core, and I used a decorative planter as a waste bin. I struggled to suck in another breath before the next wave came, while something else caught my attention. Out of the corner of my eye, I saw a cluster of small twinkling lights. I heaved again and steadied myself with my hand against the brick wall.

When I was sure my gut was empty, I looked across the parking lot and stared at the twinkling lights until my eyes adjusted and the whole dev-astating picture came into focus. A crowd had formed, much like the day before, only this time they were recording the incident with the cameras on their phones. Those bastards caught me throw-ing up on video. I marched over there and tried to collect the evidence, but it was too late. Half of them had already posted their copies online. The videos were out of my reach and likely replicat-ing in cyberspace like a virus. I was humiliated.

I grabbed one of the filming bystanders by the collar. Looking at his smug face made me want to knock his head clean off his shoulders. I gnashed my teeth while the civilians were still filming.

"Stop! Someone, help! What are you doing to him? Police brutality!" a young woman's voice cried out from somewhere within the crowd. I drew in a deep breath. *Calm down and choose your next move wisely.* Deciding he wasn't worth the risk of being on the wrong side of the news, I let go of him and marched straight into the bank.

As soon as I stepped back in there, I knew I couldn't do it. The boy was gone, but the stench of death and the image of his face were too much. I took one look at the brownish red mess on the floor, now smeared with the prints of where his mother had been sitting, and I dry-heaved. The entire room went silent, and all eyes turned to me. I didn't realize I had made a sound, but Mayberry excused himself from the interview he was conducting with a witness and walked over to me.

"We got it from here, man. Go back to the station and start filling out your report," Mayberry said, clapping me on the back. I hoped he didn't see me wince, but I gave him a curt nod and left, grateful to be getting out of there.

58 BLAKE JONES

November 8

Oh my God, oh my God. What happened? I couldn't breathe. It was some time after 6:30 PM when I came barreling down the street on my bike. I was pedaling like the devil was chasing me, frantically swiping my sweaty hair out of my eyes. It was dark, and though this was the neighborhood I grew up in, I felt disoriented and struggled to see where I was going. Everything looked different. Or maybe I was different. Jay and Paul - they promised me no one would get hurt.

I rounded the corner, and I could see that someone had left the front lights on for me. The soft glow called to me like a lighthouse to a sailor lost at sea. For the first time in months, I was glad to be home. A small wave of relief washed over me as I rode up the driveway.

I jumped off my bike while it was still in motion and let it crash down onto the concrete. I took the steps two at a time and burst into the house, slamming and locking the door behind me. *Safe*. The house was warm and smelled like pot roast (my favorite), but the thought of that brown hunk of beef stewing in its juices made me gag. My throat started constricting and before I understood what was happening, giant tears flooded my eyes.

I got to my room without encountering anyone and turned my music up loud to stifle the sounds of my uncontrollable sobbing. *They said the guns weren't loaded. Why did that lady have to struggle with me so hard? I was about to let her go. I TOLD her that. Why did she have to go and do something so stupid? It doesn't make sense. I told her she would be OK, and she HIT me*. I didn't mean to squeeze the trigger. I didn't even realize my finger was on it until the gun went off. It wasn't supposed to be loaded. That's what he told me. No one was supposed to get hurt. *Oh, God. I hope that kid is OK.*

59 CHARLOTTE MILLER

November 9

I was flipping through the channels on the T.V. last night and stopped to watch a breaking news update from the local station. There was a media crew at the bank again and, to my astonishment, they were showing footage of Cameron. I didn't recognize him at first because he had his head bowed into a planter. I watched, completely stunned.

"We are being told that the robbers shot and killed a young boy, just as they were leaving with what they came for. The scene inside was apparently so gruesome, bystanders filmed a local police officer vomiting outside the bank's doors. Warning. What you are about to see may be graphic for some viewers," the young male re-porter spoke into his microphone, never breaking eye contact with the camera. They rolled the clip.

I never thought something like this could hap-pen in a town like Monroe. And wasn't it just typical of the media to be denied entry into a murder scene and turn their attention to the next most sensational thing - a police officer losing his lunch? I felt guilty about how angry I got yester-day morning. Cameron was not a bastard. He was just a man trying to do his job. A man who I was comfortable with. A man who I wouldn't give up on so easily.

By morning, Cameron's footage was playing on the national stations. I couldn't imagine what he was going through right now. The poor man was so traumatized by what he saw it made him sick. It goes to show that he has a sensitive side to him, after all. I tried calling his cell phone a few times, but he never picked up. I sent him a text message to let him know I was here if he wanted to talk and that I only wanted to help. He needed me, whether he knew it or not, and if we were ever going to have the type of relationship I thought we could, I needed to be there for him.

Sitting at my kitchen table, I sipped at my steaming mug of black coffee as my mind re-played the events of the past few days. I took a large bite out of my toasted rye with butter and contemplated what Cameron had said the night he was here. He said Ophelia Clark was at the bank the day before last, and he suspected she had something to do with the bomb threat. *Was it possible she had something to do with the rob-bery as well?*

60 OPHELIA CLARK

November 9

The murder at the bank was all over the news. The local channels had been airing the story since last night. It happened on the eighth, not the seventh. I didn't understand how I could've been so wrong about the date until one of the news stations showed the surveillance footage of the robbery. Despite the chaos of the three armed guys entering the doors and forcing people to the ground, I couldn't take my eyes off of the calendar on the courtesy desk in the background. It still read: Today is the 7th. Someone forgot to flip it. *Maybe the stress of going into work the day after a bomb threat had something to do with it*. I could barely get myself out of bed this morning.

"Mom, I really don't feel well. I think I should stay home from school today," I said, as I rummaged through the kitchen cabinet in search of my migraine medication.

"Oh, honey. Let me help you," Mom said, reaching past me to pull out the bottle. She twisted it open, tapped two pills into my outstretched hand, and grabbed a glass of water for me. She studied me as I popped the medication into my mouth and washed it down. "You knew, didn't you?" she murmured.

"Hmm?" I knitted my eyebrows, unsure of what she was talking about.

"You knew that something bad was going to happen in this town. You saw it in your dreams - the ones you call your *shadow* dreams," she said. It was the first time she'd ever talked about my abilities without using the word nonsense. My eyes welled up, and my lower lip trembled. "Come here." Mom wrapped me in her arms and held me as I sobbed.

"I tried to change it," I said, wiping the hot tears as they rolled down my cheeks.

"I'm sorry that we never believed you. I'm so, so sorry." She hugged me even tighter. "We didn't want to believe something like this was possible, but now I see that it's true. You see things others can't." She smoothed the back of my hair before pulling away so she could cup my face into her hands and look into my eyes. "You tried to tell me, and I wasn't there for you. I want to do better, O. After what we saw on T.V. about that poor boy, I kept imagining what his mother was going through and it made me think about how much I love you and how I wish things were better between us."

"I want that too, Mom," I said, my voice still shaky. She gave me a strained smile and said, "I think it's best if you go to class today. It might help to take your mind off things. C'mon. I'll drive you." Though I was sure nothing could distract me from the grief and failure I felt, I nodded and finished getting ready. *After all these years, she finally believes me.*

I slumped over my desk in the front row of comp science class while Mr. Everets was explaining and drawing out the syntax for declaring a three-dimensional array in C++ programming language: *int three_d[10][20][30];*

My puffy, tired eyes blinked slowly. I couldn't be less interested, but my grades had slipped so badly I figured I should write something down. I jammed my hand into my backpack and felt around for a notebook and as I looked around the classroom; everyone was taking notes. Everyone except Blake Jones.

Something was off with him. He didn't seem like his regular aloof self, and when his empty gaze met my stare, I turned away quickly, freeing the pad of paper from my bag and setting it down in front of me. Mr. Everets turned around just in time to see me scribble. He opened his mouth, but before he could make a sound, there was a knock at the door.

All of us watched as our teacher made his way across the room. When he opened it, there were two uniformed officers waiting on the other side. Mr. Everets stepped into the hallway and closed the door behind him.

"Oh, *shit!*" one student who also saw the men in blue whispered too loudly.

"Did you see that?" another student asked his table partner.

The roar of a room full of teens chatting at the same time was cut down to a deafening silence the moment Mr. Everets opened the door and the two officers stepped in. I recognized them right away. These were the same two officers who responded to the bomb threat at the bank. *Oh, no. They found me.* As careful as I was to mask my IP address, they tracked me right down to the classroom I made the call from. There was no other explanation for it.

Mr. Everets walked toward me. Panic set in, and I started hyperventilating. I looked at him for help, but he ignored me completely. My teacher moved past my desk and put a hand on Blake's shoulder.

"Blake, I'm afraid you'll have to go with these men." Blake's red-rimmed eyes flashed with terror, and his entire body shook as he watched the two officers approach him.

"I'm sorry," Blake stuttered as he stood up from his chair. Tears were streaming down his splotchy, red face. "It was an accident. I didn't mean to," he sobbed. Mr. Everets leaned in close to Blake's ear and whispered:

"Blake, the school will contact your mother. Don't say another word until you have an attorney present. Not. Another. Word."

"Blake Jones," one officer said as he freed a pair of handcuffs from his utility belt. "...you are charged with the murder of Trent Walker." He clicked one cuff around Blake's wrist, then reached for the other.

"No," Blake groaned between sobs.

The sound of the second handcuff clicking into place snapped me out of it, and I realized I had forgotten to breathe. As the officers flanked Blake on both sides, they read him his Miranda rights and escorted him out of the classroom and down the hall. The entire class was dumbfounded and silently stared at the doorway, trying to process what had happened.

"Class dismissed," Mr. Everets announced. He tossed his dry-erase marker on the white-board ledge. It bounced off, fell on the floor, and rolled across the room as he walked out.

Blake? Arrested for murder? I felt like I would be sick.

61 CAMERON CAITIFF

November 10

It was 4:00 AM. I'd been at home since the shooting at the bank, but I hadn't slept in 3 days. The Sergeant told me to take the rest of the week off. I felt like a piece of shit accepting the time away, but I couldn't bear the thought of going back. I was tired. *Exhausted, actually*. I wanted to sleep, but I just couldn't. Scrolling through my phone, I cringed at the number of missed calls from Charlotte's number. She probably knew what had happened by now, but I didn't want to talk to her. Especially not while I was attempting to drown my memories in Canadian Club. I was hoping the liquor would numb the pain. Maybe get the smell of blood and vomit out of my head, but it just made me dizzy every time I got up to piss. I must've blacked out for a few hours because the next thing I knew, Marge was calling. I hit the 'Ignore' button. I couldn't talk to her either, but she left me a voice message.

"They caught them," she said. Apparently, it was two young men and a minor - the same boys I pulled over in the Firebird not two weeks ago. I recognized their names. I let them off with a warning, but I couldn't help wondering: *If I had searched that car that day, would I have found anything suspicious? Would I have found the gun that would shoot and kill that ten-year-old boy?*

Dammit. Why does Charlotte insist on calling and calling? Take the hint, lady. 'Send to voice mail'.

Every time I closed my eyes, I saw that little kid's face. His eyes that looked open but saw nothing. His screaming mouth that didn't make a sound. I saw that boy and then the blood. So much blood. No amount of rye would help me forget how that sticky mess felt under my shoes. The sucking sound it made as I bolted out of the building so I could get sick.

And then there was the media. All I ever wanted was a little recognition. A little adoration from the people I protected and served every day. Well, now I was freaking *famous*. They were calling me "Officer Upchuck" all over the Internet. Some clever son-of-a-bitch spliced a bunch of audios from news reports and auto-tuned a song called "Blowing Chunks". It was only posted for 24 hours and already had over 2 million views!

It wouldn't be long until everyone in the entire country watched me fail at my job. I could never go back to the station and face Marge and those guys. They were probably laughing their asses off at me right now. And I sure as hell wouldn't ever make it into the force in Atlanta. My career as an officer was the only thing that mattered to me, and now it was over. I was ruined. The ice in my tumbler clinked as I took another deep drink.

I'm done with this. I'm done with everything.

62 GLORY WALKER

November 14

The hospital gave me some meds to help me sleep and keep calm, but they didn't work much. Every time I closed my eyes, I only saw that face smilin' at me.

Momma and Daddy flew in from Minnesota to help plan the funeral. The military granted Cooper special leave, and he was on the next flight home. We pushed the date out so Coop could be here, though it terrified me to see him.

Daddy met him at the airport and brought him home. He'd never looked so old and broken, and I wondered if it was his service or the death of our son that had stolen the light from behind his eyes. He gave me a great big hug when he walked in and immediately broke down in my arms. How could he still love me after our baby got killed on my watch?

Momma had to give Coop the details about what happened. I didn't have the strength. Nanna used to say that the strongest metal was forged in fire and beaten over and over and then re-fired again. With each beatin', the metal got stronger. Momma was metal, but not me.

The day of the funeral was warm and sunny, so we held the ceremony outdoors at the gravesite. There were at least two hundred people in attendance. I didn't recognize most of them, but I was too sedated to care. I could barely pay attention to the sermon.

"... and in God's infinite wisdom, he calls another one of his angels back to heaven," the minister read from his book. He wore all black except for the pop of white in his collar.

I couldn't do anythin' but stare at the pearl-white casket sparklin' in the sun. It sat in the center between two large flower arrangements made up of white and blue carnations with baby's breath. The little boy in the box looked small and perfect in the new suit Momma got him. His eyes and lips were glued shut, and his body was motionless. Trent was never so still, not even when he was sleepin'. That thing inside the casket was not my boy. It was a poor imitation of him. A lifeless doll. It had nothin' in common with Trent except his size. Even the hair looked wrong.

I stood up and stumbled over to the casket as the minister was wrappin' up his eulogy. A few folks gasped when I wobbled a bit in the grass, but everyone stayed seated. I looked down at the thing everyone was sayin' was Trent and tried not to let the feelin's of relief overtake the feelin's of guilt and remorse. I wasn't fit to be his mother and now he didn't have to suffer me. Just when I was sure my chest would explode, I felt Cooper's hand on my shoulder.

"No, don't!" I slapped his hand away. "You don't get to pretend to be here for me now."

The minister stopped talkin' and all eyes were on me. I turned to face the lot of them. "None of you do! Why are y'all even here? *None* of you were kind to us when we needed it! Y'all sittin' there, starin' at me, but you sure as *hell* didn't want anythin' to do with me or my son last week." Cooper tried to pull me away, but I wrenched my arm out of his. "Y'all are a bunch of hypocrites and *gawkers*. That's what *you* are."

Momma hugged me while Cooper wiped at his face and walked away. As I watched people leavin' through blurred tears, my eyes stopped on an elderly woman wearin' a long black dress. I couldn't remember how I knew her, but I'd definitely seen her before. She walked up to the small casket.

"Fly away home, brave little angel. You were too good for this place," she told the thing that looked like Trent before she approached me, now standin' off to the side and next to momma. The woman looked me in the eye and bowed her head before turnin' her attention to the casket. I followed her gaze and noticed another two people I did not recognize from the crowd. Another older woman and a young boy peered into the pearl-white box, each of them with their hands clasped. The woman was platinum blond and sharply dressed with a fuchsia pill box hat, matchin' wool blazer, a black wool skirt, black stockin's, and black leather shoes. The boy had a slender build and wore a nicely tailored black suit with black patent shoes. His head reached the height of the woman's chin and it made me think of the last day I took Trent to the park.

As my lower lip started tremblin' and my sore eyes watered, a light breeze brought a waft of White Diamonds perfume across my nose. I blinked hard to clear my tears and tried to get a closer look at the two mourners. I walked toward them, but the old woman in the black dress grabbed my arm and pulled me back.

"Shhhhh," she put her index finger over her lips and whispered, "Watch," still holdin' my arm. I squinted at the boy, who now pulled somethin' out of his pocket. He looked up at the blond woman and smiled as he brought it to his mouth and took a bite of a cookie as they walked back down the center aisle. Stuffed up and swollen as my nose was, I could taste oatmeal and sugar on my tongue. *Could it be?*

"Nanna?" I yelled across the rows of empty chairs. The woman and the boy continued walkin' and never looked back. I watched as they faded away with every step they took. "Trent?" My voice caught in my throat before Momma wrapped her arms around me again and kept me from fallin' to my knees. The pair of them completely vanished, as if they had never been there at all. "Momma, did you see those two?" I asked.

"Oh, honey. It's just us. Your father went to go check on Coop."

"No. That's not right. This woman saw them." I pulled away from her to point out the woman in black with the cloud of white hair, but she, too, was gone.

63 CHARLOTTE MILLER

November 15

Cameron had returned none of my calls or text messages. Even if he wasn't ready to talk, I just wanted to know he was OK. I decided the best thing to do was to stop by for a wellness check, so I picked up some lunch and headed to his house. When I arrived, there were two police vehicles parked in the driveway, one of which was Cameron's. I parked on the road.

Balancing two coffee cups in one hand and a bag containing two chicken salad sandwiches in the other, I walked to the house, rehearsing what I would say to Cameron once he opened the door. "I'm so sorry about what you are going through.

The media are treating you unfairly. I know things went a little fast between us, but I'm here to support you. If you want to talk, we can, but there's no pressure. I brought sandwiches." I even practiced my smile and sandwich-holding pose.

As soon as I got close to the front door, my hands went numb. The cups of hot coffee toppled onto the porch, the plastic lids popping off on contact. The scalding liquid splashed up onto my jeans, but didn't feel it. I threw the brown bag down and ran up to the door, which was hanging wide open.

"Cameron?" I shouted into the doorway. "Cameron?" I pulled down the yellow police tape that stretched across the entrance and stepped inside.

"CAMERON!"

A police officer stepped into the hallway from another room.

"Ma'am, you can't be in here. These premises are under investigation," he said. *Under investigation? Why would Cameron be under investigation?* I had to see him and took a few more steps inside.

"Ma'am!" The officer moved toward me with his arm held out, stopping me in my tracks. I was close enough to read the name on his badge.

"Um. Yes. Hello, Officer Mayberry. What happened? Is Cameron OK?" My ears and cheeks were getting red as my heartbeat quickened with panic.

"What is your name, ma'am?" he asked. I gave him my information. "And what is your relationship to Officer Caitiff?" He cocked his head to the side and stared, pencil poised.

"I... I'm Cameron's girlfriend," I exaggerated, hoping this would grant me access to more information from the officer.

"Oh, dear. Oh, my. Miss Miller, I'm very sorry to tell you this, but Cameron Caitiff took his own life yesterday."

I covered my gaping mouth with both hands. I was speechless. As my lips quivered and a lump grew in my throat, Officer Mayberry shared some details, though I was not in a state to hear anything more than fragments of what he was saying. "... shot himself ... No note... Trying to keep things quiet for now..."

How did I not see this coming? For all my training, I should have known that what happened at the bank would have had a major psychological impact on Cameron. *If I had come here a day sooner, would he still be alive?*

I went home and opened a bottle of wine. Sitting in my therapist chair, I stared at the gray couch across from me and drew long sips of Cabernet, letting the bold flavor seep into my tongue and the alcohol do its work to numb my pain. I craved mental stillness after the emotional roller coaster

I had been on over these past few days. Instead, my head swooned with strange and random thoughts; ridiculous thoughts that didn't feel like my own, like a second voice whispering in my ear. The notions felt foreign and against everything I had learned, but the longer I sat with them, the more logical they sounded.

Cameron was more than just a one-night stand. Cameron was a real chance at happiness for me in this town. The only reason he was curt with me that morning was because he was late for work. That really was my fault. I should have woken him up. I never even apologized to him.

This all feels very familiar. Why am I thinking of my ex-boyfriend, Ted? Is it because at the time we broke up, I was so focused on Daniel Larson's case that I left no space to make Ted feel loved or appreciated? Maybe that's why we didn't work out.

That can't be right.

And besides, this situation is totally different. I focused on Cameron fully, and Ophelia wasn't even my patient anymore.

But she and Daniel shared a similar trait profile, and they were both convinced they had special powers. In Daniel's case, he got himself killed, but in Ophelia's case...

... she got Cameron killed.

But Cameron died of suicide.

Cameron never would have taken his own life if he hadn't responded to that stupid bank call.

All the police training in the world couldn't have prepared him for the horror that he saw there. All he wanted was for people to respect him and the media chewed him up and spit him out like yesterday's trash. They mocked him to death.

I poured the last of the wine into my glass and drank, listless and solemn, in the dimming light with nothing but the swelling shadows to keep me company. I let the darkness of the room overtake me and experienced the emptiness and sadness Ruth Rivers felt when the man she loved died and left her alone in this place. *Ruth, you poor, dear soul.*

Before long, dusk transitioned to dawn, and I hadn't moved a muscle all night. I was so lost in thought; I hadn't so much as blinked, though my seat was damp with urine. I should have been disgusted, but I remained unphased. As I worked my stiffened joints to stand up, the motivational picture fell off the wall behind me, and I grinned. My mind had worked its way toward a singular and obvious conclusion that I needed to take action on. *Ophelia Clark had to pay for what she'd done to Cameron and for taking away my true love.*

64 OPHELIA CLARK

November 16

A week ago, Isra and I stood outside the Neelan Thomas bank watching the cops look for an imaginary bomb. I haven't seen or heard from her since. Though she said she'd come for me if I passed her challenge, I still thought I'd see her one last time. I felt horrible about the way I'd failed Trenton Walker. The boy's death would haunt me for the rest of my life. I knew I wasn't *directly* responsible - Blake Jones would have to answer for that, but I was at least partially to blame. And Isra too. I'll never understand how she could just let something like that happen. If I had powers like hers,

I'd use them to help as many people as possible. And maybe I still could.

While the blue covellite necklace was still in my possession, I continued to wear it every day. Its essence was strengthening my waking visions, and I was getting pretty good at these. Mostly, I was gaining insight into the kids at my school. I didn't even have to touch them to have a vision now. All I needed was to place my hand on an object and I would get a sense for the last person who touched it. It's amazing what you can learn about someone when they don't have their defenses up. All this time, I thought I was the only one who felt alone and insecure, but it turns out that most kids were just like me. They showed up at school, went to class, and tried not to be singled out. Once I understood this, it was so much easier for me to relax and just be myself. I even found someone to sit with at lunch. Her name is Cheryl, and all I had to do was be the one to ask first. Who'd have guessed?

When it came to the covellite and my shadow dreams; however, it didn't seem to work at all. Lately I'd been having a new dream, but it was even more confusing than the last.

Ophelia stood alone in the woods, arms folded across her jean jacket to keep it closed, though she was already shivering. The night sky withheld its stars, allowing only the waning moon to cast its soft light upon the sparse branches of the trees and fallen leaves on the ground. The wind was low and steady and when Ophelia listened closely, she could hear the tree trunks creaking as they swayed back and forth. But something wasn't right. *Where were the sounds of chirping crickets and croaking frogs? Where were the scuttling foxes, rabbits, and rodents? There were plenty of creatures who should be out and about, both predators and prey. I wonder which am I?*

A shadow interrupted a spot of moonbeam just in front of her and crossed from left to right. The shadow was large enough to be a grown person, but there was no sound of a footfall on the dry, crunchy forest bed. Ophelia's eyes grew wide, and her heart raced. She stood perfectly still and held her breath as she looked and listened. Another shadow passed from one tree trunk to another as if it were trying to avoid being seen. Motionless, Ophelia trained her eyes on the tree trunk where she thought the thing was hiding, hoping to glimpse it the next time it moved.

"I'm done with this. I'm done with everything," a man's voice said, far off in the distance. Ophelia's body stiffened. *That voice sounds familiar. Do I call out to it and ruin my chance of sneaking up on the shadow?*

"Hell-" Ophelia started, but the moment she made a sound, a pair of hands clamped around her throat. Caught completely off guard, she began clawing and hammering at the dark figure. As Ophelia gasped for air, the shadow leaned into her ear and, in a dry, croaky voice, it whispered:

"You took him from her. You took him from *us*. Now you must pay the price."

65 BLAKE JONES

November 17

I laid on the bottom bunk of a two-tiered, steel framed bed with my arm folded across my forehead. If I had to guess the time, I'd say it was close to 3 AM. I wouldn't be falling asleep soon and, much like the night before, it was just me, alone with my thoughts. It was dark, and the entire prison was quiet except for the shuffling of the guard at his desk and my cell-mate, who was snoring. He sounded like a lawn mower with engine problems, but was a pretty quiet guy during the day. In fact, he hadn't said more than a couple of words since I got here, which was fine by me. The reality of the past 9 days still hadn't sunk in, and I didn't want to talk to him (or anyone else). There was no way this was my real life. I did my best to convince myself that this was all just a horrible dream; that I could wake up in my bed at any moment, and that kid would be alive and well. But this version of reality became less and less likely each time the sun came up. Tomorrow would probably be no different.

I've only seen my mom once since everything got turned upside down, and it was the day the cops brought me into the juvenile hall. She looked tired and her face was red, like she'd been crying. Mom made a huge scene and accused them of harassment and abuse of power. She insisted that they'd made a mistake and that I couldn't have possibly done what they said I did. But when they finally let her see me, she took one look at my face and knew it was the truth. I could pinpoint the exact moment when her heart broke by the change in her eyes. Maybe she deserved it for breaking my heart first when she chose Garry over her own family. I bet she never thought about that.

I was in juvie for five days before seeing the judge. Between my state-appointed representation and what the officers told me, I learned they caught Paul first. The cops linked his gun to the one that went off and killed the kid when that lady struggled with me before I let her go. Paul said he would get rid of it the night of the bank robbery, but I guess that didn't happen. It didn't take him long to give me up, though. He surrendered the money to the cops and saved himself from any serious charges, even though it was his gun, and he led the whole thing. Maybe he thought I'd end up serving some time in juvenile detention. Maybe he didn't care at all. But since the crime was *3rd degree murder,* and I was *seventeen*, the judge decided I should be tried as an adult and set my bail at $250,000. It might as well have been ten quadrillion space bucks. Nobody I knew had that kind of money, so I ended up getting transferred to the Baldwin State medium security prison for men while I awaited my trial.

All I can think about is how much I want to go home.

66 CHARLOTTE MILLER

November 29

I paced outside of Morson County High and checked my watch for the third time in five minutes. School was about to let out, but it was already getting dark, and I hoped I could spot Ophelia in the crowd of students once they had come bursting through the exits. I waited by the South wing so that she would need to walk toward me if she were on her way home. *Patience is key, Charlotte. Like the spider to the fly.* The bell rang and my body tensed. Teens poured out of the doorways, vacating the premises as fast as they could. My eyes darted back and forth, but there were no signs of Ophelia. When the rush slowed to a trickle, I was sure she had slipped by me. I nearly gave up, but just then, her dark hair and jean jacket caught my eye. I was right where I needed to be. With my back turned, I waited for her to walk by.

"Ophelia? Is that you?" I called out to her. She turned around, a look of confusion transforming into a flash of recognition on her face.

"Oh. Hey, Dr. Charlotte." She offered a thin smile.

"It's good to see you. How are you doing?" I kept my tone pleasant and casual, though my heart filled with rage at the very sight of her.

"I'm alright, I guess." She sounded casual, which only fueled my anger, but I remained calm.

"I'm glad to hear it. I know how difficult being a teenager can be." *Especially for a manipulative narcissist like you. Controlling everyone around you for your own amusement.* I allowed space for some silence. "Are you going home? I'm heading this way too. Let's walk together."

"Um. Yeah, sure. That's fine," she said.

"Great. I could use some company. It's been a tough few weeks, hasn't it?" I synchronized my steps with hers.

"Yeah." Ophelia walked with a confidence I hadn't seen in her before. *How cocky and full of herself.*

"For me in particular," I added.

"Oh? How come?" Ophelia looked up at me. *The fake concern in her eyes is as hollow as her soul. Do not fall for this act, Charlotte.*

"Don't you know?" I marched on for a while. "Officer Caitiff tragically died by suicide." The word suicide came out as a whisper, as I still couldn't say it without getting emotional.

"Really? Oh, no. I didn't know that," she said. *Quite the little actress indeed.*

"We were in a relationship. Well, it was only the beginning, but it was the start of something *very* special." I held back my tears while picking up an odd expression on Ophelia's face. *Was SHE judging ME?*

"I'm so sorry for your loss, Dr. Charlotte. Are you okay?"

"Well, the short answer is *no*." I grimaced. "I have a lot of unanswered questions that I need to sort out. For example, why was Cam-, sorry, I meant Officer Caitiff. Why was he so suspicious of you and your strange friend, Isra?" I stared at the girl with expectant and unblinking eyes. Ophelia's own eyes welled up, and large tears spilled down her cheeks without her making a sound.

"I dreamed something bad would happen," she whispered. "I told you about it. Remember? I told *him* too. I thought if he was there, at the bank, he could stop it. But it didn't work."

"So you admit it, then. You set him up based on nothing but a stupid nightmare and figured out a way to get him to the bank," I pressed as Ophelia wiped the water from her eyes. "You called in that stupid bomb threat, didn't you?" I pushed again. Ophelia said nothing. "You were messing around with him to validate yourself and your shadow dream bullshit."

"It *wasn't* bullshit!" Ophelia cried, her face turning red. "That little boy *really* died!" She slowed her pace as her face grew red with anger.

"It *was* bullshit, and a *man* died too. A man of the *law*. *My* man!" I yelled.

Ophelia dried the last of her tears with the sleeve of her jacket and turned the corner to head home, but something inside me took control and I grabbed a hold of her wrist with an intensity I didn't realize I had. She looked shocked and confused, and as she struggled to pull away, I maintained my pace and dragged her along with me, though I wasn't sure where I was going.

"Alright then, little miss psychic. Did you know what would happen?" I asked. As I pulled the girl down the road, I saw the signage for Armitage Park. *Perfect!* "If your dreams weren't bullshit, did you know Cameron would take his own life after being humiliated all over the news?" I yanked Ophelia's arm, pulling her into the wooded trails.

"What? No! I didn't-" Ophelia stopped herself and I could see her eyes flicker as if a light bulb had gone off in her head. "I didn't *know*. The visions were too confusing." She sucked in a long breath in between her sobs.

"You little *bitch*!" The forcefulness and raspy sound of my voice surprised me, but it was time for me to take a stand. "You knew something! You played your stupid games with Cameron and I, and it cost him his *life*. I tried to help you get better, but you betrayed me. *You* did this!" I dragged Ophelia, twisting and struggling, farther down the path. Before I knew it, we were under the complete cover of darkness, the trees allowing only the smallest amount of moonlight to trickle through.

"Dr. Charlotte, *stop!*" Ophelia squealed as she looked around and realized how isolated the two of us were. "I'm *sorry*. I didn't know. I swear, I didn't." Her voice was shrill, but easily absorbed by the dampness of the night woods. *Ophelia Clark has to pay. Ophelia Clark has to pay,* the voice in my head repeated over and over. Then everything went black.

67 OPHELIA CLARK

November 29

"Please let me go. You're *scaring* me," I pleaded, as I struggled to pull my wrist free from Dr. Charlotte's powerful grip. The wooded trail was getting darker by the minute, and there was no one else in sight. No one to hear me scream for help. I fought her and tugged as best I could. We struggled, but she overpowered me. I might as well have been a rag doll.

Dr. Charlotte grabbed my neck with both hands, straining the chain holding the covellite stone. She thrashed me and, as I gasped for air, my eyes rolled to the back of my head, and I started seeing images in my mind's eye. *Flash.* A smiling young woman with a 40s pin-curl hairdo dressed in a tight-fitting sweater, pencil skirt, and low heels. She stood arm-in-arm with a clean-cut man in an army uniform on the front porch of the Victorian house. The house still looked old, but the paint was fresh, and all the shrubs and trees were small and neatly trimmed. *Flash*. A gloomy day. The same young woman behind a window inside the Victorian house. She was reading a letter and crying as she held her clenched fist up to her chest. *Flash*. An old woman with gray, scraggly hair, all dressed in black. She sat in a rocking chair on the porch and stared out into the distance, her eyes dead and joyless. *Flash*. The same old woman, still dressed in black, digging a hole in the garden in front of the porch. *Flash*. Dr. Charlotte pulled up to the old Victorian house in a Taxi. The house was run down, and the gardens were overgrown and half dead. She wore a troubled look on her face. *Flash*. Inside Dr. Charlotte's home office, a strange black shapeless shadow expanded and slithered up the wall and seeped into the ceiling until it disappeared. Flash. Dr. Charlotte in the front garden. She put a dead cat into a hole she had dug and covered it with dirt. *Flash*. Dr. Charlotte and Officer Caitiff were asleep in her bed. She lay naked with her arm across his chest and smiled cozily as she slept. *Flash*. Officer Caitiff sat on the floor with his back against a wall in his house. He was in uniform, except for his bare feet. There were empty booze bottles all around him and his face was red and swollen from drinking and crying. He pulled out his gun. There was a bang.

I twisted and squirmed until I could draw another small breath. The flashes had stopped, but the last shadow dream I had popped into my head. It was here, in the woods. The last thing I remembered was the croaking voice saying: "You took him from her. You took him from *us*. Now you must pay the price."

Though I still didn't understand what was happening, I was certain Dr. Charlotte was about to kill me. Her nose and lips curled into a snarl, and the rage that burned through her eyes shone brightly by the light of the moon seeping into the woods through the trees. I clawed at her hands, trying to loosen her grip on my throat, but I could feel myself drifting out of consciousness. My vision was closing when I saw the shadow of a person move out from behind one tree and sneak behind another. I gasped, but the thin amount of air was not enough to keep me awake. Everything went black and my body went limp. Then I heard a cracking sound.

Suddenly, I was free. Dropping to the ground, I doubled over and drew in a deep, but ragged, breath. The cool fall air made me cough, causing excruciating pain for my raw throat. My vision came into focus just in time to see Dr. Charlotte collapse onto the dirt and leaves on the trail floor while a dark figure stood over her. The shadow dream hadn't shown me this part. As I squinted to get a better look at the stranger, relief washed over me as soon as I saw the shock of white hair. Isra was still holding the thick, fallen branch she'd used to club Charlotte over the head with.

"Are you alright, child?" Isra asked me as she crouched down to feel for Dr. Charlotte's pulse.

"I... think so." I rubbed at my neck.

"Let's go. We have to hurry." Isra said, tossing the branch into the brush behind me. "She'll be up any second now." She took my hand to support the step I needed to take over the doctor's crumpled body. Terrified that she might suddenly wake up and grab my leg, my eyes never left her wilted hands. But Dr. Charlotte lay perfectly still, and Isra and I walked out of the woods. Neither of us said a word.

As we reached the clearing and made our way to the sidewalk, Isra broke the silence:

"You can clean yourself up at my house."

"Shouldn't we report this to the police? My ex-therapist just tried to *kill* me. And you... you saved my life!"

"*No police*," Isra said.

"But-" I started and was immediately cut off.

"No police! You need to trust me when I say that things will work out the way they need to."

I was quiet for a moment before I changed the subject.

"Did you know this would happen? With me? With her?" Isra only had to glance at me, and I understood. "Thank you," I said. "I thought you gave up on me."

We walked for a while before another question popped into my head. "Hang on a second. I need to know something. It's about the challenge. Did you know my vision about the shooting at the bank would show me the wrong day?"

Isra slowed her pace and looked at me. "I knew you became certain of something when you hadn't had the time to trust your diviner skills to take them so literally. You didn't consider that the calendar could be wrong - a mistake you will, undoubtably, have learned from."

"Then why didn't you save him? If you knew I would fail, why didn't you save the boy?"

"My child, there was no better way to show you what being a diviner means. There are real life and death consequences for each of our actions or inactions. I chose Trenton Walker to be your test because it was his path to die that day. It was an incredibly tough case, as his destiny was practically set in stone. I knew there was nothing you could do to make things worse. When I told you that your diviner gift was underdeveloped and that you would be tested, the actual test was to see what you would do. The lengths at which you would go to. With no help from me, you used everything you had. You showed you had a logical mind, and you also showed that you were humble enough to ask for help by involving others. I would have hoped you would have kept the fact that you are a diviner to yourself, but you used things that were *outside* your gift. You swam against the current with no training, and you got creative. You scored very high in that regard," she said. "And by involving Officer Caitiff, you bent the divine. It just wasn't how you had expected." Isra pulled a set of house keys from her pocket as we approached her front door.

"What do you mean?" I asked as we stepped inside and moved to the kitchen. Isra turned on the light, filled a kettle with water, and set it on the stove to boil as I took a seat at the dining table. When she joined me, she said:

"The old Victorian house where Dr. Charlotte lives."

"Yeah?"

"You've spent some time inside. Did you notice anything *interesting* about the place?" Isra asked.

"Interesting isn't the word I'd use, but I definitely felt uneasy. Like, all my senses were being confused. I zoned out while Dr. Charlotte was talking and had a strange daydream. I even saw a massive shadow moving around the wall when it was only me and Dr. Charlotte in the room."

"You saw her." A grin spread across Isra's face.

"Saw who?"

"Ruth Rivers."

"Who is Ruth Rivers?"

"Ruth was once one of our most promising students and became the designated watcher for this county. The academy purchased the old Victorian house, but they convinced her to register it in her own name so that the organization could maintain anonymity. It had always been our intention to have Ms. Rivers set up a private school for diviner children in that location, but personal tragedy left her heartbroken, and she suffered a mental break. The academy took pity on her, relieved her of her duties, and allowed her to stay in the home, where she eventually died, and where her essence has been trapped ever since."

"I've heard the rumors about the lady that lived there. People called her 'the witch', but I thought it was because she was older and wore black all the time." I shrugged. "But what does any of this have to do with Officer Caitiff? I'm confused."

"I was just coming to that. You see, Officer Caitiff was never meant to be involved in the bank robbery. Despite the man's ambitions, he was never where he needed to be. But when you went to the police station and spoke with him, you tilted both his trajectory and Dr. Charlotte's. You gave them a reason to connect with each other so they could discuss *you*. Through that connection, the officer visited Charlotte at her house where they had intimate relations."

"So I caused two people to hook up?" I scrunched my face in confusion as the tea kettle sounded off. Isra popped up from her chair, poured us each a cup, and returned to the table, setting the steaming porcelain down in front of me.

"Ruth's already mad essence witnessed and re-lived the trauma of being enamored with a man in uniform and then losing him. Her agitation and her madness were so great it seeped its way into her living granddaughter, Charlotte. This is the reason she attacked you tonight. Ruth needed someone to blame for her own miserable life and she twisted Charlotte into thinking you should be the one to pay. Charlotte is not in her right mind, but she will start feeling better as soon as she gets home, packs her bags and leaves that house for good."

"Wow. That's some pretty dark stuff." I blew on my tea to cool it down, though Isra was already sipping at hers. "What makes you think she'll leave? She just finished restoring it and setting up her business there."

"I *know* she will leave because there are documents containing a fair offer (which includes our discretion about what just happened in the woods), waiting for her on her front porch," Isra said. I furrowed my brow, confused.

"*You're* going to buy that old Victorian house?" I asked.

"Technically, I will buy it back for the academy, but yes. It needs a fair bit of cleansing, but it is where I will start my next school for young diviners." The corner of her mouth turned up into a slight smile. "Recruiting starts now." She peered at me as she took another sip from her cup.

"Really? Does that mean...?"

"Ophelia Clark, will you accept my offer to join the Monroe chapter of the Academy of the Divine Arts?" Isra's lips stretched into a full out grin.

68 OPHELIA CLARK

January 2

I walked into MC High and made my way to my locker on the second floor. Having spent my entire Christmas break writing extra credit assignments to bring my grades back up, I was confident that I wouldn't let school get away from me this semester. I had also started mentoring under Isra on the weekends at the small cottage house she was renting. Dr. Charlotte ended up selling the old Victorian house back to the academy, but Isra said it wouldn't be ready for students until the spring. I guess getting rid of Ruth Rivers's shadow would take some time.

In the meantime, Isra was really helping me take control of my visions and dreams. She also helped me manage my sleep better. I'd forgotten what it was like to walk around feeling so clear-headed and rested. I even discovered I had enough time in the mornings to run a curling iron through my hair and put on some makeup. With the new clothes I got over the holidays, I felt like I was coming back to school a new person, and others were taking notice. Instead of trying to duck through the crowds and avoid being knocked down, I marched through the halls with my head held high, my long black coat flowing around my kitten heel boots. The kids moved out of my way, some of them stepping aside just to watch me walk by. *Is this what confidence feels like?*

I pulled the books I needed out of my locker and hung my coat, revealing my fitted green sweater paired with a short black skirt and black leggings, another update to my look. Just as I locked my stuff up, I heard a group of girls laughing behind me. I turned around and came face to face with Jessica and her crew: Stephanie, Rachael, and Rebecca.

"Aw, look how adorable. Someone's mommy went to Target and got a fancy new outfit for the first day back at school," Jessica mocked in a nasal voice. The girls eyed me up and down, their smiles like something out of an insane asylum.

"I'm glad you like it. Maybe you can borrow it sometime," I said.

"Ick. As if I would want to share anything with *you*." Jessica rolled her eyes as her friends contorted their faces to support her disgust.

"Why not? You seem to be good at sharing. Just ask Stephanie over there. She knows how generous you are, don't you?" I stared into the curly blond headed girl's eyes until her smirk melted like ice cream on a hot day.

"I don't know what you're talking about, nerd," Stephanie said, furrowing her eyebrows and shifting her stance.

"Sure you do. You and Jessica are sharing her boyfriend. He comes to visit you on Thursday nights so you can make out in your parent's hot tub while they're at bible study." I watched as Jessica's mind ran through all the instances she tried to hang out with her boyfriend or Stephanie on a Thursday and never found either of them free.

"What is she talking about?" Jessica whipped around to look at Stephanie, who started trembling.

"He... he said he was breaking up with you. He was just waiting until the right time." Stephanie fidgeted with her necklace as she backed away from the group. Jessica balled up her fists and closed the distance between them.

"You, BITCH!" She screamed, taking a swing at Stephanie. She missed.

"He doesn't love you," Stephanie shouted back and pushed Jessica into the lockers. I stepped aside as Rebecca tried to split them up. Rachael got out of the way, instinctively placing a protective hand over her flat stomach. I smiled as she looked her nose down at me. As the commotion of the brawling girls behind us grew, I leaned over to her and whispered.

"Congratulations. It's a girl." I didn't need to see the look of shock on her face as I strode away and headed to my first period class.

This semester was going to be awesome.

69 OPHELIA CLARK

A gray, starless sky hung behind the old Victorian house as it slumped miserably beneath the light of the moon. Abandoned for the second time, its windows sagged like down-turned eyes which longed to weep, but could not find the tears. The twisted and overgrown garden crept along the porch and up the columns while the branches of the large oak tree clawed at the home's trim.

Barefoot and in her white nightgown, Ophelia watched the house from the sidewalk as the faint glow from above bathed its facade in a soft yellow light. Moments later, a loud, thunderous boom echoed across the sky and shook the earth. Ophelia wrapped her arms around herself, still feeling the vibration in her ribs. The clouds shifted strangely and pushed past the old Victorian rooftop with unnatural speed. Ophelia trembled in fear. Something sinister was approaching, and she could feel it. She kept her eyes trained on the house until the horror appeared. A black, shapeless shadow descended from the sky, swallowing the building from its chimney down to the foundation.

As Ophelia strained her eyes to make out the silhouette of the structure, a light came on in the second-floor window. The girl's heart pounded out of her chest, as she was certain the house was vacant, but as she watched, an old woman dressed all in black appeared behind the pane. Ophelia's blood ran cold. She tried to run, but her terror kept her frozen in place. Then another light flickered on in the house. This time, it illuminated a room on the first floor. There was someone pounding on the window with their fists and yelling something, though Ophelia couldn't hear it. She squinted as she puzzled over the mysterious sight. Finally, the figure inside, palms flat against the window, got close enough to the glass for Ophelia to see who it was. Dread rushed through the young girl's core as she watched her trusted mentor mouth one word: Run.

"Isra!" Ophelia cried before all the lights in the house went out, leaving her alone in the dark.

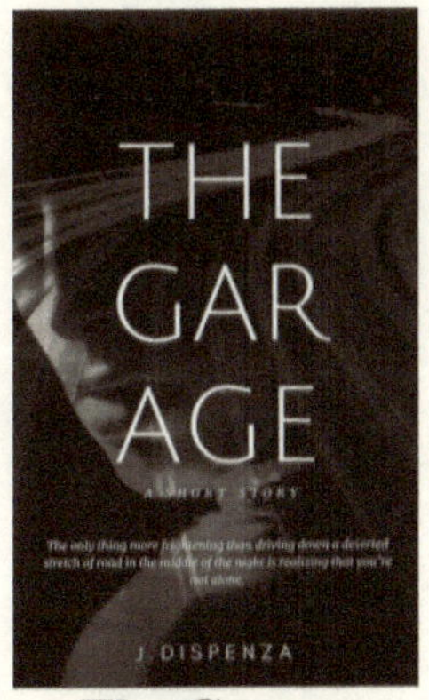

The Garage

The only thing more frightening than driving down a deserted stretch of road in the middle of the night is realizing that you're not alone.

Download your copy of this short story for FREE by visiting jdispenza.com

ABOUT THE AUTHOR

Canadian author, J. Dispenza loves all things
paranormal and is obsessed with the afterlife, the
multiverse, and all the exiting possibilities that lie
in between. She currently lives in North Texas
with her two yorkies.